CRIMES MOST MERRY AND ALBRIGHT

PRAISE FOR LARISSA REINHART

THE FINLEY GOODHART CRIME CAPER SERIES

"This is as fun a novel as it is moving and at times heart-breaking, never the more so when the final page comes and readers are only left wanting more."

CYNTHIA CHOW, *KING'S RIVER LIFE MAGAZINE* ON THE CUPID CAPER

"Another great mystery by Larissa Reinhart. Con artists, murder, a cast of sinister characters, and some laughs along the way. Loved it."

TERRI L. AUSTIN, AUTHOR OF THE *ROSE STRICKLAND MYSTERIES* ON THE CUPID CAPER

THE MAIZIE ALBRIGHT STAR DETECTIVE SERIES

"Fun characters, a perfect setting, and a mystery that will keep you guessing until the end, this book truly has it all!"

SHANNON VANBERGEN, USA TODAY BESTSELLING AUTHOR OF THE GLOCK GRANNIES MYSTERIES ON 20 CARATS

"Fans of humorous mysteries like Janet Evanovich's Stephanie Plum, and Elle Cosimano's Finlay Donovan should pick up this series. We all need some fun in our reading lives!"

SARAH CAN'T STOP READING ON 19 CRIMINALS

"I loved this very fun romance mystery novel. Five out of five stars."

BIG READER'S SITE ON 19 CRIMINALS

"I love the characters in this series, they're what keeps me coming back. If you're looking for a fun series that will keep you turning the pages, you've found it here."

SAMANTHA, COZY TEA COTTAGE ON 18 1/2 DISGUISES

"I highly recommend this series and definitely start with Book 1 you won't be sorry!!! Well written characters and a great mystery. I cannot wait to see what happens next!"

MISS W BOOK REVIEWS ON 18 1/2 DISGUISES

"The perfect combination of mystery, romance, and laughs."

DEVILISHLY DELICIOUS BOOK REVIEWS ON 18 CALIBER

"18 Caliber was my first Maizie Albright Star Detective Mystery-- I'm hoping it won't be my last. This was a fun read--a fast-paced caper that kept me entertained until the end."

TERRY AMBROSE, AUTHOR OF THE SEASIDE COVE MYSTERIES ON 18 CALIBER

"The mystery and detective cases drive the story, but Larissa Reinhart's characters steal the show every time."

THE GIRL WITH BOOK LUNGS ON NC-17

"NC-17 is simply fabulous. Fans of cozy mysteries, southern chick lit, hick lit, crime capers, and humorous mysteries will love it."

JANE READS ON NC-17

"If you love southern settings with plenty of sweet tea and eccentric characters, the meet up of these two heroines is epic."

— BARB TAUB, HUMOR WRITER AND AUTHOR OF THE *NULL CITY* SERIES ON A VIEW TO A CHILL

"Maizie's missteps make each of her successes an absolute joy, and I encourage readers to delve into this lively, funny, and genuinely satisfying series."

CYNTHIA CHOW, *KINGS RIVER LIFE MAGAZINE* ON 16 MILLIMETERS

"With visually descriptive narrative, humorous quips, witty repartee and a quirky cast of characters, this was a such a fun book to read."

DRU ANN LOVE, DRU'S BOOK MUSING ON 16 MILLIMETERS

"Larissa writes a delightful book. Suspense, romance, and some funny situations. [Maizie's] a teen star grown up to new possibilities."

SHARON SALITURO, FRESH FICTION ON 15 MINUTES

"I love Larissa Reinhart's books because they are funny but they also show the big heart of the protagonist."

LYNN FARRIS, HOT MYSTERY REVIEW ON 15 MINUTES

"Hollywood glitz meets backwoods grit in this fast-paced ride on D-list celeb Maizie Albright's waning star. Sassy, sexy, and fun, 15 Minutes is hours of enjoyment—and a wonderful start to a fun new series from the charmingly Southern-fried Reinhart."

PHOEBE FOX, AUTHOR OF THE BREAKUP DOCTOR SERIES ON 15 MINUTES

"Maizie Albright is the kind of fresh, fun, and feisty 'star detective' I love spending time with, a kind of Nancy Drew meets Lucy Ricardo. Move over, Janet Evanovich. Reinhart is my new "star mystery writer!"

PENNY WARNER, AUTHOR OF DEATH OF A CHOCOLATE CHEATER AND THE CODE BUSTERS CLUB ON 15 MINUTES

"Child star and hilarious hot mess Maizie Albright trades Hollywood for the backwoods of Georgia and pure delight ensues. Maizie's my new favorite escape from reality."

— GRETCHEN ARCHER, USA TODAY BESTSELLING AUTHOR OF THE DAVIS WAY CRIME CAPER SERIES ON 15 MINUTES

THE CHERRY TUCKER MYSTERY SERIES

"Anytime artist Cherry Tucker has what she calls a Matlock moment, can investigating a murder be far behind? A Composition in Murder is a rollicking good time."

TERRIE FARLEY MORAN, AGATHA AWARD-WINNING AUTHOR OF READ TO DEATH ON A COMPOSITION IN MURDER

"This is a winning series that continues to grow stronger and never fails to entertain with laughs, a little snark, and a ton of heart."

KINGS RIVER LIFE MAGAZINE ON A COMPOSITION IN MURDER

"Cherry Tucker is a strong, sassy, Southern sleuth who keeps you on the edge of your seat."

TONYA KAPPES, USA TODAY BESTSELLING AUTHOR ON THE BODY IN THE LANDSCAPE

"Because of Cherry's experiences, she knows that—Super Swine notwithstanding—man has always been the most dangerous game, making her the perfect protagonist for this giggle-inducing, down-home fun."

BETTY WEBB, MYSTERY SCENE MAGAZINE ON THE BODY IN THE LANDSCAPE

"The perfect blend of funny, intriguing, and sexy! Another must-read masterpiece from the hilarious Cherry Tucker Mystery Series."

"Artist and accidental detective Cherry Tucker goes back to high school and finds plenty of trouble and skeletons...Reinhart's charming, sweet-tea flavored series keeps getting better!"

"Like front-porch lemonade, Reinhart's cast of characters offer a perfect balance of tart and sweet."

"Reinhart manages to braid a complicated plot into a tight and funny tale. The reader grows to love Cherry and her quirky worldview, her sometimes misguided judgment, and the eccentric characters that populate the country of Halo, Georgia. Cozy fans will love this latest Cherry Tucker mystery."

"Reinhart's country-fried mystery is as much fun as a ride on the tilt-a-whirl at a state fair. Readers who like a little small-town charm with their mysteries will enjoy Reinhart's series."

DENISE SWANSON, *NEW YORK TIMES* BESTSELLING AUTHOR OF THE *SCUMBLE RIVER MYSTERIES* ON STILL LIFE IN BRUNSWICK STEW

"This mystery keeps you laughing and guessing from the first page to the last. A whole-hearted five stars."

DENISE GROVER SWANK, *NEW YORK TIMES* AND *USA TODAY* BESTSELLING AUTHOR ON STILL LIFE IN BRUNSWICK STEW

"*Portrait of a Dead Guy* is an entertaining mystery full of quirky characters and solid plotting...Highly recommended for anyone who likes their mysteries strong and their mint juleps stronger!"

– JENNIE BENTLEY, *NEW YORK TIMES* BESTSELLING AUTHOR OF *FLIPPED OUT* ON PORTRAIT OF A DEAD GUY

"Reinhart is a truly talented author and this book was one of the best cozy mysteries we reviewed this year."

– *MYSTERY TRIBUNE* ON PORTRAIT OF A DEAD GUY

"It takes a rare talent to successfully portray a beer-and-hormone-addled artist as a sympathetic and worthy heroine, but Reinhart pulls it off with tongue-in-cheek panache. Cherry is a lovable riot, whether drooling over the town's hunky males, defending her dysfunctional family's honor, or snooping around murder scenes."

— *MYSTERY SCENE MAGAZINE* ON PORTRAIT OF A DEAD GUY

CRIMES BOTH MERRY AND ALBRIGHT: A Maizie Albright "Between Cases" Holiday Omnibus

Copyright © 2021 by Larissa Reinhart

ASIN B099Q7RWFQ

Ebook ISBN 9798201918217

Paperback ISBN: 978-1-7377550-0-5

Author photograph by Scott Asano

Original cover design by James of GoOnWrite

https://www.goonwrite.com/

A VIEW TO A CHILL

A Maizie Albright Star Detective and Cherry Tucker Mystery Novella

Previously published in THE 12 SLAYS OF CHRISTMAS (2017)

Original Copyright © 2017 by Larissa Reinhart

ISBN: 978-0-9985484-5-6

ISBN: 978-0-9985484-4-9

17.5 CARTRIDGES IN A PEAR TREE

A Maizie Albright Star Detective "Between Cases" Holiday Novella

Copyright © 2019 by Larissa Reinhart

ePub ISBN: 978-0-9978853-9-2

Past Perfect Press

BOOKS BY LARISSA REINHART

MAIZIE ALBRIGHT STAR DETECTIVE SERIES (IN ORDER)

15 MINUTES

16 MILLIMETERS

NC-17

A VIEW TO A CHILL

17.5 CARTRIDGES IN A PEAR TREE

18 CALIBER

18 1/2 DISGUISES

19 CRIMINALS

20 CARATS

21 GUNS

A CHERRY TUCKER MYSTERY SERIES (IN ORDER)

A CHRISTMAS QUICK SKETCH (prequel)

PORTRAIT OF A DEAD GUY

STILL LIFE IN BRUNSWICK STEW

HIJACK IN ABSTRACT

THE VIGILANTE VIGNETTE

DEATH IN PERSPECTIVE

THE BODY IN THE LANDSCAPE

A VIEW TO A CHILL

A COMPOSITION IN MURDER

A MOTHERLODE OF TROUBLE

A FINLEY GOODHART CRIME CAPER SERIES

PIG'N A POKE (prequel, short story)

THE CUPID CAPER

THE PONY PREDICAMENT (coming soon!)

THE HEIR AFFAIR (coming soon!)

THE PIG'N A POKE

A Finley Goodhart Crime Caper prequel

LARISSA REINHART
Wall Street Journal Bestselling Author

When a winter storm traps ex-con Finley at the Pig'N a Poke roadhouse, she finds her criminal past useful in solving a murder.

Free for my VIP Readers!

Join Larissa's email group where she shares exclusive content, news, and giveaways — **www.larissareinhart.com/larissasreaders** — and receive *The Pig'n A Poke* as a gift.

Note: Larissa will not share your email address and you can unsubscribe at any time.

CRIMES MOST MERRY AND ALBRIGHT

A "BETWEEN CASES" HOLIDAY OMNIBUS: A VIEW TO A CHILL & 17.5 CARTRIDGES IN A PEAR TREE

MAIZIE ALBRIGHT STAR DETECTIVE

LARISSA REINHART

Past Perfect Press

A VIEW TO A CHILL

A CHERRY TUCKER & MAIZIE ALBRIGHT
INTERCONNECTED MYSTERY

A Romantic Comedy Mystery Novel
Maizie Albright Star Detective
A VIEW TO A CHILL
Wall Street Journal bestselling author
Larissa Reinhart

ONE
MAIZIE ALBRIGHT

#LASTCHRISTMAS(I'MGLADIT'SNOT)

WHO COULD TURN down a grandmother's request to find a missing granddaughter at Christmas? This is not a rhetorical question. The answer is Jolene Sweeney. Half-owner of Nash Security Solutions.

I'm Maizie Albright. I worked for the good half (as I call it) of Nash Security Solutions. To punish Wyatt Nash, as crazy ex-wives are wont to do, Jolene opened her own private investigation office. (She's competing against herself. Jolene's more into revenge than logic.) When a little, old lady — aka Celia Fowler — appealed to Jolene to help her find her granddaughter, Jolene estimated Mrs. Fowler's community and net worth and told Mrs. Fowler "Sweeney Security Solutions only deals with an exclusive clientele."

Too bad, so sad. A big no to finding her granddaughter. At Christmas, no less.

Besides acting as a pretender in the private eye world, Jolene's also a high-end real estate agent and a Who's Who in Black Pine society.

And nominated for Grinch of the year. By me.

Not just for turning down poor Mrs. Fowler. Jolene's one of the most spiteful women I'd met, and I recently moved to Black Pine from Hollywood, so that tells you something. Hollywood did spite for curtain calls. Jolene's spite would be lauded with an Oscar. Except it's not a performance. She had permanent RBF (resting bitch face) of the soul.

Enough of the dastardly Jolene Sweeney.

Who else would turn down a grandmother's request on Christmas?

Wyatt Nash. My boss at Nash Security Solutions and the man of my dreams.

Wait, what? I meant, the job of my dreams.

After playing the lead in *Julie Pinkerton: Teen Detective*, I longed to be a real private investigator when I grew up. It just took me until age twenty-five to get there.

I digressed. Why would Nash turn down Mrs. Fowler? Nash did a good Southern gentleman. Normally he's concerned with the plight of the less fortunate. Not so big on helping the more fortunate, but we'd been burned by the more fortunate in recent investigations. My old therapist, Renata, would say he had a white knight complex. He also had a hard body, a wickedly sexy smile, and cool blue eyes, à la Paul Newman. Total PI McDishy. If you're into muscle-y men who rarely smiled (despite the sexiness) and created dictums against dating their subordinates.

Which evidently, I was.

Anyhoo, it seemed Mrs. Fowler was an oldy but a goody in the private investigation world of Black Pine—a world comprised of Nash Security Solutions and now Sweeney Security Solutions. Every Christmas for the last five years, Mrs. Fowler asked Nash to find her missing granddaughter. He obliged her the last four but not this year.

"It's a wild goose chase," Nash had said. He took a turn from the front office, into his inner sanctum.

Maybe inner cubby would be a better definition. A smaller office comprised of a wooden desk, an ancient computer, and file cabinets holding Nash's wardrobe and surveillance gadgets. It smelled of old paper, dust, and a spicy, manly, pheromone-filled fragrance I like to call Eau de Nash. When working reception and billing, I took yoga breaks to pull that scent into my lungs. It's like a scent hug from Nash.

Don't tell him. It sounds weird when I say it out loud.

Also, don't judge. Nash had a rule about hugging. He has way too many rules. Taking direction was in my wheelhouse, but the man needs to allow improv every once in a while.

On the other hand, the outer office, although dusty and run down, smelled like donuts. Nash Security Solutions is housed above Dixie Kreme Donuts in an old brick building on Black Pine's original main drag. Working for a private investigator housed in a donut shop was like an unrealized dream come true. Until my hips started to show the reality.

Nash strode back through the inner office door and stopped before the sagging couch where I sat. He's a pacer. Like a caged animal. But I'm not going there because it makes me want to pick up a stool and whip.

"Krystal Fowler doesn't want to be found," Nash continued. "At sixteen, she ran out on her no-account mother and has been running ever since. All I can ever tell her grandmother is Krystal's not reported dead or in prison. I can't do that again."

"Prison?" I gasped. "How can you be so cold-hearted?"

"Miss Albright, you need to toughen up if you want to be a private investigator. Krystal Fowler dropped out of school at sixteen. Her dad's been in prison most of her life. Meth addict mom. Krystal's been caught shoplifting numerous times and suspected of various other petty theft but was never charged. I talked to the local shop owners, and they said she was able to talk her way out of the arrests. Around here, she was considered something of a con artist. The most positive thing her neighbors and teachers had to say about Krystal Fowler is that they're surprised she's not in jail. Classic making of a felon. That's why I checked the prison records."

"But she's so young."

"It's tragic. But the bigger tragedy is what Krystal does to her grandmother. Poor Mrs. Fowler gets a call every year this time from Krystal with a sob story, asking for a handout. Mrs. Fowler wires her the money and never hears from her until the next year. The girl is bleeding Mrs. Fowler dry, and I refuse to be a part of it any longer. I can not and will not take Mrs. Fowler's money. That girl is breaking her grandmother's heart."

I saw his logic. Mrs. Fowler was throwing away her money on finding Krystal.

Which is why I took on Mrs. Fowler's case for free. On personal time. Without telling Nash.

And now I drove a borrowed car (Thanks, Tiffany!) one hundred fifty miles away from Black Pine to Halo, Georgia — somewhere between Atlanta and Alabama — instead of spending my holiday in a cozy (surprising for five thousand square feet) cabin with my adorable, six-year-old, half-sister, Remi.

I had a day to get to Halo and back before Christmas Eve.

Remington Marie Spayberry would not forgive me for missing the wait for Santa. Remi didn't care that I had a hot lead on Mrs. Fowler's grand-daughter. Evidently, all those Christmas cartoons she'd been watching did not instill in her the generosity of the season. But then this was the first Christmas I got to spend with my sister in, like, ever. Before this year, Christmases were spent in tropical locations with my manager and mother, Vicki Albright. She likes the twofer of a getaway with our "Celebrities Best Holiday Destinations" appearance in magazines like *Hello!*, *InStyle*, and *People*.

Vicki didn't have anyone but me. Daddy had Remi and his wife, Carol Lynn. And all the extended Spayberrys in Black Pine, Georgia.

Except for this year. This Christmas, Vicki Albright had Giulio Belloni. I thought. Not exactly sure what's going on there and didn't want to know. Giulio had been my on-screen boyfriend on our reality show, *All is Albright*. I'd thought off-screen, too, until I left the show. His role was rewritten, by my manager — I mean, mother — as her new paramour. (I know, ew.) Ratings. Anyway, they're in Fiji and I got to stay in Black Pine for Christmas.

Except I wasn't in Black Pine. I was in a whole other part of Georgia where Mrs. Fowler's sister lived. And unlike the dry and hazy gray North Georgia Mountains, west Georgia was windy, sleety, and freeze-y. I cranked the heater in Tiffany's Pontiac as high as it would go. I might have been born in Georgia, but I was raised in California. I was not cool with the cold. I mean, boots and sweaters were fun. But on my current salary (a pittance), I couldn't afford a last-minute, real winter coat. At least not one with natural fibers. Lucky for me, I already had boots and sweaters because we liked to pretend winter in Hollywood.

When I spoke with Mrs. Fowler at her home earlier that morning, she had said Krystal wanted money wired to Atlanta (natch) but had also asked her grandma about her great aunt's health. It'd made Mrs. Fowler hopeful that Krystal was interested in turning back to her roots.

I wasn't as skeptical as Nash, but I was also not stupid (despite the way my body makes me look).

"Does she have a relationship with your sister?" I had asked Mrs. Fowler. I followed her home after witnessing Nash's gentle yet disap-pointing rejection. She lived in a small, run-down ranch in a mid-century subdivision in Black Pine.

"No." Mrs. Fowler played with the edge of her Christmas sweater. "I barely saw Krystal. My sister saw her once or twice, I guess. Maybe at a family reunion and when she was born?"

"Why would Krystal be interested in her aunt?"

"They're family? It's Christmas." Mrs. Fowler blinked at me through her glasses.

I didn't think Christmas had anything to do with Krystal's interest in her aunt. "Do you have a picture of Krystal? Something current?"

While Mrs. Fowler hurried into another room, I took a stroll around her living room. The room was crammed with stuff. Mainly boxes from QVC, Amazon, and eBay. Not many photographs. I happened upon a crystal sugar bowl full of gumdrops just before Mrs. Fowler returned. I crammed a wintergreen in my mouth and fast chewed.

"Here, Maizie." She handed me a photograph.

The picture showed a young girl. Dark-haired, oval-faced, and pre-teen-ish. She wore cutoffs and a t-shirt, sitting cross-armed on the steps of a house. Looking aggrieved. I tried to imagine her older, less colt-ish, and less hostile. But then realized, after what Nash had told me, most likely, she was still antagonistic.

Or who knew? People changed. Maybe Nash couldn't find her because Krystal had become a nun. Like in *Sister Act*. My therapist Renata said to imagine the most positive outcome before focusing on the worst-case scenario. Of course, almost-worst-case scenario seemed to happen to me a lot. But that's better than the worst case, right?

"Do you have anything more recent?" I asked. "That's what I meant by current."

Mrs. Fowler shook her head. "I'm not good at remembering to take pictures. I was never sure when I'd see Krystal. Her mother wasn't reliable."

"Does Krystal know where your sister lived?"

"I think so. She's lived in the same house all her married life. Her husband's from Halo, Georgia."

"Did you tell your sister that Krystal might pay her a visit?"

Mrs. Fowler's forehead crinkled. "No. Why would Krystal visit Martha Mae?"

Oh boy.

Mrs. Fowler paused. "You don't think Krystal intends to get money from my sister?"

I did think. But I patted Mrs. Fowler's hand and told her to call her sister. If Krystal hadn't already visited Martha Mae, Martha Mae might want to avoid her great-niece until we caught up with Krystal.

We meaning me since Nash had turned down the case.

I got the sister's address and phone number. "Tell Martha Mae I'm coming. If Krystal calls, have Martha Mae wait to invite her over until I get there. I'm going to talk to Krystal and see if I can get her to come back to Black Pine with me."

Mrs. Fowler threw her arms around me. She smelled like lavender and gumdrops. I hugged her back, pressing her bony body against my soft form. I probably smelled mostly of gumdrops.

"Maizie Albright," she whispered. "You're my Christmas angel. I know you'll get Krystal back."

Now, one hundred miles and several hours later, despite the icy rain descending on this part of Georgia, I still felt the warmth of that message. I intended to do my best to get this wayward granddaughter back into the loving arms of her grandmother. I'd do the same for any grandmother. It might take a miracle, but after all, it was Christmas.

TWO
CHERRY TUCKER

IN MY TWENTY-SIX YEARS, I'd experienced broken ribs, a bullet's grazing, and a goat hit-and-run. Add to that plenty of hangovers, food poisoning, and a bout of the chicken pox at age seven. But I'd never experienced the gut-aching, head-throbbing, bone-chilling misery that I'd felt since early this morning. Feeling puny, I'd skipped the Christmas sing-a-long with Todd's band at Red's County Line Tap the night before. Worse than puny. Tired, achy, and with a gnawing in my belly that wasn't hunger.

A big surprise, because I was always hungry.

"Cherry Tucker," my BFF Leah had said to me, "I can understand not wanting to hear Shawna Branson karaoke the 'Twelve Days of Christmas.' But if you don't even want to eat Red's turkey dinner, you best get yourself to bed."

And to her shock, I did.

Actually, I don't know who was more astonished: Leah, me, or the rest of my friends and family. They'd arrived at Red's for the second annual Christmas sing-a-long and found me missing. All my kin and kith were there except Grandpa Ed, who didn't do such silliness. And Deputy Luke Harper, who was working.

The weatherman promised an abominably icy Christmas, unusual for our area, so all available deputies were on call. Our winters tend to be cool and dry for the most part. But send us one snowflake and the town shuts down. We can't cope. Or drive. Luke had already broken up a fight in the Tru-Buy parking lot. It seemed there'd been a run on batteries, milk, and bread. Words were said. Which led to fists. And a pack of Pampers used as a weapon.

"A first for Halo," Luke had said. He'd been left with diaper cleanup.

The next morning, I lay, staring at my painting, *Snug the Coonhound,* above my bed. Willing Snug to stop whirling. Snug was making my stomach cramp. Closing my eyes made it worse. I felt incapable of doing more than opening or closing my lids, but I was burning from the inside out. I eased back, pushing my warm, limp pillow with me until I could feel my bed's brass spindles cooling the back of my head. The chill tore through me like a two a.m. freight train. Trembling, I reached for the blanket I had recently kicked away.

Licking my parched lips, I wished Santa would put me out of my misery.

I needed some centering to stop the dizziness and stared out the window at the opposite wall. The previous night, I hadn't bothered to close my curtains. The lights from my neighbor's Christmas tree winked and reflected on the window. I watched them dance and glow from across our short property divide, hoping their syncopation would bring me the focus to keep my stomach in check. Mrs. Boyes never bothered to shade her windows this time of year. She liked to share her Christmas spirit with her neighbors. Also, her fruitcake.

The thought of her fruitcake made me nauseous. And not just because Mrs. Boyes's fruitcake often had that effect. I refocused on the blinking lights.

Mrs. Boyes's living room was brightly lit against the gray and gloom hanging between our homes. Someone was sitting on the couch. I blinked, then narrowed my eyes.

It looked like a reindeer sitting upright, legs crossed, and drinking from a mug. He wore a blue sweater, which seemed unnecessarily warm for an inside reindeer. I felt unnecessarily warm but couldn't seem to stop watching him.

Rain pattered against the window, causing the reflected Christmas lights to crystallize. The reindeer bent forward, its attention fixed on the window. Or the rain. Or maybe he saw me. Watching him from my bed.

A wave of fear flipped my stomach sideways.

"Don't be a fool," I said. "That reindeer can't see you. You've got no lights on." I turned my attention from the creepy reindeer. My stomach shifted back in place, and I heaved a sigh of relief.

I closed my eyes, opened them, and checked the window. The reindeer had disappeared. Wearing a blue sweater, Mrs. Boyes stood near the window, a package in hand. Probably ready to deposit it beneath the tree. My lids felt heavy, and my chin dipped to my chest. Rain pelted the window, lulling me to sleep.

My head jerked up. The rain had stopped. The Christmas lights continued to blink. And another figure emerged from behind the couch. Santa.

Had I slept my way to Christmas Eve? I licked my chapped lips, flexed my achy limbs, and wondered if these characters always appeared in flu-induced dreams.

Maybe just at Christmas.

On this side of the room, Mrs. Boyes was gesturing to Santa. Her wild arm waves made me queasy. I had enjoyed her more as a reindeer, as disconcerting as that had been. At least the reindeer hadn't made sudden movements. And now Santa was approaching the reindeer.

Maybe he needed the reindeer to help with his sleigh?

No, Santa seemed to be talking to the reindeer. Calming her.

"Thank you, Santa," I whispered. "She'll give you cookies." Mrs. Boyes always had cookies. Unfortunately, the cookies were a better fit for skeet shoot practice than consumption. But she meant well.

At that thought, another bilious wave washed over me. I shut my eyes, waiting for the wave to crash. Rain splattered against the pane. I opened my eyes and refocused on the window, now oily with raindrops.

The reindeer pointed toward her front door and turned from Santa. Santa retraced his steps to the door and opened it. I struggled to keep my watch.

This odd Christmas special was wearing me out.

Movement caught my eye. Santa hadn't exited the door. He crept around the couch while Mrs. Boyes faced her tree.

She half-turned. Santa lunged. Grabbing a string of Christmas lights, Santa wrapped them around Mrs. Boyes's neck. She flailed against Santa. He jerked the light cord. Lights sparked and went out.

I jerked upright and leaned forward, fighting the vicious churning in my belly and the spots in my vision.

Her arms clawing at his suit, Mrs. Boyes slid down Santa's body. She yanked at his beard, ripping it sideways. Santa bent over her. And Mrs. Boyes disappeared beneath the window sill.

My head felt like it was going to explode. Heat scorched my neck. The churning in my stomach became a razor-sharp clawing I couldn't ignore. I rolled to the edge of the bed, slid to the floor, and crawled to the bathroom.

On my return, I dragged myself to the window and gripped the sides to stay upright. Leaning my perspiring forehead against the chilled glass, I searched the house next door. Once again, the Christmas lights blinked in a syncopated rhythm on the tree. In my rectangular frame of reference, the living room was empty of people. A red blanket had been folded over the sofa's back. No reindeer. No Santa.

Sleet splattered against the roof and struck my window. Shivering, I lurched back to bed, burrowed beneath the blankets, and tried to make sense of what I saw. I had no idea how long I was in the bathroom. Unfortunately, I had passed out on the floor and woke up shaking from the cold. My room was dark. Maybe some trick of light since the bathroom had been so bright. Or maybe it was the rain. Or sleet. Or whatever was going on outside.

An icy gust rattled my pane. I shivered. Had I seen a crime or had it been a dream?

Unsettled, I pulled my sketchbook off the nightstand and drew Santa and the poor reindeer from memory. My recollection seemed clear despite the morbidly odd subject. My eyes grew hot and itchy, my body languorously heavy.

"I've got to report it," I muttered. "And I better do it now. I can't stay awake for nothing. Lord, help me. I don't know up from down."

Reaching outside the blankets and into the biting chill, I snatched my phone from the bedside table and stole it under the covers. I thumb-dialed a number.

"I need to report an attempted murder," I mumbled. "I saw Santa strangling a reindeer."

THREE
MAIZIE ALBRIGHT

#WINTERNOTSOWONDERFULLAND

SLEET PELTED the windows of Tiffany's Pontiac as I pulled off the slippery interstate and took the local highway into Halo. Halo's not a big town. On the outskirts are a few fast food places, an old Waffle Hut, and a Ford dealership. There's a train track that'll give you whiplash bumping over it and two boulevards that intersect into a kind of town square, which consisted of churches on each corner. Very old-school Southern with bungalows, Victorian-type houses with deep porches, and some bigger homes that probably were once stately but now appeared ragged around the edges.

Twenty-first century Mayberry. Kind of sad.

Black Pine would be like that if it wasn't a resort town with a lot of old money. And new money. The newest money being the film industry. Bad luck for an ex-celebrity who was told to stay away from the industry by a kind, yet firm judge in California. So hard to keep up with probation requirements when your reality show follows you to Georgia and stays because it's cheaper to film in Georgia than in California. They're not allowed to film me.

Unless, apparently, I'm on the B-roll.

Martha Mae, Mrs. Fowler's sister, lived in one of the cottages leading away from the square, closer to the train tracks. It was a cute house squeezed between two other similarly-aged bungalows. Lights swayed from the porch, a big wreath hung on the door, and poinsettias lined the porch steps. The cottages on either side weren't as kept up as Martha

Mae's. It gladdened my heart to see someone caring so well for the historic home. It was probably as old as the tracks.

The poinsettias didn't look any happier than I did about the crap-tastic weather. I dodged icy raindrops that pelted my puffy UNIQLO jacket as I dashed from the curb to Martha Mae's porch. Slipping on the top step, I smacked a poinsettia with my boot, tipping the pot. I knelt to right the pot and placed it back in the saucer where a key lay. I guessed Martha Mae no longer kept her doors unlocked like small-town people used to do in the old days. But Martha Mae certainly didn't go to extreme lengths to keep her home protected from burglaries.

Nash would have a field day with Martha Mae's lack of security. Most of our (few) jobs were security systems. The private investigation side of the business had taken a hit with two notorious cases we (I) had been (inadvertently) (sort-of inadvertently) involved in. Nash would have recommended trip alarms on the doors and windows with a keypad entry.

But then Martha Mae would have to key in her code every time a neighbor stopped by for coffee or a cup of sugar. She'd end up leaving the alarm off to simplify things. Ah, small-town life. Wouldn't it be nice to live in a place where everyone knew where you kept your key?

Or would it?

From her porch, I gazed out at the wet neighborhood where bright lights blinked from porches and gutters. Yards were decorated (including a humongous inflatable polar bear), and wreaths hung on the doors. Halo may not be glamorous, but it was cozy and safe. Black Pine wasn't much bigger, but the wealth invited greater vices and bigger crimes.

Which made me worry about Martha Mae. Krystal the con artist might take the sweet old lady for a ride. I turned back to the door and rang the bell. Rubbing my hands together, I waited and still getting no answer, knocked. Leaned out the porch and double-checked that I had seen a car in the drive. Yep. A Buick LeSabre sedan. I wondered why she hadn't parked in the garage on a day like this.

Martha Mae's front windows were not shaded. I'd had some bad luck with peeping in windows and seeing things I shouldn't (a dead body for one), so I hesitated. Then peered into the picture window, shading my eyes with my mittened hands. Her tree blinked from the far corner of the room, gifts piled beneath. A sturdy couch and two wing-back chairs surrounded a coffee table and faced, I presumed, a TV in the opposite corner from the tree. My heart stung, knowing Martha Mae was a widow with no children.

I'd have to wait until Martha Mae arrived to find out if I had missed Krystal. One thing I'd learned from Nash about sensitive information, it was better to get it in person. It's a lot harder to lie, skirt the truth, or hang up when you speak face-to-face.

Plus, I had driven all this way, and Martha Mae looked like the type who would have Christmas cookies on hand.

In the meantime, I figured I might as well continue the Peeping Tom routine. I crossed the porch to the smaller set of windows. Christmas window clings — snowflakes, angels, and snowmen — and lack of light kept me from seeing much. A dining room. Table not set for company.

Avoiding the slippery sidewalk, I crossed the wet grass to Tiffany's car waiting on the curb, and slid inside. Huddled inside my coat, I pulled off my hat and shook out my damp hair, and used a tissue to blot rain from my face. Rubbing my hands together, I gave myself over to warm thoughts.

Roasting chestnuts on an open fire. Yule logs. Tahiti.

Didn't help. I was wet and cold. I needed a hot shower, dry clothes, or at least a cup of coffee. Martha Mae's garage door was closed. Maybe the Buick was an extra car. Or a neighbor had picked her up. Martha Mae didn't have a cell phone, she had a landline.

Who didn't have a cell phone anymore? Besides me. Until Nash had given me the burner because I couldn't afford a smartphone. Aha. Answered my own question.

I'd have to wait for Martha Mae's return. Wet, cold, and in need of coffee.

Near the highway, the Waffle Hut had looked enticing. The sign said they had a Christmas waffle. Red velvet with whipped cream cheese. More importantly, they had a bathroom with, hopefully, a hand dryer.

But what if Krystal showed while I was gone? Back in Black Pine, Mrs. Fowler's home phone didn't have a call log read-out. Her phone was attached to the wall with an actual cord. Avocado Green. Her sister probably had the same one. Perhaps in harvest gold. So no phone number for Krystal. Google and social media hadn't revealed anything about the young woman either. She was off the grid.

I couldn't contact Krystal, yet Waffle Hut had red velvet waffles and hot coffee.

A dilemma.

I glanced at the house to the right of Martha Mae's. The cottage looked the most decrepit and the covered drive was filled with junk. It also wasn't decked out with Christmas decor like the others. An old yellow truck rested in the driveway, but it didn't look like it ran. The house was dark, and I assumed unoccupied. On the left, a cheerier cottage had a car in the drive and a Christmas tree in the front window. Also, the inflatable polar bear in the front yard.

I pulled on my wet hat and mittens (yuck), shot out of the car, and quick-stepped through the drizzle to the polar bear's front porch. A woman answered her door at my knock.

"Hello," I said. "My name is Maizie Albright. I'm waiting to talk to Martha Mae Boyes. She's not answering her door but is expecting me. Do you know where she went or when she'll be back?"

She squinted at me. "Maizie Albright?"

"Yes, ma'am."

"Did your parents name you after the actress?"

Considering the actress was me and born on the same day, I didn't know how to answer. "No. I'm Maizie Albright."

She smiled the smile of those speaking to the less intelligent. "Maybe you don't know her. Maizie Albright's an actress."

"I know her. I was named after myself. Because that's me. I live in Georgia now."

"Of course, you do, hon'." She nodded indulgently. "What did you need?"

"Martha Mae Boyes. Where is she?"

"Martha Mae doesn't buy anything. She's on a fixed income. We get a lot of solicitors this time of year. Are you selling windows or magazines?"

"I'm not selling anything." The sleety drizzle was turning into a soak. The raindrops smacked the edge of the porch and splattered. I took a step closer to the door. "I work for a private investigator in Black Pine. Martha Mae's sister is my client. She's expecting me. I need to talk to Martha Mae about her grand-niece."

"Martha Mae doesn't have a grand-niece." The lady began to shut her door. "I don't like the sound of this."

"I'm worried about Martha Mae—"

"Merry Christmas." The door shut.

I faced a wreath made of tiny Woodstocks surrounding Snoopy. Snoopy wore a Santa suit. "Snoopy, do investigators get coffee breaks? Nash didn't teach me that yet. But I really need one."

In answer, a rush of raw wind blew rain across the porch. I yelped and ran back to the car.

AT THE WAFFLE HUT, I ordered the Christmas special and a large coffee — extra hot — to go, then waited in line for the bathroom. The woman exiting the bathroom looked about as dry as I felt.

"Y'all go in, but the floor's a mess," she said. "They need to mop. This weather is just awful, isn't it? Supposed to get worse as the day gets on. You better get your shopping done and get home."

I nodded and smiled. Maybe that's where Martha Mae had gone. Shopping before the weather got worse. With hope in my heart that she'd be home soon, I entered the wet bathroom, skirted the muddy puddle, and hung my coat over the broken dryer. I dried off as best I could with paper towels and warm thoughts.

Red velvet waffles. Extra hot coffee. I mentally added sausage to my order.

Renata had taught me that you could make yourself happy from the outside in. Look good to feel good. Yanking off my soaked beanie, I shook it out in the sink and ruffled my wet hair, now darkened to auburn. I quickly parted and double-braided my hair.

And looked like Rebecca of Sunnybrook Farm after a weekend bender.

Wiping off my raccoon eyes, I touched up my mascara. My sea-glass green eyes blinked back at me. Better. I sneezed. But I still looked cold, wet, and miserable.

Vicki, my manager (and mother), taught me that actresses should never reveal their inner misery "because nobody really gave a shit. You were hired for a job. Do the job and be miserable on your own time." This was speaking to a fourteen-year-old who didn't want to work. She'd found out her daddy was remarrying and wanted to move home to Black Pine. Have a normal life. With normal Christmases.

But Mrs. Fowler needed my help. I wasn't fourteen. I was just wet and cold.

I cocked a hip, fixed a teenage sneer, and mustered up enough snark until I saw the character from my most famous role, Julia Pinkerton, staring back at me. This Julia Pinkerton didn't look fourteen, but she did have spunk. "Get over yourself, girl. You've gotta bust this case. I'll make it happen."

I never understood that line. The writers loved a catchphrase. But it worked.

Maybe it would for this case as well.

FOUR
CHERRY TUCKER

I WOKE to find a hand covering my eyes. My body jerked, but I didn't have the strength to buck. I opened my mouth to scream but could only muster a low howl.

The hand jerked off my eyes.

"What in the hell was that?" I recognized the voice of my sister, Casey. "Is she dying?"

My vision cleared. Grandpa Ed's woman, Pearl, loomed over me. She wore a concerned look and a Christmas sweatshirt. The sweatshirt had a pyramid of goats, each with an ornament hanging from its mouth. The kid on top held a star between its hooves.

"She's burning up with fever. Bet it's the flu." Pearl held her hand away from her sweatshirt. "I need to wash up. Don't want my goats to get sick with this. Looks ugly."

I moaned and rolled over, eyeing Casey's lean against the doorway. On a cold and wet December twenty-third, Casey wore a tank top, yoga pants, and flip-flops. In keeping with the season, the tank top read, "One of Santa's Ho's." It was stretched over a rounded belly that didn't quite meet the top of the yoga pants.

"I'm sorry you're feeling so bad," said Casey. "But I don't want the baby sick, so I'm not coming into your room."

"You should go," I whimpered. "Let me die in peace."

"Who dies from the flu?" She rolled her eyes. Casey wasn't much of a history or science buff, but I could tell she was concerned. Enough that she'd brought Pearl to check on me. The sort-of step-grandparent we never wanted. "I made you chicken soup."

My parched mouth oozed drool, causing my stomach to roll. "No food talk. And stand still. You keep rocking, and it's making me nauseous."

"I'm not moving. I'll leave the soup in the—"

She backed into the kitchen until I returned from the bathroom. During that time, Pearl had stripped the bed, remade it, and placed an assortment of Gatorades on my nightstand.

Red, blue, and green. Christmasy. My stomach took another roll.

"Now then." Pearl placed a cool cloth on my head, tucked me into the hospital-cornered quilt, and squirted her hands with sanitizer. "What's all this about reporting a crime?"

I stared at my *Snug the Coonhound* painting above my bed. The last few hours were hazy. Snug was no help. He continued to undulate. "Ma'am?"

"Honey, you called the police. Beth Ann Simmons is filling in for Tamara and couldn't understand a word you said. Everyone knows you're sick, so they sent an ambulance over. Not an ambulance, really. That was needed with...well, never mind that. You don't need the details. The town is just a mess. And Line Creek has all their emergency people on the interstate because of a pileup. Anyways, Sheriff Thompson sent June Peterson in her minivan in case you needed transport. But you didn't answer the door, so June went home. That's when she called Casey. Casey called your Grandpa Ed, and he sent me. Here we are."

"Good thing I'm not dying," I croaked. "I'd have to haunt June Peterson."

"Of course, you're not dying," said Pearl. "You just have the flu. Didn't you get your flu shot?"

"No, ma'am."

"Where's the sense the Lord gave you? Goodness knows I get a flu shot every year. I get one for the shingles, too. Now that's a disease you don't want to get."

I rolled, searching for a cool spot on my pillow. "I guess I'm lucky to only be dying from the flu then."

"Nonsense. Who dies from the flu? Now don't be calling 9-1-1 anymore. Leave the emergency responders to the real emergencies. You can call me. Or Casey, although she shouldn't come near you. I mean, look how she's dressed. Half her body is exposed to all sorts of germs not to mention the cold."

"I'm hotter than Hades, Pearl," said Casey. "I'd walk around in a bikini if I could get away with it in this town. I feel like I'm having a Kenmore electric range."

"She acts like she's the first person ever to experience pregnancy, I swear," whispered Pearl. "But still, she shouldn't risk it. Casey shouldn't be near this house. You don't even have a can of Lysol. People die from the flu, you know."

I opened my mouth, then closed it.

"Now I'm going to run to the store and get you some Lysol. Also, some Tylenol. Then I'm going to clean your bathroom. It's like you don't even know how to take care of yourself. You could have children by now, Cherry. And what will you do when those poor babies get sick without Lysol and Tylenol?"

I didn't have the energy to defend my mothering skills to imaginary sick children, so I lay back on the pillow and waited for her to leave. "Casey, you still here?"

She waddled into the doorway. "Yep."

"Did I really call 9-1-1?"

"Yep."

"Where's Luke?"

Her gaze circled the room and drifted down the hallway. "Busy. You know. Working."

"If I had called the sheriff's office, I know Luke would come. He said he'd check on me."

"With the weather and...and everything, the sheriff's office is hopping. It always is this time of year, you know that as well as anybody." Casey stroked her belly. "Just focus on resting and getting well. We'd all miss you if you couldn't come to Grandpa's on Christmas day. I'm making a turkey and—"

"No food." I rolled onto my back and panted. Snug panted with me. "I kind of remember calling 9-1-1 now."

Casey turned in the doorway to face me. "What'd you tell Beth Ann? Uncle Will said it was gibberish. He's worried about you."

"I thought I saw—" I rubbed my head, slid to ease against the bedstead, and checked Mrs. Boyes's window. In the corner, reflected lights from the tree blinked. Her living room was dark, but I could see a glow in the back of the house. "I don't know what I saw. Mrs. Boyes next door. Remember her?" I pointed toward the window.

"Yeah, sure." Casey glanced in the direction of my point.

"I was watching her through the windows. You can see straight into her living room. She looked like a reindeer, but never mind that. I think the flu's messed my brain. She had a visitor. Santa."

"Santa?" Casey snorted. "He's got one more day until he shows."

"And I thought Mrs. Boyes and Santa were arguing. Except she was a reindeer. And then Santa left. But he came back and strangled her with the Christmas lights."

Hugging her belly, Casey doubled over with laughter.

"I know," I said. "I don't believe it either. But Casey, it looked as real as you. Except it was raining. And kind of blurry. And…I don't know what I saw."

"So, you reported it anyway." Casey rolled her eyes. "Only you would report a crime on her deathbed."

I slid under the covers. "I thought you said no one dies from the flu."

"Not healthy young folks like you."

"I'm not healthy," I whimpered. "I have the flu. And I feel like death."

"Better than Mrs. Boyes felt getting strangled by a reindeer." Casey snorted.

"Santa," I whispered. "She was the reindeer."

Casey crossed the room to peer out the window. "You want me to go check on her?"

I stared at Snug. He still made me dizzy. Maybe I shouldn't have painted the coon dog in cerise and tangerine and stuck to browns. I swung my gaze to Casey. "Yes, I guess I do."

"You got any cookies to bring her? I need to have some reason to knock other than asking her if Santa visited early."

I double-blinked at the word cookies and felt my stomach bubble into my throat. I rolled onto my side, slid out of bed, and crept to the bathroom.

"Never mind," called Casey. "I'll see you in a minute."

WHEN I RETURNED from the bathroom, the room was empty and dark. I turned on the light, crept back into bed, and huddled beneath the heavy quilt. My eyes crept to the window. Mrs. Boyes's overhead living room light flashed on. Remembering Casey's mission, I forced myself to sit up and focus.

A man was crossing through the living room from the back hall. He wore a white t-shirt. No Santa suit. I sighed and rested my chin on my knees. The man opened the front door, and after a long pause, Casey shuffled into the living room. She'd pulled on a knit hat over her long, dark hair and covered up with a jacket but left it hanging open. She glanced around the living room as she talked. The man waved at the back hall entrance.

After a moment, Casey nodded. She spoke then waved to the window.

The man turned toward the window and also waved.

Realizing my lights were now on, I held up a hand and let it drop.

Casey turned toward the hall once more, spoke, then exited the house.

As the front door shut behind her, the man in the white t-shirt sauntered to the window facing my bedroom. Placing his hands on his hips, he stared for a moment. Covering his eyes, he leaned against the pane. He was older. Gray seasoned his thick hair and beard, maybe giving my flu-addled brain the impression of Santa. He didn't have Santa's build, though. With his arm flexed, his forearms and shoulders bulged. No bowl full of jelly either.

The man squinted through the dark. Might've met my eyes, although it was difficult to tell through the rain and gloom filling the small space between our houses. Not-Santa grinned and waved once more.

His grin showed in his teeth but not in his narrowed eyes. Definitely not Santa.

I shivered and slunk lower into my quilt. Reached for my sketchbook and a pencil on the nightstand. Then drew a quick sketch of the man in Mrs. Boyes's living room.

FIVE
MAIZIE ALBRIGHT

#PLEASECOMEHOMEFORCHRISTMAS

RED VELVET WAFFLES are difficult to eat in a car. I don't recommend it. Particularly with a plastic spork and mittens. However, the hot coffee did the trick. I revived. Damp instead of drenched. Tiffany's car had smelled like wet boots and pine tree freshener, but now the wet pine boots had mixed with sweet waffles and coffee.

Wet pine coffee waffles. A definite improvement.

I sat across the street from Martha Mae's semi-dark house, waiting for her return. Feeling moderately cheery about my stakeout. It was about time I did some real investigative work. Although this field experience — like my past fieldwork — was not on Nash Security Solutions's docket. I wasn't sure if it counted as real. One of these days — I hoped. Prayed. Wished. — Nash and I would do for-real fieldwork together.

I took a minute to dream about those possibilities, leading me down an imaginary road (we weren't supposed to take) that involved a lot of heavy lip action between the blue-eyed PI and myself. I'd gotten a taste. Once. And it was sweeter than red velvet waffles. And that red velvet waffle had made my teeth itch. Unfortunately, the romantic detour Nash and I'd taken had been short. Brief. Temporary. Fleeting.

Unfortunately, I hadn't been the one who'd fled.

Although the memory was warming me up — silver lining there — I forced myself to stop thinking about Nash. The temperature was plummeting. And with the icy rain, I worried about Martha Mae out in this nasty weather. She was of hip-breaking age.

As I waited, vehicles pulled into the neighbors' drives. An old Firebird and a big truck stopped at the house I thought was abandoned. Two women exited the vehicles, hurried into the carport, and through a side door. The house blazed with light. Across the street, an old Cadillac pulled into the drive of a rambling Victorian. An older man disappeared into that house and a string of blinking, colored lights lit up his porch. I sipped coffee and watched Martha Mae's house.

Nothing happened.

Except for more sleet. Wind. My waffle was gone (I had better luck using my hands). And I now had to pee.

But — I reminded myself — this was my dream job. I was investigating a missing person's case. An actual granddaughter. Who might be a felon. But she also might be a nun. Life was funny like that.

Sleet pelted the car. I sipped more coffee. Turned on the radio and sang along to "Baby It's Cold Outside" (both parts) while I watched the big truck leave the neighbor's house. Did my Marilyn imitation singing "Santa Baby" complete with shoulder shrugs in my imaginary mink.

"Have A Holly Jolly Christmas" came on. I took a coffee break. A phone rang. I jerked. Coffee missed my mouth and rained on my puffy coat. My phone. I'd almost forgotten.

I had given up my smartphone when I left California (mainly so my manager/mother couldn't find me). Nash had given me a burner phone. It was rarely used (unless my manager/mother was trying to find me). But I loved the little flip that couldn't do anything but make calls and take grainy pictures. I checked the screen. Nash. I grinned.

Wait, a minute. Nash didn't know I had taken on Mrs. Fowler's case.

My hello was tentative at best.

"Where are you?" said Nash.

"Out of town? It's very seasonal here."

"And here is?"

"Not like seasonal snow," I continued, astutely avoiding his question. "But it's cold. And wet. So more seasonal than I was used to in California. But I can't say it's a white Christmas."

"I'm not asking for a weather report, Miss Albright. I'm asking for a location."

"I'm still in Georgia. Which is why the seasonal weather surprised me."

"Please don't tell me you drove your scooter out of town."

"Lucky's a dirt bike, but no. My thighs couldn't take that long of a drive. I borrowed Tiffany's car."

"Your thighs—" He cleared his throat. "How long of a drive? Where are you?"

"A little town called Halo."

A figure emerged from the neighbor's house and walked across the driveway. A woman wearing an unzipped jacket, flip-flops, and a hat.

Who wears flip-flops in sleet? Was this sleet? Not really rain, not really ice. Definitely not snow. I shivered.

"You're helping Mrs. Fowler," said Nash.

"I'm not taking her money. She already wired some to Krystal. I know you felt guilty about taking her money."

"So, you're helping her for free." He sighed. "Miss Albright."

"I know. Merry Christmas."

"Where did Mrs. Fowler send you?"

"To her sister, Martha Mae's, house. Krystal had asked about her. I thought it'd be helpful for me to come down here and see if Krystal shows."

"And did she?"

"Not yet. I don't think."

"Are you with Martha Mae right now? Did you talk to her?"

"Not exactly. Martha Mae's not home yet. I'm waiting." I bounced on the seat. "I'm keeping surveillance on her house. And since we're speaking of surveillance — you know mentor to mentee...am I a mentee? That doesn't sound right. Mentoree? Anyway, how many coffee breaks do you usually take when on a stakeout?"

His second sigh was longer. And very audible.

"Miss Albright, come home. And please drive carefully. The weather is supposed to get worse."

"What if Krystal shows up?"

"Krystal Fowler was arrested three days ago. She's not going to show."

"Oh." Why did I find that disappointing? I had really hoped she'd become a nun.

But hold on. "Wait a minute," I said. "That means you've been looking at arrest records. You're also helping Mrs. Fowler. For free."

"Merry Christmas."

"Busted." My heart flip-flopped. Nash was no Grinch. I knew it all along. "Why were you looking for me anyway?"

"I wanted to—" He was silent for a moment.

I gave him the moment. Across the street, the woman in flip-flops, looking very pregnant — What was she thinking? She could slip and fall in flip-flops. Plus weren't wet, cold feet bad for your health? I shouldn't judge. But here I was judging — had marched from the neighbor's house to Martha Mae's. In the sleet.

I almost leaned out my window to tell the semi-barefoot, pregnant woman that Martha Mae wasn't home and to warm her feet back inside her house.

But Martha Mae's living room lit up. The door opened for the pregnant woman.

Shizzles, I thought. I should have rung again instead of assuming Martha Mae wasn't home. Where was my common sense? I studied the parked car, trying to understand how I missed her. Hells. Had the Buick moved? I couldn't tell.

An older man had opened Martha Mae's door. The pregnant woman went inside. Scooting closer to the front windshield, I craned my neck to watch them through Martha Mae's living room window. My vantage point in Tiffany's car made it almost impossible to see anything. Two shapes backlit by blinking Christmas tree lights.

Who was the man? Mrs. Fowler had said Martha Mae's husband had died. Martha Mae didn't have children. Was he home when I rang? If he was, why wouldn't he answer for me? Because I wasn't from Halo?

This town was a little odd.

"And anyway…"

Craptastic, Nash had been speaking and I had forgotten to listen. I could usually multitask. Why didn't I tune in for Nash of all people?

"It's Christmas," he continued. "So, I thought it'd be nice."

"Oh." My eyes flicked back to Martha Mae's house. What was nice? Christmas?

"If you don't want to because of our situation, I understand," said Nash. "Did you already make Christmas Eve plans with Mowry? Or someone else?"

Wait, what?

"Plans?" Plans sounded like a date. Did Nash ask me out on a date when I wasn't listening? How could I have stopped listening? But he said no dating until our two-year apprenticeship was up. And he didn't actually use the word "dating." Maybe there was a Christmas loophole. What a time to focus on work instead of my love life.

Shizzles, that's not what I meant.

I opened my mouth to speak but couldn't find the words that wouldn't make me sound like a desperate nut job.

"I'll let you think about it," said Nash.

And lost my opportunity.

"Call me when you get back. Drive safe."

He'd hung up. I stared at the phone. Switched to Martha Mae's house. The pregnant woman was leaving, walking back across Martha Mae's yard. Should I call Nash back? Drive home?

But who was the man in Martha Mae's house? It'd only take a moment to find out. Maybe he would know if Krystal had called or talked to Martha Mae. But wait, she'd been arrested three days ago. When did Mrs. Fowler talk to her?

Before she was arrested? If so, must've been just before. So, no way Krystal had contacted Martha Mae. Unless… Did Nash check to see if Krystal had gotten out on bail? When I'd been arrested (Fiancé-Accessory Before the Fact), I'd only been in jail for a day before my initial appearance with the judge. She could have posted bail. We didn't know anything about Krystal.

Although I no longer believed she could be a nun.

Best not to assume anything, I thought. Just in case. Look what happened when I assumed Martha Mae wasn't home. A man had been there. Maybe he was a house sitter. And what if Krystal does get out on bail? I should probably warn Martha Mae that Krystal had been interested in her health.

In answer to my good Samaritanism, the sky opened. The icy drizzle turned into a downpour. I crawled into the backseat of Tiffany's car where she had a variety of miscellaneous goods. I flipped through the debris. Tampons. Mascara. Lotion. Nail polish. Hallelujah, an umbrella. Cracking open the door, I shoved the umbrella toward the sky and opened it. Three spokes were bent, but a half-working umbrella was better than none.

I took a step into the street, slipped, and grabbed the door. Steadied myself as the sleet rained into the car. (What Tiffany did not have in her car was a towel.) Shoved the car door closed, turned (carefully), and shimmied across the road. The umbrella protected my face. My back, however, was soaked by the time I made it onto Martha Mae's porch. Shaking off the umbrella, I set it to the side and prepared my "I'm not wet and cold but happy to meet you" face. It used to be my promo face. Very useful when you do thirty back-to-back interviews during a release.

Past acting experience can be useful when applied discriminately.

The older, bearded man opened the door halfway. "Yes?"

"I'm Maizie Al—" That hadn't worked well with Martha Mae's neighbor. I tried again. "I'm Maizie, and I work for Martha Mae's sister, Celia Fowler, up in Black Pine. Are you a relative of Martha Mae?"

"Why?" His eyebrows knitted and lowered.

Small-town people were a lot more suspicious than I imagined. I thought they'd be more open and trusting, offering me cookies and gossip. Like in The Hallmark Channel's small-town movies. What was up with Halo?

"Mrs. Fowler's granddaughter, Krystal, may try to contact Martha Mae. I wanted to speak to Martha Mae. Is she home?"

"She's resting."

"I see. Did she do a lot of shopping today? With this weather, the shopping must have worn her out." I forced a hearty chuckle. But fell flat. He was not amused. "Can I get your name?"

His gaze shifted behind me.

I glanced over my shoulder but didn't see anything.

"What do you know about Krystal?" he said.

"Are you related? Because I'm—"

"Distantly," he said. "But I know Krystal and Celia Fowler. You can speak plainly."

I wasn't sure if I could speak plainly. I had a flashback to an early *Julia Pinkerton: Teen Detective* episode. Julia's basketball-star boyfriend was involved in a drug ring. She had snuck into the boys' locker room looking for him. His friend, Will, asked more questions than answered. Julia took that as a tipoff and learned Will had been double-crossing Xavier. This man seemed as suspicious as Will.

"Your name wouldn't be Will, by any chance?" I gave him my *Cover-girl* smile — girl-next-door friendly — hoping to relax him.

He shook his head. "No. Are you looking for a Will, too?"

"Not really." Broadening my smile, my teeth gleamed (I hoped) in the porch Christmas lights. The lights had not yet frosted in a coating of ice. "Have you heard from Krystal?"

No reaction from Not-Will.

I rubbed my arms and blew on my mittens. "I'm super cold. Could I come in for a minute?"

Not-Will considered, then opened the door. "Just for a minute. Martha Mae is resting."

"Of course." I quick-stepped past Not-Will, took a fast gander around the living room, and slid a few steps toward the doorway into the hall. "So, Martha Mae's sleeping?"

"Did the gal next door send you?"

"The pregnant one?" I considered his question and took another step back toward the hall. "No. I just saw her leave. Mrs. Fowler sent me."

"But you know the gal next door. The sick one."

"I'm sorry I don't." I half-turned and glanced down the hallway. Light shone through the cracks around the door in a room at the end of the hall. "I'm from Black Pine, not Halo. That's where Mrs. Fowler lives. Anyhoo, could you check to see if Martha Mae is awake? I'd really appreciate it. I'd like to drive home before the weather gets any worse."

He nodded. "Why don't you check out the tree while you wait?"

Odd request but okay. Maybe he or Martha Mae was super proud of their tree-decorating abilities. I wandered to the tree in the far corner of the room, glanced at the colored balls and bubble lights. Spun around.

Not-Will stood right behind me.

I hopped back, bumping the Christmas tree. The tree shook, splashing colored light across his face.

"I thought you were checking on Martha Mae? Tell her I only need to talk a few minutes."

The man nodded and retreated to the hall. He needed a lesson in personal space. Also in creepy house guest behavior.

A door creaked. The man returned.

"Martha Mae's real tired," he said. "She's sleeping. She don't have nothing to do with Krystal anyway. Hasn't seen her in years. But maybe I can help. Have you seen Krystal recently? Her family'd really like to know where she's been keeping herself."

"Me, personally? No. Mrs. Fowler has been looking for Krystal for five years. So sad." I didn't feel comfortable adding our recent news about her arrest. If he were family, he'd find out soon enough. "How are you related to Krystal?"

He shrugged. "Blood's blood. Just about everyone is related in these parts."

Probably true. "And I already forgot your name. What was it again?" Because you didn't tell me in the first place.

"Jay." He folded his arms. "You need to get back to Black Pine. The weather's turning."

"I thought it already turned." I chuckled, and getting no reaction, handed him a Nash Security Solutions card. " If you see or hear from Krystal, can you call me? Please share it with Martha Mae, too. Krystal may be in some trouble, and Mrs. Fowler thought she might turn up in Halo."

"Why's that?" he said. "Krystal's never lived in Halo."

"Krystal asked about Martha Mae."

"Did she now?" He rocked back on his heels.

"Um, yes. Mrs. Fowler really just wants to see Krystal. She's worried about her. It's been five years and—"

"Celia Fowler don't care nothing about Krystal. She didn't take her in when Krystal needed her. She's the reason Krystal is in trouble now." Jay shoved me toward the door. "Now get yourself outta this house and don't come back."

SIX
CHERRY TUCKER

MRS. BOYES'S living room remained lit. I watched Not-Santa's blurry form retreat to the back hall and disappear. The overhead gleam of her living room, spangled with the blinking tree lights, shone against the gloom that had descended between our homes. In comparison, my bedroom felt cold and starkly lit. If Luke ever got off work, I thought it'd be nice to sit in that warm glow with him. Even if I was sick.

When Casey returned, I asked for a string of Christmas lights. If she could find a spare.

"You want a what?" said Casey. "You hate Christmas decorations. You're feverish."

"Maybe so," I said. "But I can't get warm, and I thought…"

I didn't know what I thought. I just wanted a string of lights. And could no longer remember why. "Maybe I am feverish."

"We'll assume so. I ain't going to touch you. Lie down and stop watching Mrs. Boyes's house. It's making you crazy."

"It's the flu."

"But now that you mention it," said Casey. "This house needs a few Christmas touches."

"No."

"You're real sick, and I don't see you making it to the farm on Christmas day. We'll come here. Therefore, we need to bring Christmas with us."

"You know I don't do Christmas."

"You give gifts. You go to church with us. You definitely eat my Christmas dinner every year. That's doing Christmas, ain't it?"

I groaned. "Please don't mention Christmas dinner. I was going to bring Luke to the farm this year. If his family will let him go. But I guess not anymore."

"Put that out of your mind." Casey rubbed her arms. "Just plan on us coming here. I'll take care of everything. But I ain't cooking Christmas dinner without Grandma Jo's Christmas china. And a few other things. You're just going to have to put up with a little Christmas in your house this year."

"No more talk about cooking. Who was that man next door?"

"Mrs. Boyes's nephew. He's visiting her for Christmas. She's fine. Slipped. She's flat on her back."

"You saw her?"

"She was sleeping. Anyway, she can't get up." Casey stretched and rubbed her belly. "I'm having the same problem lately. Nik has to pull me out of bed. Also out of Mr. Max's hot tub. But that was worth it—"

"You're going to make me sick again."

"All this talk makes me want to call Nik. And I need to check on… something," said Casey. "You rest."

Casey left and I turned my attention to the window. Sleet pounded the tin roof and frosted the edges of my window. I let the rain lull me for a moment but blinked at movement in the house next door. The nephew had reappeared from the back hall and strode across the living room.

I glanced toward my bedroom door, heard Casey's murmur, and turned my attention back to Mrs. Boyes's house.

He'd opened the door partially, blocking my view. A minute or two passed, the door widened, and a young woman walked in. She wore expensive-looking knee-high boots, jeans, and a puffy silver coat. Looked like she'd gotten the worse end of the weather. Long, red braids plastered to her jacket. She didn't look like Halo, although she looked vaguely familiar. Hard to tell through the wavy glass of our wet windows. She had that long-legged model way of walking that didn't match the heavy country trod of folks around here.

While she talked — and her mouth didn't seem to close — the woman openly looked around the room and peeked into the hallway. Pretty brazen for a guest, at least in my neck of the woods. With that swishy walk of hers, she moved toward the tree, and I got a better look.

Even drenched like a drowned rat, she was pretty. More than pretty, if I was honest. Not Shawna Branson-pretty, either. Too pretty for Halo, that was for damn sure. Not the kind of beauty I liked to paint, though. Her features were more suited for a camera lens than a painter's canvas.

Maybe the flu was making me catty. But what was someone like her doing in Mrs. Boyes's house? Looking around like that?

The nephew had crossed the living room in three, quick strides to stand behind the woman. Sweat broke out on my forehead and my hands clenched. Hadn't this happened before? Santa and the reindeer? My heart sped up. I hollered at the woman. Stupidly. She couldn't hear me. I could barely hear myself. My throat was parched, so my voice barely rose above a hoarse, exaggerated whisper.

Before the nephew reached for the tree lights, the out-of-towner pivoted and found herself eyeball-to-eyeball with the man. I couldn't see her reaction, but she backed into the tree making the lights shudder and flicker.

My stomach rolled, kicked my other organs to the side, and crawled up my throat. I made a quick passage to the bathroom.

When I returned, the beauty was gone. I added the movie star to my sketchbook and flipped back through the drawings, trying to sort the oddness in the house next door.

SEVEN
MAIZIE ALBRIGHT

#EVERYBODY'SWAITINGFOR THEMENWITHTHEBAGS

IN THE WAFFLE HUT, I held a fresh cup of coffee. And (if you want to get technical) I ordered another red velvet waffle. I told myself I was preparing for the drive back to the mountains. I was also piecing together what I knew.

Mrs. Fowler wanted Krystal to come home. Every year for the last five years. Krystal asked for money and never came home. But this year, Mrs. Fowler might have been Krystal's one phone call. The money she'd wired could have been for Krystal's bail.

Jay — whoever he was — had said Krystal was in trouble because of Mrs. Fowler. Because Celia Fowler had abandoned her and not cared for her? Or did it have to do with Krystal's recent arrest? For a distant relative, he knew a lot about Krystal, Mrs. Fowler, and Martha Mae.

And why hadn't Mrs. Fowler taken Krystal into her home if her mother had been a junkie?

That really bothered me. I didn't have a grandmother. Daddy's mother had died when he was in college. Cancer. And Vicki's had been hit by a bus sometime when I was a toddler. Which always unsettled me, so I didn't like to think about it. Vicki never encouraged me to ask about her. I'd imagined my dead grandmothers as a cross between Mrs. Werther and Mrs. Butterworth.

Maybe because I spent a lot of my childhood forced to resist candy and carbs.

A pony-tailed waitress stood before me, coffee carafe in hand. "Warm you up?"

I wish. The last time I'd been this cold had been Sundance. I had been invited to a cast party and ended the night passed out in a snowbank.

"Thanks." I shoved the cup toward her. "I guess it's pretty quiet today because of the weather."

She nodded. "That and the bank robbery. Spooked everyone."

"Robbery?" I tipped my head back to get a good look at the server. "What happened?"

"Local bank. Everyone was cashing in their Christmas bonus today, too, since most are off work tomorrow and Christmas."

"Wow," I said. "Just like in the movies."

She gave me a look that told me she thought I was about as smart as my waffle. "Cop was taken hostage, too."

"Oh no," I said. "Is he or she okay?"

"He. They've still got him as far as I know. Been trying to listen in on the local radio, but they don't like to interrupt the Christmas music for news much. And they don't let us keep a TV in here."

"Why don't you use your phone?"

She gave me another look.

"I hope the police will save him," I said. "That's just terrible."

"Local boy, too." She shook her head. "His girlfriend is something else. Damn shame on both counts."

"Sorry to hear about his girlfriend. Still, terrible."

She refilled my coffee.

"By the way," I asked. "Do you know Martha Mae Boyes? An older lady living in Halo?"

"We've got a lot of older ladies living in Halo." She gave me the side-eye. "Why?"

OMG, these Halo people were suspicious. "I'm working for her sister, Celia Fowler, who lives in Black Pine. Her sister called Martha Mae to say I was coming. I left Martha Mae a message myself, but she wasn't at home when I arrived. I waited, but now there's a man at her house. Jay. Jay said she's resting, but I don't know. It just seemed odd."

The waitress set her hands on her hips. "I don't know Miss Martha. But I doubt she'd get up to anything odd around here. Although it's been an odd day all around. This weather is terrible. And a robbery. Just don't seem like Christmas."

"Maybe it'll snow," I said helpfully.

"Good Lord, I hope not."

When the waitress had returned to lean against the counter and talk to the cook, I slid to the end of my booth and flipped open my phone.

"Where are you?" Nash's normal low rumble had pitched higher. "Did you slide off the road? I checked the reports and Atlanta's a mess. Do you need my help?"

"I'm in a Waffle Hut. I haven't left Halo."

He gusted a sigh. "Don't wait much longer. Get your coffee to go. Take it slow. I'm not sure if you should risk local highways. Stick to the interstate but don't go through Atlanta if you can avoid it."

"You're worried about me." My toes curled inside my boots.

"Of course, I'm worried about you." He'd been pacing because his heavy tromp suddenly stopped. "There's weather."

I grinned at my phone. Why did I love that he was worried? Vicki would say it was chauvinist — women doing it for themselves, you know — but I thought it adorbs. Renata would probably have something to say about that, too. "Father absence syndrome." But I didn't care. Totally adorbs.

Also, I was totally off track. Still sitting in an overheated Waffle Hut in the middle of nowhere with a suspicious man in an elderly lady's house. I told myself to focus. "Here's the thing."

"What happened?"

"There's a man at Martha Mae's house. He said Martha Mae was resting and didn't want to talk. Kind of strange, right?"

"I don't know Martha Mae, so I can't say for sure."

"Just believe me, he was strange. And he said Mrs. Fowler was the reason Krystal was in trouble. Nash, Mrs. Fowler didn't take Krystal in."

"I'm not following." He paused. "Trouble now or trouble earlier?"

"I don't know. I'm worried."

"Let's get you home, then worry. I don't like this weather."

"Nobody does. I don't think I'm ready to leave just yet. I don't like what's going on here. Did you ever check into Mrs. Fowler? Did Krystal have an arraignment yet? Could she be out on bail?"

I waited a beat. "Nash?"

"I never vetted Celia Fowler," he spoke slowly. "And I only looked up the arrest. I didn't check to see if Krystal had made bail. Dammit." Nash swore again. "Miss Albright. Maizie. It's not our problem."

"Can you do some research? I'd really like to know what Jay meant by Mrs. Fowler causing Krystal trouble. Why wouldn't a grandmother take in her grandchild if she didn't have a father and the mother was a junkie? Why would a grandmother not help her granddaughter?" I checked my rising pitch and lowered my voice. "And what about Martha Mae? She knew I was coming. Why wouldn't she talk to me? Nash, I'm—"

"I know. You're worried." The deep voice steadied into a soothing murmur. "Listen, give me a minute. I'll see if I can find anything about Mrs. Fowler for you. You might need to camp out in Halo. Is there a motel?"

"I can't afford a motel."

"We'll expense it."

Wow. Nash didn't expense anything that couldn't be billed to a customer. I felt a flush of heat in the back of my neck. "But I think I should continue to watch Martha Mae's house."

"What are the roads like?"

I glanced out the window next to me, watching the wind pelt icy rain against Tiffany's Pontiac. "Not too bad. And it's cozy in Tiffany's car."

"Don't forget to fill it up. Sometimes gas stations in small towns close down for the holidays and bad weather."

"Right." File that under things I never thought about. "Good idea. And Nash?"

"Yes, Miss Albright?" His low drawl caressed my ears.

"If I'm late getting back, I'm sorry."

"Better to be safe than sorry, right?"

"Yes." The flush heated my cheeks now. "I meant late for that other thing you mentioned earlier. For when I returned…"

He cleared his throat. "We won't worry about that now."

Hells. "We won't? But—"

"Let me work on Mrs. Fowler and Krystal. I'll call you back."

"You will?"

"Always." He cleared his throat. "I mean, of course. You have a phone charger for that car?"

"Yes." I didn't want to hang up. His voice was making me forget how wet and cold and miserable I was about to be. "Are you in the office? Is Lamar with you?"

"I guess we're predictable."

I smiled. "I like predictable. My therapist Renata says it's because I didn't have a lot of stability…never mind. But I'm glad Lamar is with you."

"Why?"

The heat rushed from my cheeks to my chest and prickled my neck. I didn't want Nash to be alone during the holidays. But telling him felt too personal. Too intimate. For now, anyway. "Um, tell Lamar he should try a red velvet for the donut shop. It's very seasonal."

He took a beat to digest the comment. "All right. Anything else, Miss Albright?"

"There was a bank robbery in town."

"In Black Pine?" I heard him tromp and the creak of his noisy door. "Lamar. Bank robbery."

Nash must have been speaking in his office with the door shut. Odd. Normally, he let Lamar hear everything.

"No, here in Halo. Surprising for a little town, don't you think? But the waitress said most people cash their Christmas bonuses today. I guess the robbers knew it. They took a local cop hostage."

"Were they arrested? Is the officer okay?"

"I don't know. The waitress didn't have an update, but last she heard, they still had the officer."

"Sounds like a standoff. It'll get ugly. The holidays are always rough for law enforcement and to combine this with the weather? Damn. I'll check the news. Atlanta might've picked up the story. Wherever that bank is, stay clear."

"I'm headed back to watch Martha Mae's house. Some other neighbors are home. I might talk to them and see if they know anything about the man in her house. He gave me bad vibes."

"Vibes." A door closed. He must have reentered his office. "It's good to trust your instincts when feeling someone out but don't jump to any conclusions. And don't rush into a situation. Just keep watch."

"But—"

"We both have a job to do. I'm going to do mine and get back to you. And when I call, I expect to hear the same from you. No — What do you call it? — no improv. This man at Martha Mae's house, Jay, does he have a last name?"

"He wasn't forthcoming with Jay, let alone a surname. That's part of the bad vibes."

"All the more reason to leave him be. You have a bad habit of following instincts instead of procedure."

"But my instincts are usually right. I've got good instincts."

"They're also dangerous. If you have bad vibes, stay away from this man, Maizie. Your bad vibes make me crazy."

That almost sounded hot. But admitting that made me sound desperate, so forget it.

DANGEROUS VIBES ASIDE, I felt it couldn't hurt to speak to the other neighbors, particularly the home of the pregnant woman. She'd gone to Martha Mae's house and spoken to Jay. These small towns were tight. Surely, they'd give me some insight into Jay's relationship with Martha Mae. Or some background into Jay. He knew Krystal and Mrs. Fowler. But something wasn't right with him.

I tried the pregnant woman first. When I returned to Martha Mae's street — fishtailing over progressively slick roads — the truck was still gone, but the old Firebird remained. I took it as a good sign and pulled in behind the Firebird. The broken umbrella made a half-hearted fight against the rain then blew inside out. I slid-walked up the drive. Shivering, I rang the doorbell and hopped from foot to foot. Although in need of paint and repair, the porch was clean. A small, brightly colored table sat between two rocking chairs, also hand-painted with abstract designs and flowers.

But no wreath, no porch lights, no Santa Snoopy. I wondered what the other neighbors thought. The absence of decorations disturbed me. In this town of wooden nativities and inflatable polar bears, it seemed a flagrant disregard of holiday spirit.

The pregnant woman answered the door. She wore a tank top that barely covered her baby bump. It read, "One of Santa's Ho's." Vicki would not approve. I wasn't going to judge. Maybe with the pregnancy, she had no time to put up a tree or decorations and chose ironic holiday slogans in maternity wear instead.

"Who're you?" she said.

"I'm Maizie. I work for a private investigator in Black Pine. Mrs. Boyes's sister hired me to check on Martha Mae."

Proud of my ability to introduce myself and my mission more coherently, I continued. "Mrs. Fowler, the sister, is worried about Martha Mae." Which wasn't really a lie. "She didn't answer her door earlier today although she was expecting me. And there's a man there now — Jay — but Mrs. Fowler didn't expect him. I was watching the house and saw you spoke to Jay, too. Do you know him?"

"I'm Casey." Her brown eyes narrowed, and she flipped her long chestnut mane behind her shoulder. "Interestin'."

"Can I come in?" I blew on my mittens.

"You can, but I don't know if you want to. My sister's got the flu. This house is probably what gave it to her. It's barely warmer in here than out there. There're leaks, too. I've got her paint pot sitting on the kitchen floor, catching drips. She won't move, though. Cherry's stubborn like that."

"Okay?" Was that an invitation or not? "I'll take my chances on the flu. You look warm enough."

"I'm hotter than a brick oven. You could bake a pizza on me." She stepped aside to allow me through the door. "My husband's sort-of Russian. Close enough to Russian for around here. Anyway, he says Slavic pregnancies are always like this. It's real cold up there in Russia. I have no idea if that's true, but I've been sweating up a storm since the second trimester."

"Congratulations?" I glanced around the room. The paint-splattered wooden floors looked original as did the plaster walls. The room was mostly bare but for a vintage fainting couch, an easel, and an old roll-top desk. The Pasadena antiquers would've had a field day. A series of portraits covered the walls. I recognized the pregnant woman in one. "Who did these?"

"My sister, Cherry. She's an artist."

"The one with the flu?"

Casey nodded, gripped her lower back, and eased onto the fainting couch. "What's it like to work for a private investigator? We don't have anything like that around here. Sometimes Cherry looks into criminal problems for friends, but she usually gets into trouble with the sheriff's office for that."

"It's wonderful." I clasped my mittens together, then wrung my hands. "Well, mostly it's kind of boring. Due diligence work. Security systems. Serving subpoenas. Maybe not any more boring than other jobs. I don't know. My previous career hasn't given me a lot of experience with other jobs. But right now, we're working on a missing granddaughter case. That's what I always dreamed of."

"You've always dreamed of a missing granddaughter?"

"Helping people find missing persons."

"I hope you don't get too many of those." She wrinkled her nose. "My uncle is sheriff. I've heard about crime my whole life. It's horrible. Especially what they're dealing with today."

I checked my excitement. "I heard about the bank robbery. Did they arrest the suspects yet?"

Casey shook her head and lowered her voice. "Far as I know, they're holed up in the bank with one of our deputies. He offered himself in exchange for the customers they held hostage."

"Oh, my God."

"The deputy's my sister's man." She folded her arms over her bump. "Keep your voice down. She doesn't know."

"Oh, no." My hand flew to cover my mouth.

"We don't want to tell her," she whispered. "She's already sick with a high fever. Seeing crazy stuff. Knowing Cherry, she'll crawl out of bed, drive to the bank, and get herself killed."

"That poor woman."

"The sheriff's waiting on a special team who works with hostage situations. FBI, too. They're coming over from Atlanta, but the weather has slowed everything down. They want to be real careful with this group. I guess they've had a lot of experience in armed robbery. Warrants out on all of 'em. They're stuck inside right now. Going on two hours." Casey bit her lip, and her eyes shone. "They shot Melanie when she triggered the alarm. She's a cashier. Part-time, too. Sumbitches. We'll get 'em, though. Luke's got a good head. He's ex-Army. And we've got them surrounded."

I hoped the deputy would be okay. The robbers would be desperate to get away.

"We're worried, though," she continued. "They won't put Luke on the phone and have threatened to kill him if the sheriff doesn't provide an escape. Their getaway driver took off when the alarm went off, near as we can figure. That was the last I heard. Pearl's gone to the Tru-Buy, hoping to get more information. I don't think Uncle Will can wait for the Atlanta team to get here."

Tears pricked my eyes, and I pinched the skin between my thumb and finger. "I'm so sorry. I hate to be bothering you at a time like this."

"Y'all want something hot to drink? Cherry don't have much, but I can rustle you up something." Casey pushed herself into standing. "I don't know why I'm telling you this. I guess I'm just desperate to talk about it, and I can't say a word to Cherry."

"Don't make anything. I just came from the Waffle Hut." I hesitated, hating to bring up the neighbors with the anxiety she must already feel. "About Martha Mae next door. Do you know her well? Or Jay?"

"The nephew? Cherry thought something was going on over there, too, but she's half-crazy with that fever. Jay's staying with Mrs. Boyes for the holiday. She hurt her back."

"Oh. Nephew." Nash was right about me jumping to conclusions. Again. But then, why didn't Jay tell me he was a nephew? Didn't he say distantly related? "I guess you know Jay."

"Naw. Never seen him before. But I went over there to see what was going on. I'm going to make them a casserole soon as I get home."

"Do you know Krystal, Martha Mae's grand-niece? She's the missing granddaughter. I was supposed to talk to Mrs. Boyes about that today."

"Never heard of her."

I moved toward the door. "I really appreciate your help. You'll probably see my car on the street. Until I know more, I'm going to watch Martha Mae's house. My partner's checking to see if Krystal's out."

"Out?"

"She was arrested three days ago. We don't know if she's in jail or out on bail."

Casey shivered and crossed her arms. "Too many criminals running around here for my liking."

"Don't worry. If I see anything suspicious, I'll call it in."

"Good luck getting anybody to help. They're all over at the bank."

EIGHT
MAIZIE ALBRIGHT

#OLITTLETOWNOFHALO

THE OTHER NEIGHBOR, Josiah Sweeton, knew nothing about Krystal or Martha Mae's alleged nephew, Jay. I say alleged because there was something fishy going on over there. Back in California, I knew a few "nephews" who helped their "aunts" or "uncles" for whatever reason. You learn not to ask a lot of questions in those cases. You just don't want to know. But this wasn't Beverly Hills. This was Halo, Georgia. And in Beverly Hills, the "nephews" were younger and better looking than Jay.

Possibly Martha Mae was into something weird. Not judging. But Jay knew Krystal. Krystal was not a nun (as far as I knew). And it sounded like nobody else around here knew Jay or Krystal, but they knew Martha Mae. If Martha Mae was into something weird, I felt certain the neighbors would've hinted at it. Or at least made the quote sign when stating, "nephew."

Therefore, I was worried about Mrs. Boyes. And she didn't answer her phone. If her back was out, maybe she couldn't pick up. But wouldn't Jay check to find out who kept leaving voicemails?

I moved Tiffany's car to a less obtrusive spot down the street where I could keep an eye on Martha Mae's house. Using a pile of napkins that I had taken from the Waffle Hut, I dried myself as best I could, cranked the heater, and watched the house. Checked my phone six times to make sure it was still charged. Then checked again to see if I had bars. And a dial tone. Played Christmas music. Imagined warm thoughts…

Maybe of me and Nash under the mistletoe.

But I won't go there. Tired of waiting, I called Nash.

"Any news?" I said.

"I can't find anything about the robbery," said Nash. "Maybe the local law enforcement is keeping the story under wraps."

"Maybe they captured the criminals, and the deputy is home. Everyone is worried. What about Mrs. Fowler and Krystal?"

"You were right. Krystal was arrested on December twentieth. Petty theft charge. Didn't have to make bail. At her preliminary hearing, the charges were dropped. Guess she hadn't changed her tune. She didn't have much of a record, surprisingly."

I chewed my lip. "So, she's out."

"Mrs. Fowler doesn't have a record. But her husband did. Hinky."

Hinky was Nash-speak for suspicious.

"I also checked on Martha Mae," he said. "She's clean. Married someone from down around Halo. He worked at a sweet tea factory. She's a widow. No kids."

"So sad. And now she has to spend Christmas with an alleged nephew. Poor Martha Mae."

He gave me a minute to get over the state of Martha Mae's life. "I don't know where this Jay fellow comes in. If he's a nephew, he's got to be from the husband's side. We know he's not on Martha Mae's side since it's just the two sisters."

"Right? And he's not a 'nephew.'" I made quote signs and realized it didn't work on a phone. At least a phone that didn't have video chat.

"I thought you said he's a nephew," said Nash.

"Never mind. But if Jay was a relative on Martha Mae's husband's side, why would he know Krystal?"

"It's hinky." He paused. "You should come home. But now you can't."

"I can't?"

"The storm's come to the mountains. And the rain you just had is snow here. It's icing over something terrible."

"Yay, white Christmas for Remi." I smiled, then frowned. "Oh no, I've got to get home tomorrow. Remi is expecting me."

"Tomorrow. Get a motel room. They'll scoop tomorrow. At least in the mountains."

"It's still early."

"I don't like you being all the way over there." He cleared his throat. "I don't have a good feeling about Mrs. Fowler. "

"Mrs. Fowler didn't help Krystal when Krystal needed her."

"That and her husband used to rob banks."

"Used to?"

"He's dead. Died in prison."

"Oh." I felt some sympathy for Mrs. Fowler even though I still felt she should have been a better grandmother. She had her own baggage. But still. "At least we know he's not involved with this bank robbery because that'd be super hinky, right?"

No sound.

"Nash?"

"Right." He took a breath. "Find a motel room. I'm going to do more research."

HALO DIDN'T HAVE MOTELS. Or inns. Or stables. I didn't want to travel to another town. I was also concerned with bank robbery traffic. There wasn't traffic in Halo, but with my luck, I'd get stuck. The neighbors didn't seem to care that I parked in front of their house. Or notice. The Hallmark Channel had given me the impression that small towns were full of nosy neighbors. Nosy but caring. Why weren't Martha Mae's neighbors paying any attention to me?

Not that I was complaining. I didn't want to get run out of town. I wanted to know that sweet Martha Mae — whom I'm sure would've made a wonderful grandmother if given a chance — was really flat on her back.

Not that I wished her a back injury. It'd just make me feel better.

All was quiet at Martha Mae's. The lights were still on in the living room. The tree still blinked. But there was no other movement. What was Jay doing? Taking a nap? The other houses showed signs of life. TVs lit front rooms. Lights flicked on and off. Shadows crossed before windows. But at Martha Mae's, nothing. The temperature continued to drop, but the rain had stopped. I took it as a sign to get out and explore Martha Mae's again. Also, my legs were cramping because I had curled them underneath myself to stay warm.

Outside the car, I unbent and did a quick yoga sun salutation. No sun appeared. Just moist, frigid air. Not a fav. But it cleared my lungs and mind. I needed to get inside the house. To see if Martha Mae was okay, I told myself. That was legit. Right? Without a car, it was difficult to tell if Jay was even home. Martha Mae's Buick still sat in the drive, but judging by the coat of ice, it hadn't moved since lunchtime.

I scooted across the street and down the sidewalk toward Martha Mae's. The sidewalk was slick. The grass crunchy. On Martha Mae's porch, I peeked into the living room window. No movement except for the bubbling lights of the tree. I knocked on the door. Quietly. Tried the knob.

Locked.

No one home. Except for Martha Mae, if her back was really out. I knew where Martha Mae kept her key.

I hesitated on the porch. The wind rattled the frosted Christmas lights. I was totally overstepping my bounds. But sometimes a girl's just got to break and enter. To help the elderly. At Christmas.

A truck roared up the street and turned at the drive into the pregnant woman's sister's house. I backed against the front door. Corrected my flattened stance to a casual lean. Waited for a minute. Sauntered to the edge of the porch to examine the Christmas lights. Heard a door slam next door. Walked back to the door and waited another minute. And scurried to the porch steps to steal — I mean borrow — the key.

NINE
CHERRY TUCKER

"THERE'S something weird going on in Mrs. Boyes's house," I told Pearl. She'd returned with weapons for battling the flu. Cans of Lysol, bottles of Tylenol, and applesauce.

"It's all in your head," said Pearl. "You're burning up with fever and we've got to get that temperature down. If you don't cool off, I'm tossing you in a tub of ice."

My skin broke into goose pimples. "You try to throw me in a tub of ice and I'll fight you." I pulled out a fist and returned it under the blanket. My teeth chattered. "Plus, I've got the Remington under my bed. Be warned."

She waved away my threat. "You can barely sit up. You don't have the strength to pull out a shotgun, let alone the *cajones*. You want to exchange threats, I'll bring Snickerdoodle over and park her in your kitchen."

Snickerdoodle was Pearl's evil goat, the terror of Grandpa Ed's barnyard. Her offspring were devil's spawn. They hated me and my truck. Snickerdoodle scared the bejeesus out of me, but I'd never admit that to Pearl.

I fell back against my pillow. "I probably have the goat flu as it is. This feels worse than the human flu."

"Goats are too smart to get the flu. That's for chickens and pigs." Pearl shoved a green Gatorade toward me. "You need fluids."

My stomach cramped. I pointed a trembling finger at my window, hoping to get Pearl off the subject of fluids. "A woman was in Mrs. Boyes's house while you were out. An out-of-towner. The nephew invited her in and she looked around like she was taking inventory."

"Martha Mae's house? Of all the nerve." Pearl dropped the Gatorade on my bed and stomped to the window. "Who is this woman prying into poor Martha Mae's house?"

"I don't know," I said. "She looked like a movie star. Except wet."

"Everyone's wet today." Pearl glanced back at me. "Are you sure you saw this woman? Not another hallucination?"

"Pretty sure." I struggled to push myself up and collapsed against my pillow. "The nephew let her in. She looked around and then left."

Pearl turned back to the window. "What's a movie star doing in Martha Mae's house? What did she say?"

"I'll go over and ask Mrs. Boyes. As soon as I'm over this flu."

"Don't get sassy with me." Pearl tapped her chin. "I wonder what Gertie Sweetley will say about this. She's Martha Mae's best friend, but a terrible gossip. We do the bingo together."

"Maybe you should ask her yourself."

"Is this nephew staying for Christmas?"

"I hope so." I closed my eyes. "Casey said Mrs. Boyes's back is out."

"Casey said?" Pearl whipped around. "What does Casey know about this?"

"I asked her to go check on Mrs. Boyes. Because of… you know, what I thought I saw."

"Casey should not be walking around in this weather. She's just about nekkid."

"Casey's used to being 'just about nekkid,'" I mumbled. "It's her signature style."

"She is carrying your niece or nephew. Casey could slip and fall. It is getting icier than a Tastee Freeze out there."

"Sorry," I muttered. "You're right."

"I'll go over there myself. If Martha Mae's back is out, she's going to need help. That nephew probably don't know up from down."

"I don't think that's a good id—"

Pearl was gone before I could get the words out.

TEN
MAIZIE ALBRIGHT

#RUNRUNRUDOLPH

I RETRIEVED the key from under the poinsettia. Shoved it quietly (as possible) into the lock. Cracked the door and whispered a "Hello? Mrs. Boyes? Martha Mae?"

Nada. Maybe due to the extra quiet nature of my call. But still. I took it as an all-clear sign.

Tiptoeing, I sped through the living room and peeked into the dining room. Glanced into the empty kitchen. Smelled like gingerbread. More evidence that if only Martha Mae'd had children, she'd get the grandmother-of-the-year award. Peeked into the hall. A double row of closed doors. I took a deep breath.

Here's where it got tricky. I had bad luck with closed doors.

I crept down the hall and placed an ear near the edge of the first door. No sound. Sniffed. Caught a hint of lavender. Rotated the knob slowly.

Bathroom. Papered in pink and purple flowers. And decorated for Christmas. Martha Mae had a Grinch toilet seat cover. Adorbs.

I left the bathroom open and sidled to the next door. This was the room where earlier I had seen lights. A low murmur, then music blared through the closed door. The volume lowered. Someone watched TV. The commercials were always louder than the shows. Maybe Martha Mae? Should I pop in? I didn't want to scare the woman. I was just looking for evidence that Jay was legit. And I needed to warn Martha Mae about Krystal.

Hello, Maizie. You're also trespassing. And on probation. Trespassing is not cool with probation officers.

Worrying my lip, I moved toward the other side of the hall. Listened. Couldn't hear anything. A bell ping-ponged. I froze before the closed door.

Doorbell. Shizzles. And there it went again.

I sensed a stirring behind the door with the TV. I yanked open the door before me and darted inside. Bedroom. I waited for my eyes to adjust to the lack of light. No one called out or moved. That was good. My heart slowed from sprint to marathon beat. I rubbed a mitten on the back of my neck.

One silver lining to trespassing: the adrenaline kick sure warmed a body up.

The bell rang again. Knocking commenced.

I placed my eye against the crack in the door. Saw nothing but the closed door opposite.

"Yoo-hoo, Martha Mae?" A woman called from the front of the house. Her voice grew louder with each word. "Y'all home? It's Pearl. I'm visiting Cherry next door."

Craptastic. I had left the door unlocked. Who was Pearl?

"I understand your nephew is there. Maybe he's gone now. I just wanted to check on you. I know you can't get up. I'll come to you."

The door across the hall opened. I squinted through the crack, but my view was blocked. Someone hurried down the hall. An exchange began between Pearl and Jay.

Holy shiz. A chill crawled up my neck. Jay was home. He could've caught me roaming the hall. My heart hammered against my ribs. Back to sprint. And I was now perspiring. I needed to get out of this house.

What in the hellsbah was I thinking? House-crashing some poor grandma and her nephew?

But with Pearl occupying Jay, wouldn't this be a good opportunity to check on Martha Mae? Just in case my intuition had been correct? Jay sounded intent on keeping Pearl from seeing her friend. Wasn't that weird?

So hard to judge weird in a town I didn't know. But I couldn't leave Martha Mae without checking on her first.

I slipped out the bedroom door. Poked my head into the room opposite where Jay had just exited. Looked like a master bedroom. A small

TV on top of a dresser provided the only light in the cavernous room. The volume was almost muted. Curtains had been pulled across the shaded windows. I squinted into the dark. The bed faced the front of the house, but the room behind it jutted out from the hall, blocking my view of the bed other than the foot. There was a shape on the bed, but I couldn't make out if it were a person or bedding.

"Martha Mae?" I whispered. "Are you in there? Are you okay?"

The voices in the front room climbed. Pearl was arguing with Jay about hot compresses and his apparent ignorance of the subject.

I took a step into the room, inching along the wall. "Martha Mae? Your sister sent me. I left you a bunch of messages. Has your niece Krystal been here? You need to know she might show at your house and she's been in some trouble."

Why didn't Martha Mae say anything? Was she hiding?

Of course. She probably thought I was a crazy person.

"I'll just take a second." Pearl's voice had grown louder. "And let me peek into your kitchen pantry to see what y'all need. I'm sure you haven't thought of everything, son. Are you prepared to ride out this storm?"

Holy Shizzolis. Jay and Pearl were going to find me in Martha Mae's bedroom. I froze against the bedroom wall. Inched back toward the door.

"What's that?" said Pearl. "What're you doing?"

Where was Pearl? In the kitchen? How was I going to explain myself? I peeked into the hall. Empty. I darted back to the other bedroom. Closed the door and leaned against it, panting.

OMG, I ran like three steps, and I'm panting?

Focus Maizie. When they go into the bedroom to visit Martha Mae, get the hells out of the house. Martha Mae didn't want your help.

Why did I still have the feeling there was something odd going on? Was Martha Mae even there?

A loud bang shook the walls. My heart leaped from my chest to my throat. Something heavy thudded against the floor.

What in the holy shiz was that?

I clapped my hand over my mouth to keep from crying out. It sounded like a piece of furniture had been knocked over. More than one. A dining set? A refrigerator? I placed my ear to the door. What was that sound? Were they moving furniture?

Pearl wasn't talking. She had talked the entire time she was here. Why wasn't she talking?

Okay. Loud Pearl was now totally silent. Martha Mae was also quiet. And weird Jay was somewhere in the house.

OMG.

"Do something, dumbass," said my snarky, inner Julia Pinkerton.

I turned on the overhead light and glanced around the bedroom. A host of Santa dolls dressed in long underwear decorated the flat surfaces. Quilts covered the walls. A box of gift bags lay on the bed. Martha Mae wrapped presents in here. Scissors. She'll have scissors. I pawed through the tissue paper and ribbons. Found a box of candy canes. Grabbed a stick.

What was I going to do with a candy cane? Focus, Maizie.

I shoved the candy cane into my pocket and rummaged through the box. No scissors.

Seriously Martha Mae? You never used wrapping paper? Sometimes it's nice to have a box wrapped in ribbon and not just a gift shoved in a bag with a piece of tissue paper.

Maizie, stop judging this poor grandma. She could have arthritis, for God's sake. You're just panicking.

The bedside table held a Santa in a rocking chair, hand on his stomach, and eyes closed. Long Winter's Nap Santa. No scissors. I opened the dresser drawers. Quilts. Folded material. Material cut into squares. Another drawer of material. This time in rolls.

Martha Mae sewed stuff. She must have scissors. Something sharp.

Another drawer revealed rows and rows of thread. One roll of masking tape. The narrow drawers on top held tiny boxes. Straight pins. Tiny gold safety pins. Needles. In various sizes but all small and slender.

OMG, Martha Mae. Unless I had a blow dart these sharp objects were useless.

I broke off the hook of the candy cane, tore off a bunch of masking tape, and wrapped the tape around the stick. Stared at the masked stick in my hand.

In my head, Julia Pinkerton laughed. Seriously? What are you going to do with that?

I shoved the candy cane back into my pocket.

Taking a deep yoga breath, I forced myself to calm. I was jumping to conclusions, just like Nash had warned. Of course, he'd also told me to do nothing but watch. Which is why I had left the phone in the car.

Craptastic. My phone was in the car.

I returned to the door. Listened. The furniture-moving sounds had stopped. All quiet. Placed my hand on the doorknob. Said a quick prayer. Rotated the knob. Heard a door slam on the other side of the house.

Took my hand off the knob, turned off the light, and set my back against the door. Blood hammered inside my ears. Sweat pooled beneath my beanie.

My eyes darted around Martha Mae's craft storage/guest room. In the dark, I felt six pairs of Santa eyes watching me. Except for Long Winter's Nap Santa whose eyes were closed.

Faint light rimmed the window.

I ran to the window, grabbed the string for the shade, and ran the louvers to the top. The window looked newish. Easy to open. There was a screen, but that could be removed. I unlatched the window, pushed it as high as it would go. Cold air whistled past me. I squeezed the screen's spring latches. Gave it a push, up and out. The screen struck something and fell to the ground outside. I stuck my head through the opening. Wind rushed past me, chafing my cheeks. There was a bush below the window. Covered in net lights.

At least the neighbors behind Martha Mae's house couldn't witness my escape. I could just make out their lights past a stand of trees in Martha Mae's backyard. If this were the side of the house, the artist's home next door was spitting distance. Silver lining.

The window was waist-high. I threw a leg up. With an over loud thud, my boot heel hit the sill and scuffed the white paint. Wind blew into the room, rattling the paper bags and ruffling the tissue paper. I turned and hoisted my seat onto the ledge, grabbed the window frame, and inched my butt through the window. When my back hit air, I angled my sit and bent my left leg. I was not going through this window backward. No trust fall into a bush. I didn't know the bush, let alone want to get tangled in a bunch of netted lights. Martha Mae had put a lot of work into Christmas-fying her house and I didn't want to screw it up.

Poor Martha Mae.

With one butt cheek in the open air and the other wedged against the window frame, I eased my left foot onto the ledge and wiggled my bent leg toward the opening. Bent the right leg and got both feet onto the ledge. My knees threatened to hit my chin. I scooted to turn toward the open air.

The bedroom door creaked.

I pushed off the window and fell into the bush. Face first. Tangled with the lights and rolled toward the house, pulling them with me. Wrapped in net lighting, I squeezed between the bush and the house. The tiny lights blinded me. And totally lit my whole body. I might as well have a blinking neon arrow pointing toward my hiding spot. I yanked on the cord and pulled a net off the next bush. Scrabbled with the net to push the lights off my face. Pulled off my mitten, grabbed a tiny bulb, and twisted. The bulb popped out.

The entire back of the house went dark.

I'll fix that later, Martha Mae.

I dropped the bulb. And lost my mitten.

Never mind, Martha Mae.

Above me, something hit the window. I looked up. Two dark hands silhouetted against the white frame. Rolled in net lighting, I flattened against the house and held my breath. A shape appeared in the window. Jay leaned out, craning his neck right and left. He retreated. The window shut with a slam.

On the frigid, soggy ground, I tried not to think about the icy mud oozing up my sides and coating my coat, jeans, and boots. I waited what seemed like hours — realistically, maybe thirty seconds — then wriggled from behind the bush. Fought the net lighting. I slithered out. Kicked the lighting behind the bush.

Then ran toward the house next door.

ELEVEN

CHERRY TUCKER

FROM MY BED, I studied the scene through the window. The movie star had returned. Uninvited. Skulking. At least that's what it looked like. No one let her in. She snuck in. Skittered through Martha Mae's living room and disappeared.

Dammit. What was she up to? Should I call the police? That's a B and E if there ever was one. Was she going to rob Martha Mae?

I glanced at the phone on my bedside table. Call 9-1-1? Maybe get Casey to do it this time. They were going to think I was like that shepherd boy who pranked the villagers with wolf stories. Even though I wasn't goofing off. Something funny was going on at Mrs. Boyes's house.

"Case." My voice warbled, frail and thin. Lord, I hated this weakness.

Casey appeared at the bedroom door. She held a string of lights in her hand.

"Found lights. And a little tree. You'd shoved Great Gam's boxes in the back of the guest room closet," she said. "Where do you want them?"

I ignored her and focused on the window opposite. "Something is going on in that house again."

"I'm going to put some lights up in here. It'll make you feel better. You seem to like looking at Mrs. Boyes's tree." She sauntered into the room. "Just don't cough on me or anything."

"Don't you want to know what's going on over there?"

"Not really." She gazed about my bedroom. "I don't know why you don't decorate. It's punishing you, not her."

I snuggled deeper into my quilt and rested my chin on my knees. "Most decorations are tacky. Or insipid. Not my cup of tea."

"I thought you were an artist. You could make your own holiday decorations." Casey stood before the window. "Paint a Christmas scene or something."

I waved a hand. "You're blocking my view."

"I don't think she chose to leave us at Christmas on purpose. Momma wasn't that mean. Maybe she thought it'd take our minds off her going."

"I'm sick." I slithered beneath the quilt. "Hang the lights or not, but I'm not up for psychoanalysis if you don't mind."

Casey held up the lights, eyeballing spots on the wall. "Just trying to help. I try to think about all the Christmases Grandma Jo made special for us. She put a lot of effort into Christmas."

"I know." Propping my head on my hand, I tried to see above the window sill. Gave up. Sat up and squinted at the window. "That makes it even harder."

"I thought you hated Christmas because of Momma. It's because of Grandma Jo dying so young?"

I sighed. "Both, I guess. I'm just tired of being lonely."

"You don't have to be lonely. Luke—" Casey cut herself off. "Maybe we shouldn't decorate your house just now."

I cranked up an eyebrow. "Why? Don't tell me it's because you're agreeing with me because I know you better than that."

"They remind you of bad times, and you're feeling bad anyway. Maybe I shouldn't push it." Casey wound the lights around her arm. "Christmas should make you happy."

"But you're right. I should think of the good Christmases we had with Grandma Jo and Grandpa Ed. Not what we missed out on." I studied the blinking tree through my window. "Everything looks warm and friendly over at Mrs. Boyes's house. But I think something cold and sinister is going on over there. Decorating can't cover that up."

Casey glanced over her shoulder, eyeing the scene on the other side of the window. "I don't see anything. And the nephew is helping Mrs. Boyes out. That's good Christmas spirit." She turned back to study me. "I think I need to close these curtains."

"No," I cried. "I need to know what's going on."

"Don't excite yourself." She bit her lip. "I'll leave them open for now. Lord knows you'll climb out of bed to open them as soon as my back is turned. I don't want you getting up. Let me hang these lights, then you rest."

I nodded, my attention fixed on the window. The rain had stopped, but the windows were icing.

Casey plugged the lights into my bedside socket. "What do you think is going on at Mrs. Boyes's now?"

"An out-of-towner's over there. Some fancy woman. She just broke into Mrs. Boyes's house."

"A what?" Casey dropped the lights and turned to face the window. "Wait. A redhead? She came over to ask about Mrs. Boyes. Her name's Maizie, and she's a private investigator. Mrs. Boyes's sister hired the investigator to find her granddaughter. The sister sent Maizie down from Black Pine to warn Mrs. Boyes about the granddaughter."

"Private investigators don't break into people's houses, Casey. She must be lying."

Casey massaged her lower back. "I don't know. I talked to her a bit. Seemed nice enough. Maybe she's in the house to check on Mrs. Boyes. The granddaughter's out on bail. Maizie seemed genuinely worried about Mrs. Boyes."

"I don't like it." I scooted to the edge of the bed and dipped a toe into the cold air. Shivering, I slipped my other foot off the bed. Pulling my blankets around my shoulders, I sat on the edge of the bed, gathering strength. "I'm going over there."

Casey whipped around. "Get back in bed."

"Don't try to stop me. There's funny business going on at Mrs. Boyes's house. I haven't seen Mrs. Boyes since Santa killed the reindeer. Now there's a movie star snooping around." Dizzy, I dipped my head and panted. "Just give me a minute."

"I'm stopping you." Casey strode to the bed, placed a hand on my forehead, and flicked it off. "You're burning up. Did you take that medicine Pearl got you?"

"I don't remember." I sniffled. "Where's Pearl?"

"Lord, if you're crying over Pearl, you're seriously ill." Casey pulled the covers off my shoulders and shoved me back onto the bed. "Now climb in. Take your medicine. Drink your Gatorade. And stop being

such a pain in the ass. You've never done what you're told when you're
sick. Not even as a child. Just lie down."

"Casey," I said. "I'm serious. Where's Pearl?"

"She went out a minute ago." Half-turned, Casey's anger faded. Her
eyes narrowed, and she shot back to the window. "Dammit, Pearl's there
now. I told her I already went over. What's she doing?"

I lay on my back, panting. "Pearl will find the movie star."

"She's arguing with that nephew." Casey laughed. "This is pretty
funny to watch. I wonder what's she saying? Probably telling him, 'Son,
you need to soak your aunt in goat's milk.' Or some such goat
nonsense."

I closed my eyes. "Prob'ly."

"Now she's marching toward the kitchen. Fixin' to cook. Or inventory their supplies." Casey sucked in her breath. "The nephew's following. He looks madder than spit."

Dreams interfered with Casey's play-by-play. I saw Santa, his eyes
narrowed, lips pulled back in a snarl. Yanking the Christmas lights tight
in his hands. Flinging it around the reindeer's throat. I drifted.

"Wake up," said Casey. "Cherry, wake up."

My eyes flew open. "What?"

Casey sat on the edge of my bed. "The nephew and Pearl were gone
for a minute, then he came back into the living room alone. I don't know
what Pearl is doing. The nephew saw me, watching. And now he's
moving the tree in front of the window."

"Serves us right, I guess." I couldn't pull my thoughts together.
Colored light shone on Casey. I looked up and saw the string of lights
had been flung over Snug. The cord dangled down the wall. "Wait a
minute. Mrs. Boyes wouldn't want anybody moving her tree. She's very
particular about decorating. She always has the tree in that corner."

"Never mind that." Casey's voice shook. She wrapped her arms
around her belly. "Cherry, he saw me watching the house. The nephew.
He pointed at me. Then drew his finger across his throat."

TWELVE
MAIZIE ALBRIGHT
#WENEEDALITTLECHRISTMAS
#LIKERIGHTNOW

I WAS FAIRLY sure Jay hadn't seen me. Soon after I escaped Martha Mae's backyard, I heard a door slam. Scooting from my hiding spot behind a sawhorse in the next-door carport, I slid-crept between the parked vehicles and watched Martha Mae's house. A minute later, Jay tramped off the porch and strode around the side of the house. He disappeared from view. Looking for whoever broke into the house.

Couldn't really blame him. Because it was a break-in.

By me.

Keeping to the far side of the artist's driveway, I used the cover of the old yellow pickup, the Firebird, then the big truck to keep myself hidden. Ran across the road and down the street. Slid and almost fell six times. Ducked into Tiffany's car. With trembling fingers, I shoved the keys into the ignition. And stopped before turning on the engine.

Pearl. I bet she's the woman with the big truck. Casey, the pregnant woman, had mentioned her.

What had happened to Pearl?

I popped up my head to peer out the frosted windows. Martha Mae's living room lights were still on. I couldn't see Jay. In the sick artist's house, someone stood before the living room window. Hands around her eyes, looking out into the dark.

Ducking beneath the driver's side window, I glanced at my phone, wanting to call Nash.

And tell him you did exactly what he didn't want you to do?

The man was already freaking out about the weather. Knowing Nash and his massive protection instincts, he'd drive hell-bent for Halo. The weather in the mountains would be much worse. I'd be risking his life.

Call the police? And tell them I — while on probation — illegally entered a woman's house and discovered…nothing useful for the police. They were busy with a serious bank robbery.

Maybe Pearl had stopped talking because she had gone back to the artist's house.

I blew on my mitten-less hand. The sweat I had accumulated running — Twenty yards? I so need to get back to the gym — now felt like a film of ice on my skin. But with Jay skulking about, I didn't want to draw attention to my car by turning it on.

I needed more information. First, see if Pearl is home.

Cracking the door, I slid out and kept low. Squat-walked on the sidewalk behind the car and peered around the side. The woman in the window was gone. I didn't see Jay.

"Coast is clear," I told myself. "Now just look normal. In case anyone is watching."

"Like it matters now," said my inner Julia Pinkerton.

Teenagers. Always the critic.

Straightening, I strolled around my car, then hurried across the street, sliding and slipping. With my arms windmilling, I reached their drive. Decided on the better traction of walking uphill in the crispy grass. I grabbed the railing on the front steps and hauled myself onto the porch. Rang the bell, then knocked.

Pregnant Casey peered out the window. I waved. She opened the door and dragged me inside.

"What in the hell happened to you?" she said. "You look like you fell into a goat pen. Why did you break into Mrs. Boyes's house? I trusted you. My sister wants to report you to the sheriff."

I raised my mittened hand. "Oh my God, please don't. I'm on probation. I'll probably get sent back to Beverly Hills to face Judge Ellis again."

Casey's penciled eyebrows hit her hairline. "I'm calling Uncle Will."

"It's totally cool. I used Martha Mae's key." I left off the part where Martha Mae hadn't given me the key. "I needed to check on Martha Mae. But I don't even know if she's in the house."

"The nephew said—"

"I know. But did you see her? Because I went into the bedroom — not all the way in, just the doorway, didn't want to scare poor Martha Mae — and called for her. I explained who I was and about Krystal. If anyone was in there — they've got the shades drawn, TV muted, lights off — they didn't respond. Does that sound like Martha Mae Boyes?"

Casey stuck a hand on her hip and sucked on her lip, considering. "It don't sound like Mrs. Boyes, I admit. She's like Pearl. Kind of loud. But in a friendly sort of way. Even to strangers. If you were already in her room, she'd say, 'Well, now that you're here, you might as well come on in. Let me tell you about my ruptured disc.'"

"See what I mean?" I clasped my hands together, then wiped my wet, bare hand on my dirty jeans.

"Maybe she took pain meds, and she's sleeping."

"But even sleeping people make some noise." I steepled my hands together and gave her my *American Girl Magazine* (circa 2000) smile. "I'm really trying to help Martha Mae. I have a bad feeling about her sister, her great-niece, and her nephew. Martha Mae's the only one in the family that doesn't set off alarm bells. She really should've been a grandma."

"Huh," said Casey.

My smile stretched, froze, and dropped. "Niece and nephew. Distantly related nephew. Hang on. Sorry." Turning my back to Casey, I pulled out my phone. "Nash."

"Are you in a motel?"

My heart fluttered. I wished. That wasn't all I wished. Focus, Maizie.

"No. I'm in a house. Next door to Martha Mae. Everything's cool." I turned and smiled at Casey. "It's my boss, Wyatt Nash. He owns Nash Security Solutions in Black Pine."

"Who are you talking to?" said Nash.

"Martha Mae's neighbor, Casey."

"I don't live here," said Casey. "My sister, Cherry, does."

"The neighbor's sister."

"What's going on?" said Nash.

"Krystal's dad. You said he was in prison? Is he still in prison?"

"Dammit."

"So you'll get back to me on that?"

I snapped the phone shut and turned back to Casey. "I might have a lead on who Jay is."

She shuddered, then wrapped her hands around her belly. "The nephew moved the tree. He knows Cherry's been watching the house. And he saw me. Kind of threatened me."

"I thought I heard furniture moving." I paused. "But the living room is carpeted."

"Pearl went over there." Casey ran her hands up and down her arms. "And she's not back."

"Hells. I heard her talking to Jay, but I took off before I could help." I stared at my muddy boots. "I should've gone back in. Somehow."

"I think I should call Uncle Will. But the bank robbery—" Casey bit her lip and hugged her shoulders.

"Still a standoff?"

She shook her head. "Sheriff had to let them go. The FBI team didn't make it in time. The robbery gang threatened to kill Luke. Uncle Will negotiated a van for them. They dragged Luke out. Bound, gagged, and blindfolded. They had all these guns aimed at him. Makes me sick. If they kill him, I don't know what Cherry will do. Why did this have to happen on Christmas?" She choked back a sob.

"What happened? Did they get away?"

Casey jerked a nod. "Uncle Will had our deputies and Line Creek police in unmarked vehicles waiting to follow them. They lost them for a minute. Then found the van headed toward the Winn Dixie on Highway Nineteen."

She took a deep breath. "But the robbers must've had different vehicles waiting. When the police followed them around to the back, the van had parked so law enforcement couldn't get around a big delivery truck. The robbers had gone inside the store, through the back, and out the front. The Winn Dixie was full of shoppers. Folks still stocking up for Christmas, worried about being totally iced over. The robbers split up and slipped out the front with the other shoppers."

"No one saw them?"

"At the bank, they were all dressed like Santa. They left the suits in the van."

"And the deputy held hostage?"

"Luke wasn't in the van. Don't know where he is. They're studying the Winn Dixie's security tapes and interviewing the employees. But they think there might have been another car that met them before getting to the Winn Dixie." Casey shook her head, her eyes filled with tears. "I should call Uncle Will. But I don't know how serious this is next door. He's got his hands full with the search."

I hugged her. She felt warm and smelled like baby lotion. I could've used a longer hug. "You should go home. Take your sister with you. If it's serious—"

"Cherry shouldn't be out. Her fever is real high. I can't leave her. Nik is working tonight, or he'd come over. He wouldn't want me to drive the Firebird in this anyway. It's rear-wheel drive."

"I'll stay with Cherry." I strode to the window and peered out.

"I'm not leaving my sister," said Casey. "No offense, but she doesn't trust you. And with that fever, I don't trust her."

"What would she do?"

"She finds you in her house, she'd probably shoot you. Cherry keeps a shotgun under her bed."

I LEFT Casey to check on Cherry — and hopefully to advise her sister not to shoot me. I'd met some crazy artists but none with shotguns — and took a page from Nash's book. I paced before the window, thinking. If Jay was Krystal's father, why would he show up at Martha Mae's? Because he knew Krystal would show? If so, that meant I really couldn't leave. Was Krystal already there? What had happened to Martha Mae? And Pearl?

My phone rang. "What did you learn?"

"Merry Christmas to you, too, dear." My mother's honey-cloaked-in-steel drawl sounded tinny. "It's morning here. The jet lag is terrible. There's no Starbucks."

"Vicki, you're in Fiji. Drink the local coffee." I paused. "I mean, Merry Christmas. I really want to talk to you? But it's not a good time?"

"You're doing that up-talk thing again. Darling, you know it makes you sound stupid. Now, I have a list of things I need you to send me. Find a pen."

"Vicki. I'm on a case. A grandmother is missing. Maybe two. And a granddaughter. I can't talk."

"First, decent coffee. Second, Neiman's had a Kate Spade bikini that I almost ordered. I changed my mind. They have the audacity to say, they don't ship to Fiji. Unbelievable. So, I need you to express it to yourself and then express it to me. We're only here a week, so you'd better get on it."

"You're not hearing me." I pulled in a deep Ujjayi breath, held it five beats, and let it out. Renata said it would help to clear my mind and focus on the message, not the mother. "I'm waiting for another call. And I have to prepare myself for breaking and entering. Again."

"Is that a play? Are you auditioning?" Vicki paused. "Don't start back with stage work. Unless it's a charity gig. Are they paying? I'll negotiate—"

"It's not a play. It's a form of trespassing. And I have to go. Merry Christmas." I hung up on my manager. I mean, mother.

I'd not done that before. First time for everything.

OMG, Vicki was going to kill me. Thank God, she was in Fiji.

Casey walked in as I stared at the phone in my mittened palm. "What're you doing?"

"Calling my boss again." I quickly thumb-dialed and cradled the phone against my ear. "Nash. What's Krystal's dad's name?"

"Jim Wiley."

"And he was in jail for?"

"Armed robbery. Got out three months ago."

Shizzles. "Krystal might be next door. I'm pretty sure Jim is Jay."

"Call the police."

"The police are a little busy with the bank robbery. The suspects escaped. And it's not illegal for Jay and Krystal to be next door. As far as we know. Although I'm not sure where Martha Mae went. Or Pearl."

"Dammit. Who's Pearl?"

"Actually, I'm not sure." I looked at Casey. "Who's Pearl?"

"Grandpa Ed's woman. She raises goats, too. That's the attraction, we figure."

"Pearl's a neighbor," I simplified.

"You're not going over there."

"Don't worry."

"Miss Albright, call the police. They can handle both emergencies. They're equipped."

"I don't think they have enough evidence to search the house," I said. "I certainly can't give them my testimony."

"What testimony? Did you—"

"Don't worry. I won't break and enter," I said, then swallowed the words, "this time."

"Did you say, 'this time?'"

"And it's getting icy. So, I'll just stick around here. If Vicki calls you, don't answer."

"I never do." He paused to add a string of curses. His voice sounded tinnier than Vicki's. Maybe it was my reception and not Fiji's. "Now listen. I'm speaking partner-to-partner here. You don't have backup. We don't know if Jim and Krystal are dangerous, but we do know Jim's been convicted of armed robbery. You're smart, and you're resourceful, kid. But you're getting in over your head. Again. We have no right to go into that woman's house unless she invites us. And you have no right to put yourself in danger. Again."

"That last part didn't make sense. Why would that be a right?"

"Do not put yourself in danger. Is that more clear?"

"Nash—"

"Dammit, Maizie. Just stay put in the neighbor's house. For once, can't you just wait it out?"

"What if Pearl's in danger? And Martha Mae?"

"And what about you? If they're in danger and you go sneaking into that house, you're in danger, too. You make me half crazy, thinking of all the—" His voice shook. His breath expanded. Or was that wind?

"I'll be careful, don't worry."

"Of course, I'm worried. You do these— I wanted to spend Christmas Eve with you. I mean, Lamar spends it with his family. And I… so I just thought…never mind. That has no bearing on the issue. The point is, don't be stupid and get yourself hurt. Or killed. And if the roads are icy, yes, stay off them. Stay there. In a motel." He paused. "I'm done."

My heart did a Parkour leap up my throat, dove to my toes, and bounced back into my chest. "Oh my gosh. You don't want to be alone for Christmas Eve. You want to spend it with me. That is so sweet."

"Let's focus on what's important."

"That is so important, Nash. That's the point of every single Hallmark Christmas movie. And everyone loves those movies. Micky tried to get me an audition for *I'll be Home*— Okay, rule number one. No talking about my former career." I took a deep breath. "Focusing."

It was super hard to focus after hearing that. But business before pleasure, like Vicki always said.

With Vicki, we never got to pleasure. I'd hoped it'd be different with Nash.

"Bank robbery or not, call the police," said Nash. "Be concise as possible. But detailed. But only detail the facts."

"Got it."

"Then stay at the neighbor's house and watch Martha Mae's. Do not leave the house."

"Uh…"

"Miss Albright."

"I need to call you back," I said. "A car's slowing down in front of Martha Mae's house."

THIRTEEN
CHERRY TUCKER

I'D FORCED myself against the grogginess and haze to evaluate what I knew against what I thought I knew. Mrs. Boyes had disappeared from view. Whether she'd hurt her back or had been strangled by Santa was yet to be determined. Pearl had gone over there and not returned. She could be helping Mrs. Boyes. Or something else had happened.

Then the nephew — Santa? — had moved Mrs. Boyes's tree. Mrs. Boyes who hadn't touched the tree in all the Christmases I remembered visiting Great Gam. Nor the Christmases after moving into Great Gam's in-town home from Grandpa's farm. Mrs. Boyes wouldn't abide the changing any of her decorations, let alone a tree. She made the exact same cookies every year. Unfortunately. Hung the same wreath on her door.

Then this man had threatened my pregnant sister. That angered me beyond belief.

At that thought, the ice melted from my toes. Heat poured off my neck. Who was this supposed nephew? Pearl wasn't here to answer that question. I wasn't sending Casey over there to ask. Then I remembered Pearl had said Gertie Sweetley was Martha Mae's best friend. I didn't know Gertie Sweetley, but she'd know me. Everyone in Halo over the age of fifty-five knew me through my grandparents.

And through stories about my notorious mother. And maybe some stories about notorious me.

This was all confirmed when Gertie Sweetley realized who was calling. "Cherry Tucker, the town council has already chosen someone to paint the water tower. We have to use a professional company that's licensed and insured. And we don't want some gewgaw painted on the side. It's a rust-proof, army-gray type of job."

"Ma'am. That's not what I'm calling about — although something as tall as a water tower would be a fine place to represent town pride, but if y'all feel Halo is only worth army gray, then enjoy. I'm calling about your friend and my neighbor, Mrs. Boyes. She's got some strange visitors."

Gertie Sweetley snorted. "And even if we were to paint an angel on the water tower, you'd give us one of those abstract messes. Or worse. I know about those nekkid men paintings you did. Angels wear robes."

I sighed. "Miss Gertie. I really don't want to paint an angel on the water tower. And even if I did, it wouldn't be a nude. Even though nudes happen to be a classic representation of the human form used in art for longer than three thousand years."

"They never painted angels nekkid. I can tell you that for sure."

"I'm not arguing with you, Miss Gertie. Nude lends itself more to gods and goddesses. Although Michelangelo seemed to enjoy it in Biblical representation." I gave into a fit of coughing. She was wearing me out, and I hadn't even gotten to the point of the conversation. "I really just want to ask you about Mrs. Boyes's nephew who's visiting."

"Martha Mae doesn't have a nephew visiting."

"There's a man in her house who says he's her nephew."

"Oh, my stars," said Gertie. "A surprise Christmas guest. I wonder if she stocked up before this weather hit. Is that why you're calling? Does she need something? I bet she didn't buy a turkey. But why wouldn't Martha Mae call me if she needed a turkey? Anyway, I don't have an extra turkey, and I'm not running out to the Tru-Buy in this weather. Besides, the Tru-Buy is out of turkeys. She needs to go to Line Creek. The Winn Dixie is still stocked."

I closed my eyes, leaned back against my bed rails, and stared up at Snug. He was bathed in multi-colored lights, like the shrine on the wall at the nail salon. "Miss Gertie. Ma'am. I just want to know about Martha Mae's nephew."

"Don't tell me you're planning on cozying up to her nephew. I thought you were stepping out with JB's stepson. The deputy. And with him involved in this awful mess in town. Are you not seeing him no more? That poor man. But maybe it's for the best."

I opened my mouth and shut it before I said something I regretted. "I am not looking for a date, Miss Gertie. This nephew is old enough to be my father anyway. I am concerned that he is not a good sort. He moved Mrs. Boyes's tree."

"No, he didn't."

"He did. In front of her side window."

"Martha Mae wouldn't allow such a thing. She always places it in that corner opposite the front window so everyone can see her tree but not block the window, so she can see out. Martha Mae thought a lot about the tree placement over the years. She's tried it centered on the opposite wall, but then it interferes with the placement of her couch and she likes to watch her shows in the evening. Plus, you shouldn't put a live tree near a fireplace. That's asking for trouble."

"Exactly. Which is why I want to know who this so-called nephew is."

"I have no idea. But I can tell you this. He better not move any more of her things. She's not going to be happy when she finds her tree moved."

"Do you mean she's not at home? Do you know where Mrs. Boyes is?"

"No, hon'. But she can't be home if he's moved her tree, now can she?"

After hanging up, I watched Mrs. Boyes's tree lights blink and thought about the likelihood of Mrs. Boyes not being home. Casey had said her back was out. Maybe I should have mentioned that fact to Miss Gertie, but it was a road I didn't feel like exploring. Partly because the conversation exhausted me. And partly because I didn't want Miss Gertie getting any bright ideas about visiting her friend with the weather, bad roads, and Pearl already missing.

Come to think of it, Pearl would have told off the nephew for moving his aunt's tree, too.

The cost of the conversation was the creeping heat of fever. I shuddered with bone-aching chills and slid below my quilt. I pulled the quilt around my head and lay on my side, trying to analyze our conversation. Something else she'd said had bothered me. But now I couldn't remember. And it was getting difficult to stay awake again. I reached for my sketchbook to add a tree and Pearl, then closed my eyes for a minute.

Damned flu.

MY DREAMLESS SLEEP was interrupted by Casey, who claimed we'd have our own unexpected guest. The movie star. Who was as suspicious as Mrs. Boyes's nephew in my book.

I couldn't believe Casey had let that woman into my house. I couldn't stay awake for the life of me. And somewhere during my last slumber, Casey had invited the movie star to spend the night.

"The roads are iced over," Casey had said. "And Maizie's stuck. We can't let her sleep in her car. It's Christmas time, ain't it?"

"If it's that bad, I hope you're not planning to drive home," I said. "You take the guest bed, it's got a better mattress to support that extra weight you're carrying. The movie star can have my room. But we'll have to change the sheets."

Casey laughed at me. "She's fine with the couch. I've got Great Gam's plastic tree up, by the way."

Can you put it in here? I'd almost said, then caught myself. I'd almost forgotten I didn't do Christmas trees. "Keep it out there. Did you see Mrs. Boyes's bubble lights? You could take some pointers from her."

Then I'd fallen asleep. Again. I hated this flu. I was so damn weak it was pitiful.

After waking, I glared at glowing Snug. And then at Mrs. Boyes's tree, which I could see much better as it was pushed up against the window.

Also, something else was going on. Casey was acting extra nice. She didn't do extra nice. Even with child.

I tried calling Luke, but couldn't get through, figuring the bad roads must keep him extra busy. I didn't want him to see me like this. But then again, I really wanted to see him. He'd snuggle in bed next to me to rub my shoulders and stroke my hair. Tell me about all the accidents and arrests he'd handled. I loved cop stories. But mostly, I just wanted him here. For no apparent reason.

Damn flu making me addle-brained.

Casey appeared in my doorway with a steaming mug. "You want to try some chicken soup?"

My stomach rolled, but my mouth felt parched. "Maybe. What's the movie star doing?"

"She ain't a movie star. Maizie's a private investigator. I have her business card."

"Anybody can make a business card, Casey. Thank God we got nothing worth robbing in this house."

"I know you don't mean it," said Casey. "You're just worried about—"

"What am I worried about?" I squinted at her.

"Pearl," she spit out the name quickly. "And Mrs. Boyes. Someone else showed up at her house. Maizie's gone over there to see who it is."

"Who does that kind of thing?" I took the mug and let the steam heat my face. "Sneaking around someone's house like that?"

"You, for one," said Casey. "On a number of occasions. When you think somebody's up to something no good."

"Well, that's different." I sipped the soup and eased back, letting the savory heat trickle down my throat. My head wanted more, my stomach wasn't sure. "In those circumstances, I had evidence of criminal wrong-doing and was helping friends in need."

"That's exactly the same thing, except this Maizie is a professional. And you're not."

I gave Casey my best stink-eye.

She snorted. "What was that?"

I guess the illness had also weakened that effect.

"I found more boxes of Christmas lights," said Casey. "And there's a box in the guest room closet with your name. It also has decorations. Can I use them?"

"No." I chewed my lip. "Whatever. I'm too sick to care. There's a stocking in there that Grandma Jo made for me. You can have it for the baby."

"When's the last time you hung up that stocking?" Casey folded her arms. "Grandma Jo embroidered it with an angel carrying a paintbrush, right? I haven't seen that in years."

"Fifteen. I thought I was too old for Santa."

"Fifteen is how old you were when Grandma Jo died."

I looked up at the lights wrapped around Snug. "You can use it this year. I'm sure Santa visits those in utero."

As soon as Casey had left, I wrapped the blankets around my shoulders, turned off the lights, and crept to the window. With their soft glow,

Snug's Christmas lights held off the edge of complete darkness. Hanging across the room, they didn't hinder my ability to see out the window. I left them on. I didn't have much of a view with the Christmas tree blocking Mrs. Boyes's living room.

But the glow from her house lights still illuminated the window, creating a hazy spotlight on the winter wonderland outside. And I could see a shape, crouching on the ground at the corner of Mrs. Boyes's house. The shape appeared to be watching the front of the house. Movie Star. Getting herself into trouble, likely.

I crossed back to get my mug of chicken soup. I needed to get over this flu fast. She was going to need my help.

FOURTEEN

MAIZIE ALBRIGHT

#BABYITSCOLDOUTSIDE #REALLYCOLD #REALLYREALLYCOLD

THE ARTIST'S drive was on the opposite side of the house from Martha Mae's. I had to leave the house and cross to Martha Mae's to see anything. The wind had died down, but the air felt thin and sharp. Woodsmoke from nearby fireplaces stung my lungs, but I also tasted wet pine from the surrounding trees. Casey had lent me another pair of mittens, which helped. A little. I felt like I'd never feel warm again.

If I'd been thinking I would have borrowed Carol Lynn's DeerNose weather apparel. Smelling like deer pee would be the least of my worries now. Frostbite, yes. Also, the camo would have come in handy with all this prowling.

Next time I see Daddy, I might advise him on a Christmas camouflage collection. Maybe poinsettias and holly? And to skip the scent. Deer don't celebrate Christmas.

A car — a Toyota sedan — had inched along the street, fishtailed, and slowed to a crawl as it reached Martha Mae's. The Toyota now idled behind Martha's parked car. Had Krystal finally shown?

I felt and heard the rumble of the garage door. My heart pounding, I backed from the edge of the house and flattened against the wall. Hearing nothing more than the garage door and the still-running car, I peeked around the corner.

Jay tramped into view. With a scraper, he chipped off ice, then entered Mrs. Boyes's Buick. He backed into the grass, around the idling car, and parked on the street. Exiting the car, he shoved his hands in his pockets and tread up the drive. Stopping at the visitor's car, he leaned in. The car's window rolled down and the murmur of voices hung in the still air. It looked like a single driver. A moment later, Jay turned to face the house.

I shrank back against the wall.

Maybe another relative was coming to take care of Martha Mae. So nice, right? No doubt, Pearl was in the bedroom with her. Too busy applying hot compresses to talk. I could go back to the artist's house and drink hot chocolate with her pregnant sister. Their house might be chilly and leaky, but it wasn't the ice bath I felt out here.

"Yeah right." Julia Pinkerton sneered. "Here's how this is going down. You need to get inside that garage to look around. Then you can get inside the house. Keep low. Nobody's watching. I've done this a million times. Which means you've done it a million times, acting as me on the show."

"Are you insane?" I thought. "That wasn't even real. The writers made sure you weren't killed. There are no writers in real life."

Oh, my God, I was the one who's insane. Arguing with a fictional character inside my head.

Taking a deep breath, I peered around the edge of the house. The waiting car pulled into the garage. Jay followed, stomping and rubbing his hands together. Martha Mae's car remained on the street.

I held my breath, stood, and sidled around the edge of the house. With my heart pounding in my head, I darted across the front yard. Ducked as I crossed before the porch. Before reaching the drive, I leaped behind a bush next to the garage.

This was the stupid Nash had spoken of. So stupid.

Keeping my back against the house, I glanced inside the garage. Two cars. The visiting vehicle plumed exhaust and cut off. The car door opened, but the driver had bent into the passenger seat to retrieve something. Jay circled the car and stopped at the back.

I dropped to the icy, wet ground, sliding to hide my body beneath the hedge. A holly. Prickly. And full of berries. Under the holly, fallen leaves rustled and rattled. I halted my slide. My shoulders and chest didn't fit beneath the shrub. If Jay and the other driver stepped outside the garage, they'd see me, lying Sphinx-like beneath a holly.

What was it with me and bushes today?

Someone was speaking. A woman. I didn't dare peer around the side of the garage.

"Unlock it," said Jay, followed by a thump.

"What're you doing?" called the woman's voice. "I told you it's not your business."

Did he want her to open the trunk?

A metallic pop and a creak answered that question.

"Shee-it," muttered Jay. "Why'd you get stuck with this mess? And now we're stuck here. Damn ice."

I held my breath and clamped my jaw to keep my teeth from chattering. My flattened stomach shot flames into my chest. Warming as well as painful. Cranking my head, I could just see the opposite edge of the garage. A pair of men's boots faced the car.

The trunk door slammed shut. "I'll take care of this mess. As usual."

"Don't give me that crap," said the woman. "I've been taking care of myself long enough. And done pretty good with what I've been dealt, I'd say."

A tremor worked its way through my legs. My shoulders shook, making the metal zipper on my coat jingle. Ducking, I placed my forehead on the corner of the drive to push my chest against the ground and stop the noise.

"Fine way to spend Christmas," said Jay.

"Right." Her forced laugh sounded brittle. "Because our other ones were so great."

"What were you doing asking Celia about Martha Mae? You put her on our tail. Celia sent a woman down here, and she's asking questions."

"We'll be gone soon enough."

"We ain't going anywhere with this ice. And we don't need you getting hot-headed again."

"I don't need *your* advice, of all people," said Krystal. "I've been doing just fine on my own."

The woman had talked to Celia Fowler. She must be Krystal. I found myself feeling pity for Krystal. She was a product of her upbringing.

"You can't get yourself out of this without my help," said Jay. "You wouldn't have called me otherwise."

"What do you want? A thank you note? You know what you're getting from this."

"I thought you were headed in the right direction for once," said Jay. "I told you to steer clear of her."

"Had no choice."

Who was her? Mrs. Fowler? But Krystal only took money from her grandmother. She didn't steer near her grandmother at all.

Unless her grandmother hadn't told us the truth. That thought made my chest hurt. It felt the equivalent to Vicki's "Let's talk about Santa and who really buys the toys around here" speech.

"Well, now I ain't got a choice either, do I?" Jay's boots clomped, stopping near my edge of the garage. "I couldn't do you right back then, I'll have to do you right now."

"Whatever."

I slithered backward, pushing myself into the corner of the house and garage.

A car alarm bloop-bleeped followed by another heavy, metallic pop. A trunk opening. Jay was checking the other trunk. A moment later the lid slammed shut. Boots tromped toward the far end of the garage. The garage door rumbled. An inside door slammed shut.

Scooting closer to the garage, I peered around the side. Flattening on the drive, I peered beneath the descending door. A woman walked toward the back of the garage. In a bulky coat and hat that hid her completely.

The garage door clanged against the cement, sending a cloud of dust into my face.

RETREATING to my holly bush corner, I regrouped. I needed to be certain that the newcomer was Krystal. But I really needed to find Pearl for the neighbors. And Martha Mae for myself.

I could watch from inside the artist's house like I'd promised Nash. Except I wouldn't be able to see anything. Sorry, Nash.

Stretching, I noted my silver jacket had gone camo. Streaks of brown and orange mud covered my puffy coat, pants, and boots. Private investigator work was so hard on my wardrobe. I tried not to think of the cost of my Gianvito Rossi boots. At least I had chosen leather over suede.

"Cheer up," I thought. "The Rossi's were last year's design anyway.

Remember the distressing fad a few years back? Maybe mud camo will trend."

I feared my trending days were over. My shopper at Barney's would be so disgusted with me.

Biting my lip, I continued around the garage. On the back side of the house, I glanced at the unlit bushes (sorry Martha Mae), then studied the backyard. Martha Mae had a small, fenced vegetable garden. In the distance, a copse of trees hid the house from the neighbor's yard behind her. A screened-in porch decorated with boughs, lighted stars, and tiny Christmas trees flanked this end.

Lights were on in the kitchen, seen through the porch. Figures moved, but the porch blocked the view. There was a smaller window, set higher than the bedroom windows, probably placed above the kitchen sink. I was tall enough to peer through it, but I'd have to get close to the house and possibly expose myself. I'd have a better view of the kitchen on the porch. But a much greater chance of getting caught.

Kitchen sink, it was.

Creeping along the house, I thought I heard the muffled sounds of an argument. Arguments made my stomach clench but so did sneaking around houses. It's a good sign, I told myself. Jay and She-Who-Might-Be-Krystal would be preoccupied with the dispute.

However, they'd also have heightened emotions. Which, if spotting someone skulking outside their house, might cause a rash action. For example, they might call the police.

Or try to hurt me.

I increased my speed around the screened porch and darted beneath the window. I rose slowly, angling to keep my body on the side of the window. From the side, I saw a door, a fridge, and part of another doorway. Martha Mae had a cute chicken border and oak cabinets. I ducked below the window and popped up on the other side. Someone sat at a kitchen table, but they were blocked by Jay's large body. With his back to me (Hallelujah), he stood in a wide-legged stance. Arms folded. Immobile. Go figure, if they were still arguing.

The person at the table was shouting. A woman, judging by her arms. The only body parts I could see, unfortunately. The arms moved, pointing toward one end of the house and the other.

I pressed my ear against the wood frame, hoping to hear something useful, but could only make out the rise and fall of her voice. Occasionally, her high pitch was cut off by a low murmur. Which I took as Jay's response.

Not a very talkative guy. Kind of a one-sided argument.

Jay swung around. I sucked in my breath and shrank back against the house. His eyes, dark and angry, had darted toward the window.

OMG, had he seen me? My heart pounded. Blood rushed inside my ears. I couldn't move.

Water turned on. Jay had to be standing at the sink. He spoke again, a low rumble muffled by the water. The water turned off. A door slammed. The wall behind me vibrated.

I pivoted slowly, inching toward the window. Scooted back at the sound of a second door slamming. Took a deep breath. And peeked.

The woman had disappeared from view. Jay stomped through the kitchen carrying a bag and a shovel. A big one. With a pointy end. He cut around the kitchen table and out of my view. Metal scraped, and something heavy dragged then rolled.

Craptastic. The sliding glass door. He was coming outside. My heart leaped into my throat. I pulled away from the window and flattened against the wall. Had he seen me? Was he coming to knock my head in with a shovel?

Jay slammed the sliding door shut, making the wall behind me shudder. Inside the screened porch, he used the shovel to knock down Martha Mae's little trees. Swiped at the lighted stars swinging from the porch rafters. Littered the ground with tiny ornaments.

Pressed against the wall, I fought off shudders. Poor Martha Mae. All her decorating work ruined with a few swings of a shovel. I tried not to think what the shovel also might do to my head. Jay hadn't given an indication that he knew I was out here. But he would see me if I ran.

He'd see me if I didn't run. I felt like crying. The thought of frozen snot kept back the tears.

Taking a break from his Christmas demolition, Jay shoved open the screen door on the opposite side of the porch. It swung back and crashed into the frame. With a final swipe at an angel hanging above the door, he lumbered into the yard.

Slowly, I sank toward the ground. Keeping my back to the wall, I sat on my haunches in a tight huddle, hoping the shadows would keep me hidden. Above me, the light from the kitchen shone through the window.

Jay tromped through the icy grass, the bag swinging from one hand, the shovel dragging behind him. It made an eerie ringing, cutting across the cold, bumpy ground. At Martha Mae's garden, he unlatched and opened the gate, more carefully than he'd done on the porch. Dropping the bag on the ground, he began to dig. Jay strained against the frozen top layer. His labored breathing grew louder with his muttered curses. Eventually, the sound of shovel hitting clay and the flung dirt smacking the frozen garden became rhythmic.

I couldn't move. I needed to move. Jay was preoccupied. There was a chance he wouldn't see me. The front half of the garden fence had lights hanging from it. I could see him, he probably couldn't see me.

There was also a chance he could see me. And he had a big, wicked shovel. Plus, he was making a very large hole in the ground.

For a body?

My thighs shook. My knees felt close to exploding. Cold had set into my bones.

A new fear. Frozen joints. I'd be permanently stuck in this crouch like an overlarge, frosty garden gnome. Jay would find me, pick me up like he was carrying a super-sized pretzel, and toss me in the hole. They'd find my skeleton, bones contorted and fused together, and wonder what monster had been buried in Halo years before.

I didn't want the fate of an unwanted garden gnome.

Summoning all my courage and Julia Pinkerton's swagger (nine years younger, she was also lithe and flexible), I kept my back against the house and crab-walked. With the speed of a large, ancient tortoise. At the corner of the house, I slithered. One appendage, then the next. Dropped on all fours. And crawled until I felt more safely out of sight. Did a quick round of cow-to-cat yoga to loosen my muscles, pushed into downward dog to relieve my calves, and unfolded (slowly, creakingly) to upright. I leaned against the house wall, panting.

Felt a little better. Except for feeling like an idiot.

Jay was burying something in Martha Mae's kitchen garden. Guns? A stash of money? Bodies?

And what was I going to do? My plans had gone from convincing Krystal to return home to visit her Grandma, to doing what? Saving two elderly ladies from possible bank robbers? Who shot people and kidnapped cops? Come on. Even Julia Pinkerton didn't do stuff like that on the show. Nobody had guns. They mostly shot off their mouths. The writers couldn't risk a rating censure.

I ambled forward, stopping at Martha Mae's living room window. Her Christmas tree blocked the view into the house. I stared at the bubbling and blinking lights for a moment and listened to the distant ring of shovel on dirt.

Big hole.

What if it was for a body?

Yanking off my hat, I ran my fingers through my hair, then caught myself in the window's reflection. Someone I didn't know looked back at me. Her eyes had a hard, calculating set to them. Her former Colgate smile had vanished for a grim scowl. And let's not talk about the woman's hair. I did not want to go there. I pulled the beanie back on.

I'd always been impetuous — borderline reckless — but more like, the imprudent "rich kid from Beverly Hills" type. That was embarrassing enough to admit. I couldn't save anybody from bank robbers. Not when the bank robber might shoot them. Or me. What would that do to Daddy? Find out his daughter was shot at Christmas? And Remi? I'd promised her I'd be home for Christmas Eve. I'd ruin Vicki's Fiji holiday. I didn't have high hopes for getting her a bikini in time, but no chance of that now if I was dead.

Also, Nash. He wanted to spend Christmas Eve with me, too. I was more excited about that than a visit from Santa.

Plus, Nash would kill me if I got shot.

I RAN (SLID) to Tiffany's car and laid flat on the back bench seat. For a long moment, I stared at the ceiling, panted, and wiggled my numb toes. I assumed Jay continued his (literal) skullduggery and the woman-I-presumed-was-Krystal did whatever she deemed necessary after a bank robbery (Showered? Counted money? Renewed her passport?).

"You don't know for sure they're bank robbers," I told myself. "Possibly, this is all one big mistake. They're visiting Aunt Martha Mae — who they'd never visited previously — to help her with her back. And Jay is digging a coffin-shaped hole in her garden because people with bad backs shouldn't be digging."

"Yeah, right," said my inner Julia Pinkerton. "That hole is *for* Martha Mae."

I was in way over my head. I had to call the police. As soon as they showed to protect the sick artist and her pregnant sister, I'd drive to the twenty-four-hour Waffle Hut, spend the night in a booth, and drive home in the morning. Surely in the morning, the sun would come out, melt the ice, and I'd be on the road with plenty of time to binge-watch all the Rankin-Bass Christmas shows with Remi. She went to bed early. I'd have time to see Nash. Did he have an office Christmas party planned? Would we drink eggnog and do a Secret Santa exchange? Mistletoe in his office door?

Kind of hard to do Secret Santa with two people. Maybe he'd include Lamar. Hopefully not Jolene Sweeney, because that's a sure way of knowing I'd get coal. But if Lamar and Jolene were invited, I doubted there would be mistletoe.

Hello, Maizie. No secret Santa until I knew these people were safe.

I dialed 9-1-1.

"9-1-1. What's your emergency?"

Nash had said concise, but detailed. But detail only the facts.

"Possible violence," I answered. "I don't think you'd call it a domestic, but it is in a domestic domicile. 213 Loblolly. Martha Mae Boyes's house. Not Martha Mae. I don't think she'd hurt a fly. I'm not positive, but her nephew and grandniece might be armed. Possibly they're bank robbers? In any case, I'm concerned for Martha Mae and Pearl. I don't know Pearl's last name. She raises goats? Also for her neighbors, Cherry and Casey. I forgot their last names. One is sick. The other is pregnant. We're talking the endangerment of the elderly and the infirm. Not that pregnancy is an illness. Casey looked pretty healthy to me. In any case, we haven't heard from Martha Mae or Pearl for quite a while. They could be held hostage."

"Your name, please?"

"Maizie— Does it matter?" I said, thinking of my probation officer and her hearty dislike of my job. "I'm just visiting."

"Visiting Cherry Tucker?" The voice hardened. "Did Cherry tell you to call?"

"No. I'm supposed to be visiting Martha Mae? But she never came to the door? Just the nephew. And he's a convicted felon. Although he served his time. His daughter is out after an arrest. But she wasn't charged with anything."

"And you saw them with weapons? Did you say they're armed?"

"Not totally sure on that point? But I know the bank robbers are armed."

"Have you heard any gunshots? Any evidence they're using the weapons?"

"No."

"Where are you now? I'll send an officer out to talk to you."

"In a car…" I chewed my lip.

"What's your business there?"

"Martha Mae's sister sent me to talk the grandniece into coming home for Christmas?" My nerves were making me up-talk. This was not going well. I sounded crazy. "I heard about the bank robbers and—"

"Yes, we've gotten a lot of calls about the bank robbers today. I'll send an officer to speak to you—"

"I'm leaving. I need to get home." All I needed was for a Halo deputy to look me up and learn I'm on probation. And contact my probation officer. Who was scary. "Can the officer just go to Martha Mae's house and check on her?"

"They'd like to talk to you first."

"I've got to get home," I said. "Never mind me. Just send someone out to keep an eye on Martha Mae's. And the house next door, 211 Loblolly. I'm worried they're not safe. The officer needs to make sure Martha Mae and Pearl are okay. Pearl went to check on Martha Mae, and she hasn't come back."

"Thank you for your information. As soon as an officer is available, they'll be there. The roads are bad, so please wait. Remain where you are so they can speak to you. Are you at the house?"

"No." I hung up.

Craptastic. I lowered my head to the steering wheel and jerked back. Freezing cold and with me sweating bullets, I might have stuck. That's all I needed, my forehead stuck to a steering wheel. Finding a candy cane in my pocket, I pulled back the plastic on the end that wasn't covered in tape and shoved it in my mouth. I needed sugar in a very bad way.

My therapist Renata and my trainer Jerry would be so disappointed. One for needing a crutch and the other for eating chemically treated high-fructose corn syrup. Jerry said I might as well eat poison.

I'd take candy cane poison over getting killed any day.

Sucking on the candy cane, I stared out the window. In the artist's house, the pregnant sister was decorating a small tree she'd placed in the window. That looked normal. Pleasant. Christmas-y. Giving me hope that this was all just some crazy storm of coincidences that meant nothing.

Why did I agree to help Mrs. Fowler? She was a terrible grandmother.

Granted I didn't know that at the time. Nor was I even sure about that now.

At Martha Mae's, there was movement. I squinted and fast-sucked my candy cane. The door opened. Light spilled onto the porch.

Oh, my God. Jay was leaving the house again. Did he finish digging? Was he coming here? Was the hole for me? I slid halfway down my seat, keeping my eyes on Jay.

Using Martha Mae's porch posts, Jay banged the mud off his shoes. I hated to think what he'd done to poor Martha Mae's floors. I took the candy cane from my mouth, pulled the plastic over the now-sharp end, and shoved it into my pocket. My heart beat in my throat.

Still on the porch, Jay lit a cigarette. Slowly, he scanned the street.

I dropped beneath my window. Blood pulsed inside my ears. I felt dizzy. Realized I was panting again. Deliberately slowed my breathing.

At least my puffing made the car smell minty.

I wanted to look up, but fear kept me crouched beneath the seat. Possibly Jay was taking a smoke break. Rewarding himself after the hard work. Hard work of burying bodies.

Santa, I want a patrol car for Christmas. Early. Like right now. With flashing lights and a siren.

I peeked through the driver's window. Jay was no longer on the porch. I inched my way up the door, peering right and left. Climbed onto the seat. No Jay.

A tiny orange light between the houses winked and went out. Was that Jay? In his neighbor's yard? The sick artist's house.

Hells. What was he doing there? Did they have a garden for burying bodies, too?

I quietly opened the door and set a foot on the road. My boot slid sideways. I hit the road with both hands. Bit my lip to keep from crying out. Kicked the door shut and crawled forward. Prayed no one would drive down the street and splatter me. At the artist's driveway, I pushed up, slid toward the Firebird, and hand-over-hand, vehicle-by-vehicle, trekked up the driveway. In the carport, I ran to the kitchen door and stopped.

I didn't want to freak out a pregnant woman and someone sick with the flu. I knocked. Quietly.

Casey appeared. I sidled past her and shut the kitchen door.

"Did you find Pearl?" she said.

"Not yet." I didn't want to tell her what I did find. "I just wanted to let you know that I'm going to be checking out your yard? Just ignore me? But, maybe stay away from the windows and lock your doors?"

"What in the hell is going on?"

"I'm being cautious. Checking the perimeters. But maybe get out your sister's gun and stay in that room with her?" I opened the kitchen door, shut it behind me. The lock clicked.

I was alone in their yard. With Jay. Again.

Worst Christmas ever.

FIFTEEN
CHERRY TUCKER

MY EYES FELT tight and dry. My head foggy and full. I shook with chills. But while Casey busied herself decorating for the Christmas I didn't want to have, I had pulled on layers to free my body of blankets and positioned myself before the window.

I'd seen Santa. Creeping around my house.

Casey didn't need to know. She'd fight me, knowing I was out of bed, let alone what I planned on doing. Luke wouldn't call me back, which told me the sheriff's office was in over their heads between the weather and the domestic disturbances that always happened this time of year. If I called the dispatcher, she'd just think the flu had melted my brain. Besides, I had nothing much to report other than a tree that had been moved and two missing women who might just be watching *A Charlie Brown Christmas* rerun in Mrs. Boyes's bedroom.

I'd unplugged Snug's lights, darkening the room, and half-hid against the wall. The light next door gave the nephew away, but even in the shifting shadows, the glowing end of a cigarette drifted near his face. He'd strolled around the edge of the house. Stopped in the corner of Mrs. Boyes's house, where he dragged on the cigarette, then let his arm drop and hang. Facing my house. Like he was studying it.

My eyes narrowed. I no longer felt the chill. Heat poured off me, damp and angry. My sister and her baby were at my house. And this man had threatened her. For what? Watching our Pearl argue with him through his aunt's window? What was he hiding with that tree? And where the hell was Pearl?

I wanted in that house. But I couldn't leave Casey alone with Creepster Santa hanging outside my window. A light knock in the kitchen startled me. Creepy nephew was still standing next to his aunt's house, smoking. I left him to sneak down the hallway and peer into the kitchen.

The movie star was back. Casey had let her in. Dammit. It was going to be harder for me to sneak out with the prying eyes of the so-called PI in the house. But then, she'd keep an eye on Casey while I could see what the nephew was doing.

I swiped at the sweat dampening my neck and listened.

What in the hell? Movie Star knew about Pearl? And she was checking our perimeter? Did she know the nephew was out there? Idiot. She'd get herself into trouble. That one did not look capable of taking on a killer Santa.

If the nephew had strangled Mrs. Boyes with Christmas lights. I still wasn't sure.

But Movie Star was plenty worried about Pearl. I could hear it in her voice. She shook with tension. Or maybe with cold.

Why didn't Casey offer her a cup of cocoa or something?

She left. Movie Star was out there with creepy Santa.

It was time to pull out the Remington. For Casey and the baby's sake.

MY HAIR FELT SLICK with sweat and my hands clammy, but I ignored the fever. Keeping an eye on the window, I busied myself with a half-cocked — as Luke would call it — plan. After I had checked and filled the Remington with shells, I placed the shotgun on the guest bed. I'd make Casey spend the rest of the night in there. She and I had been raised with hunters. Casey knew her way around a shotgun. Anyway, Uncle Will had made us take gun safety classes every year. His responsibility as sheriff, he'd said.

In my bedroom, I had plugged the Christmas lights back in and piled my pillows beneath the blanket. From the outside, if anyone cared to peek in my window, it'd look like I was sleeping. Found the trigger and door stop alarms Luke had gotten from a home security seminar. Then pulled out the lights from Great-Gam's box of Christmas decorations and took a moment to admire the thick wiring and heavy-duty bulbs.

I had a few surprises set up for Santa. Just in case he tried to come down my chimney early this year.

While I stretched Christmas lights between eye screws, the ping-pong of my front doorbell startled me. Casey, still working on the tree, answered. She kept her voice hushed, but I recognized the fear in her rushed whisper. Whoever was there, she wouldn't allow in the house.

Dumping the lights, I leaped into the guest room, grabbed the Remington, and half-slid down my hall. Tearing around the arched doorway, I ran into the living room.

"Get out of the way, Casey." I racked the shotgun and swung it up to my shoulder, pressing my cheek against the stock. "Whoever you are, I am armed, and this gun is loaded."

Casey cried out and spun around, hugging her belly. A man stepped into the doorway and shoved her aside. A handgun rose, pointed at me.

"Drop your weapon," he yelled. "Police."

"Cherry, it's Deputy Fells," called Casey. "What in the hell are you doing? Please don't shoot her, Fells. She's crazy with fever."

My finger slid off the trigger guard. Raising my left hand, I bent to lay the Remington on the floor. "I thought you were the creepy nephew." My voice faltered. "Oh, Lord forgive me. I swear on my life, I would never knowingly aim a gun at law enforcement, Jake."

Clouds swam across my vision. I felt, more than saw, Casey at my side, walking me to the sofa.

"You should've stayed in bed. You shouldn't be out here." Casey glanced behind her. "Jake, why don't we talk on the porch?"

"You sure?" The deputy looked up from his squat, the Remington in his arms.

"No," I yelled. "All y'all, stay inside. He's out there. Santa. He's watching the house."

"What?" Jake popped a cartridge from the shotgun, checked for the next round, and looked up. "Was that your call, Cherry? I know you've got the flu, but you've got to stay off the lines. We're still on a manhunt and the roads are terrible. We're making shitty progress."

"Call? Cherry called?" Casey's voice sounded sharp. "Fells, I thought you were coming out here to tell us about Luke— Never mind. Let me get Cherry to bed, and we'll talk."

"Luke?" I said. "Why would you come here to tell us about Luke?"

The heat drained from my body. Cold seeped in, turning my fingers white. I stared at my hands, then at Casey.

A fat tear rolled down her cheek. She swiped at it, raised her chin, and looked away.

"What happened?" I turned toward Fells.

His body vibrated with tension. Pulling the action bar back on the Remington, he popped out another round and set the cartridge on the floor. Keeping his eyes on the shotgun, he continued to unload it.

"Fells, I'm really sorry. I didn't know it was law enforcement at the door. What manhunt? Where's Luke? Is he on a manhunt?"

The deputy's jaw twitched. His eyes moved from the shotgun to Casey. Lines had tightened around his eyes as he switched his gaze back to me. "You can't go waving a gun around, Cherry. What if I were a neighbor kid? I could call you in on that."

"Please don't make this worse," said Casey. "It's already bad enough."

"I know. I know. I'm really sorry," I said. "I thought someone was threatening Casey and the baby. I have to protect her."

Casey clamped a hand over her mouth. Her eyes squeezed shut, and tears bled from the corners. Sniffling, she lifted her hand. "I know you have to tell his family first," she said, her voice a raw whisper. "But can't you tell us something?"

"I don't know anything for sure, Casey. I can't tell you what I don't know." Holding the shotgun, Deputy Fells rose. Shotgun shells stood in a row at his feet. "What's Cherry talking about?"

She sighed. "The weird neighbor next door caught me watching him through the window, and he gave me the finger across the throat sign."

Fells held up a hand and backed out the doorway. After leaning to look at the house next door, he stepped back inside. "Your neighbor did that? Who lives there?"

"Martha Mae Boyes. Not her. Her nephew." Casey rubbed her eyes with the back of her arm. "Martha Mae hurt her back. Her nephew is creeping us out."

"You want me to talk to him?"

"Forget it." She shook her head. "You better tell us what you know."

Dazed, I looked from Deputy Fells to Casey. I couldn't stop shaking. A pit had formed inside my chest. Afraid of what would fall in, I shouted, "Tell him about Pearl."

Casey spoke woodenly. "Pearl went over to check on Martha Mae and hasn't come back."

"Did you call her?" asked Fells.

"Of course, we called her. She didn't answer," I said. "And I called Gertie Sweetley."

"I'm taking away your phone," snapped Casey. "Why can't you just rest in bed like a normal person?"

"I'm not normal," I yelled. My voice broke. A lump rose in my throat, and I thought I might choke. "Go next door, Jake Fells. There's something going on. I saw Santa choking Mrs. Boyes with the Christmas lights."

"You did not," hissed Casey. "It's the fever. You got me all worked up, too. I didn't want to think about Luke, so I played along. Stop it. Just let Deputy Fells say what he's got to say. There's no point in waiting anymore."

"The nephew threatened you. You saw that." I gasped. My chest constricted. I couldn't catch a breath. "Pearl's over there. The nephew moved the tree. And Mrs. Boyes's car is on the street. Did you see that?"

"You think Grandpa wanted to hear Grandma Jo's cancer had come back? He listened to the doctor anyway, even though the doctor was an ass." Casey took another swipe at her tears. "I know it's Christmas. I've been trying to protect you from the news. But your man is a deputy. You know what can happen. Don't make this harder on Fells."

Fells had taken his hat off. Held it between his hands.

I slid back against the wall. My bones hurt too much to sit up. I nodded for him to continue while the pit inside me widened. I teetered at the edge, noting the darkness beneath.

Deputy Fells started with the bank robbery. Told me Luke was a hero. Explained the gang's escape and the reasons why they'd lost the van. Then lost the perps.

And lost my man.

Numbly, I took the last step and fell into that pit.

SIXTEEN

MAIZIE ALBRIGHT

#FROSTYTHESNOWWOMAN

I HOPED Casey and her sick sister would be safe. Possibly, Jay had just picked a strange place to smoke. Nash would accuse me of jumping to conclusions. But he'd also say the situation was hinky at best.

From the artist's carport, I tiptoed to peer around the back of the house, but I couldn't see Jay nor the burning embers of his cigarette. The artist's backyard had a fence running around it. Unless he'd returned to Martha Mae's, Jay still watched from the side of her house.

In the artist's drive, I positioned myself between the old truck and the Firebird, squatting in the shadow between them. Spotted Jay still at the corner of Martha Mae's house, smoking. Innocently. Or smoking was a pretense for something else. Why would he stand on the side of the house in the freezing cold and not on the porch?

Was he watching the artist's house? Or waiting for someone?

After thirty minutes of squatting, I thought I'd lose my mind. They don't teach you stuff like this in the Criminal Justice courses at U Cal, Long Beach. The temperature continued to drop. I couldn't feel my toes. Under the streetlight, the neighborhood yards looked coated in sugar. The street glistened and not in a good way. Beneath me, a thin layer of ice covered the cement. I had to remind myself that I'd have more heat loss standing than squatting. Silver Linings. However, I could see glute exercises in my future.

A depressing thought so close to Christmas.

I'd make it a New Year's resolution. I couldn't disappoint Carol Lynn by turning down all the cookies she'd spent weeks baking. Not to mention the holiday dinner she'd planned. There'd been a mention of green bean casserole. Which, I'm pretty sure, is illegal in California. Anyway, I'd never tasted it. But I liked any food with the word casserole in the title.

My Christmas dinner reflections were interrupted by a car's engine. The motor gunned and slackened in choppy repetition. Eventually, the vehicle appeared, creeping down the street. Sliding and recovering. A patrol car. Forks County Sheriff.

Hallelujah. The cavalry.

They didn't use lights and sirens, but Santa must have heard my prayer. Soon, this would all be over. The pregnant sister would tell the cop about the black hole in Martha Mae's house where people keep disappearing. They'd quickly figure out Jay and the woman-who-may-be-Krystal must be connected to the bank robbery, giving them the legal impetus to search the house.

Unless, of course, Krystal turned out to be a nun, wrongly accused of a crime. The judge had dropped her earlier charges, after all. I still had hope for Krystal.

But finally, I'd be warm. And I could make my way home to Remi and Nash. As soon as the roads cleared.

Julia Pinkerton never let the police take over a case unless she'd already solved it. That's the difference between TV fiction and real life. I was happy to turn over this mess to the cops. Nash would be proud of me. Not only did I find Krystal (I think), but I helped solve a bank robbery (maybe). I was too cold to pat myself on the back, but props is props.

If the police needed extra testimony, I'd crawl out of my hiding spot. For now, I (and, by default, my probation officer) would stay out of their way.

The poor deputy was having difficulty parking at the curb. The car kept sliding into the street. Oh boy, black ice.

Speaking of ice. I glanced at the sheen below me, hoping my boots hadn't stuck. Not that I was doing anything wrong, but it didn't seem smart to stay crouched between cars on someone's driveway with a police officer about to walk past me. I scrambled up the drive, grabbing vehicles to pull myself along. Under the carport, I crept toward the fence. Put my hand on the gate, changed my mind, and circled outside of the fence.

Following the fence, I plodded along in the crunchy grass. Passing Martha's dug-up garden, I headed for the group of trees that hid her house from the neighbor's. It was too far to see anything well, but a good place to stakeout (or hide) while the police did their thing. I figured bank robbers trying to escape the police would run out of the back of the house. The police would surround the house. I'd get to see the action from this safe vantage point.

And could melt into the backyard behind me if the action looked a little too hot.

For a good forty-five minutes, I waited, shivering next to a tree. A copse of trees is much colder than hunkering near a house. Tried calling Nash, but he didn't answer. Thought about calling Lamar, but he went to bed super early due to owning the Dixie Kreme Donut Shop. I stood then squatted, willing myself to think warm thoughts. Tried on a very merry Nash Christmas fantasy, but when he took off his shirt (in my head), I broke out in goosebumps, making the cold worse. Even the memory of his Jessica Rabbit tat flexing over his massive deltoid did nothing for me. Except wish Jessica into a sweater.

Throwing a blanket over the dream of near-naked Nash, I added a roaring fire. And a space heater.

I was having a blue Christmas. Literally. My fingers were going to fall off. My nose felt a shade similar to Santa's. I was pretty sure my internal organs had a coating of frost. No longer numb, my toes actually hurt. *The Shining's* ending kept flashing through my mind. Which didn't help me feel any warmer.

Forget it, I thought. I'd rather get in trouble with my probation officer than hide from the police. At least a California prison was warm.

I trudged across the backyard, angling toward the artist's house. On the way, I checked the garden where Jay had been digging. The string of lights provided enough illumination to see the hole had been filled in. Which was a little comforting. Also, a little disconcerting, not knowing what had been in the hole. I thought about a quick dig (one way to warm up), but the shovel was gone. I'd just point the police toward the lovely mound full of evidence Jay had left for them.

Nearing the artist's fence line, I halted to check the side of the house. Jay had disappeared. He'd seen the patrol car, obviously. I crept between the houses, hoping I didn't look as suspicious as I felt. Peered into the front yard.

No patrol cars. Not even one.

What happened to my cavalry? Had Jay been caught quickly and quietly and taken back to the sheriff's office? But wouldn't I have heard something? All was calm. Not so bright. I could see well enough into the house. Lights were on in the back, but there was no movement.

Wait. If the police hadn't arrested Jay…Or hadn't searched the house for bank robbers…Or missing people…

That meant I was the cavalry.

Supershizzles.

SEVENTEEN
CHERRY TUCKER

FOR WHAT FELT like a long time, I couldn't make myself move from the settee. I lay slumped against the wall, feeling but not feeling the ache in my bones. I stared at the little tree Casey had put in the front window. Hating it. Hating the cheap ornaments and the blinkety-blink lights and the tacky gold tinsel she'd draped over the branches with little care. An end dangled from the bottom branch, swaying as the heater kicked on beneath it. Tiny bits of tinsel and fake pine needles vibrated on the wooden floor. She'd tacked my stocking to the window ledge. Grandma Jo's artist angel smiled at me.

I didn't smile back. I wanted to walk across the room and throw the tree out the door. Rip the stocking down. Once again Christmas had brought me nothing but pain and heartache. Even my quickie marriage and even quicker annulment from Todd had happened at Christmas. And this year I had the flu.

The damn pit inside me yawned, but I refused to think about *that*.

"You want anything, Cherry?" Casey called from the kitchen. "Tea?"

I wanted Christmas to be over. I wanted this flu to be done. I wanted Deputy Fells to believe me about Mrs. Boyes's creepy nephew. I wanted Pearl to stroll in and tell me she'd helped Martha Mae slip her disc back in place.

I wanted Luke back.

But I wasn't thinking about *that*.

Pushing myself into sitting, I considered the creepy nephew, Pearl, and Martha Mae. I shuffled into the kitchen. We'd waited too long to check on Pearl.

I'd waited too long. Damn flu.

"When exactly was the bank held up?"

"What?" Casey glanced over her shoulder. She stood at the stove, stirring a pot. Barefoot and pregnant.

I shook that thought from my mind. "What time was the bank robbed?"

"Around noon." She paused her stirring, then resumed to a furious whisking.

"Why didn't you tell me?" I hugged my arms across my chest to keep from shivering.

"I didn't want to ruin your Christmas."

"Too late for that." I couldn't keep the vehemence from my voice. "I already had the flu."

Her head dipped and body trembled. She turned slowly, fighting tears. "If it weren't the flu, it'd be something else. You're bound and determined to find something wrong with this time of year. And we have a lot to be thankful for."

"Not me. Not anymore." I stared at her belly, hating my argument. From inside the pit, I could only see dark walls.

She turned back to the stove. "I'm sorry I didn't tell you about the bank robbery. And...Luke. But you were laid flat — should be still — and I don't trust you. You've already been talking crazy today about what's going on next door—"

"Crazy? Pearl's not back, Case. Despite what Deputy Fells said, things are not right over there." My voice rose, and I forced myself back to calm. "That man's been acting weird all day. I know what I thought I saw. You telling me you're not worried about Pearl? You want to call Grandpa Ed and tell him that Pearl could be in trouble and we're doing nothing to help her?"

"Pearl can handle herself."

"You sure about that?"

Casey spun to face me. "She's over there helping Martha Mae. You've been delusional. Half of what you've said today has made no sense."

"We don't *know* that Martha's hurt her back. You tried to talk Deputy Fells out of going next door. It's his job, Casey."

Her bottom lip trembled. She wrapped her arms around her belly.

"For the same reason you should have, too. Because he needs to be out there looking for Luke Harper's—"

"Don't you say it," I hissed. "Don't say body."

"If there's a situation next door, they'd pull deputies off the manhunt." Casey sniffed. "But you know procedure. Uncle Will lectures us on it enough. Procedure means even if they have probable cause, they need a warrant to search the house. And Fells did go next door. He didn't get invited inside, but he said he talked to Pearl himself."

"I don't believe him. Maybe the nephew threatened her or something. Why wouldn't Pearl answer her phone? And why's Mrs. Boyes's car parked on the street? They moved her tree and the car, Casey. It's weird."

"The nephew was with Mrs. Boyes when the robbery happened. The nephew's just creepy. Pearl's not in any trouble. She's staying with a sick friend."

"The nephew could be involved with the bank robbery."

"You're ridiculous."

My sister was ridiculous, too. But the hollows beneath her eyes were purplish-blue. Her shoulders had bowed like she'd wilted. Her normal cock-of-the-walk demeanor seemed more like scared hen.

Casey'd never been a Luke Harper fan. Hated his family and him by default. Motherhood had filled her with a crazed yearning to see me settled. And since she couldn't convince me to take back my sort-of-ex, Todd, she'd turned her hurry-up-and-get-my-sister-married sights on Luke. And now her heart was breaking for him. A man, seven months earlier, she'd claimed to hate.

Hormones. Rotting her brain and revving her emotions. Probably what drove Eve to take that damn apple.

"Why don't you lay in the guest room?" I said. "I'm feeling better. I'll look after myself."

She yawned. "I'm making cocoa."

"You can reheat it later. Take a nap or something."

She didn't argue but shuffled toward the guest room.

I followed her, carrying the Remington. "I'll leave this with you. Be careful because it's loaded."

"I thought Fells unloaded it." Casey gave me a look but took the shotgun.

I strolled to the single window that looked onto the porch. Double-pane with built-in muntin bars and plantation shutters. Front-facing windows with a couple of layers of wood and glass. It felt safer than my bedroom. The side windows on my house didn't have muntin bars. I locked the shutters with the hook and eye. Closed the louvers.

"Don't do anything stupid, Cherry."

I turned from the window. Casey stood cradling the shotgun over her belly.

"I'm not about to start stupid now," I said. "But keep the lights off, just in case. I've taken some security measures."

She arched an eyebrow and climbed into bed. "You're still sick."

"I'm being careful."

This wasn't my first rodeo, although it was my first with the flu. Maybe Casey had hoped Movie Star would take care of business. But who knows where the PI had gone?

It was time for me to get back in the saddle, flu be damned. I might have lost Luke, but I wasn't going to lose my sister and Pearl.

OUTSIDE, the cold just about knocked me over. Followed by the ice. I slip-slided my way to Mrs. Boyes's, glad I had bundled up. If I crashed, at least my layers would prevent the fall from hurting too much. On Mrs. Boyes's porch, I glanced in the front window, noted the empty room and the placement of the tree. The tree fueled my anger. Anger forestalled my flu symptoms. Shoving my finger into her buzzer, I rang long then with repeated jabs.

Nothing.

I pounded on the door. "I know y'all are in there," I hollered, cupping my hand over my mouth and aiming my voice at the glass. "I demand to see Pearl."

Grabbing the doorknob, I rattled it. "I've no patience for this today."

I stomped to the steps, knelt, and lifted the poinsettia pot, looking for Mrs. Boyes's key. No key. Everyone knew Mrs. Boyes kept her key under that pot. Rage surged through me. First the tree, then the car, and now the key.

I kicked the door with my boot and hammered with my fist. "You know that deputy who was just here? Did you see him while y'all were slinking around my yard? I'll get the law back here. I'm giving you to the count of five before I call 9-1-1. And if you're really related to Mrs. Boyes, you'd know my uncle is the sheriff."

A light flipped on in the kitchen.

Figured.

A woman answered the door. Brunette with short hair.

That I wasn't expecting.

"Who're you?" she said.

"You're kidding me, right?" I said. "Because I know you don't live here. You've got no business asking me who I am. Who're you?"

"Martha Mae's niece."

"Miss Martha Mae doesn't have a niece." I narrowed my eyes.

She narrowed hers back. "She damn well does. It's me."

"Then can you tell me your name? I've known Mrs. Boyes my whole life and she's never once mentioned a niece."

"It's Krys. I'm here for Christmas."

"Isn't that nice? Bless your heart." I scanned her slim body, looking for odd lumps that might indicate a weapon. If this were only summer. Krys wore a bulky sweater that halfway covered her jeans. No way to tell. "Krys, get out of my way. I need to talk to Pearl."

"Who's Pearl?" she said.

"Who's Pearl? The woman apparently taking care of Mrs. Boyes's alleged back condition. When she's supposed to be helping me get over the flu. Now if I find Pearl's caring for Miss Martha Mae, I'll mosey back home. But if something's happened to her, you're in for it."

"Am I?" she arched a brow. She placed a hand on the frame, blocking my passage.

"Don't mess with me," I snarled. "I'm infecting you with influenza as we speak. And it's the stomach kind. If you were smart, you'd get out of my way."

"If you were smart, you'd go home."

"No one's ever accused me of being a brain surgeon." I placed a hand on my hip. "But they do accuse me of being fearless." Also, foolhardy, but I wasn't going to add that. "I'm not leaving."

"Fine." She dropped her hand from the door frame. "I'll show you where they are."

I followed her inside. My eyes cut to the dark dining room entrance to my left then to the blinking tree pushed against the window. "Why'd you move the tree?"

Krys shrugged and waved a hand toward the hall. "They're in the bedroom. Naturally."

"You lead the way. Since you're the niece and all." I didn't trust her. And I didn't know where the nephew had gone.

She rolled her eyes and strode toward the hall.

"So, after all these years, Miss Martha Mae has a visit from her niece and a nephew." On the same day as the Forks County Savings and Loan was robbed. But I kept that part to myself. At the hall entrance, I hung back to peek into the kitchen. My eyes gravitated toward the back porch. Mrs. Boyes's star lights that had hung from the rafters now lit the floor and her trees had been knocked over. "What happened out there?"

She glanced over her shoulder. "Wind, I suppose."

"When'd you get here? I didn't see you earlier."

"Got here this morning."

"Didn't see you. Saw the nephew. Looks too old to be your brother. Where'd he go?"

"He's out," she said, skipping the family tree.

"Kind of surprising, since the roads are a sheet of black ice."

Krys shrugged and pointed to the door on the far right. "They're in there."

"Go on in," I said. "You best announce me."

"I don't think it's necessary." She reached beneath her sweater and pulled out a pistol. "Since y'all know each other so well, no introductions are needed."

Dammit. Of all the times to be right.

I lifted my hands. "You held up the bank. You and the nephew?"

"I don't believe I said any such thing." She unzipped my jacket, ran her hands down my sides, and pulled my phone from my coat pocket. "If you thought we robbed the bank, why'd you come in here? You are a stupid woman."

Also, a sick one. I hoped she picked up a good amount of germs, patting me down. She knelt, feeling inside my boots.

"You had something to do with the bank," I said. "Maybe you technically didn't rob it. Driver?"

Her eyes flicked up, giving her away.

"Left them high and dry? That's some honor among thieves. They got lucky with the weather. Otherwise, the FBI would have taken over. Now you're on the run, and you don't even have the money. You know the deputy your partners took hostage? He's mine." I gritted my teeth. "Where is he?"

"I don't know what you're talking about." She jerked to standing and motioned with the gun. "Go. Bathroom's inside."

I planted my feet, stared her in the eye. "If y'all hurt a hair on that deputy's head, I'll get you. All y'all. Every single last one."

"Kind of hard to do that now, isn't it?" Her brows rose with her smirk. "I heard he barreled right in that bank, just like you did this house. Got yourself in the same predicament, didn't you?"

EIGHTEEN

MAIZIE ALBRIGHT

#HARKYOUHERALDANGELANDLISTENUP

I RETURNED to the artist's house, fighting panic. The patrol car had parked there. They must have spoken to the police. Was an arrest made or not?

At the kitchen door, a bright spotlight blinded me. Shielding my eyes, I couldn't squint past colored lights backlit by a stark, white beam. Inside the door, rows of Christmas lights stretched across the frame. Someone had positioned a lamp just behind the door to beam through the squares of glass. The glare reminded me of professional camera lighting. Bright, stark, and hot. The artist might use something similar for her portrait painting. What was she doing beaming it at the door now?

Backing from the door, I carefully picked my way through the piles of junk and carefully stepped my way across the icy drive. More lights blared through the window and door. Old-fashioned Christmas lights had been wrapped around the porch and across the entrance at knee height. Like holiday lighting for elves.

I stepped into the grass and checked my watch. It'd been a little over an hour since I'd last talked to Casey. Someone had been busy. And now I couldn't get back in the house.

Circling between the two houses, I glanced into the bedroom window. Christmas lights shone above a bed where it looked like someone slept. She didn't look well protected, not like in the kitchen and front porch. An air conditioner unit stood under the window.

Climbing on top, I reached to knock on the glass. Just before my knuckle rapped, I stopped. Some instinct caused me to focus on the window itself. I cocked my head, adjusting my focus, and spotted the thin wire stretched across the inside window frame.

Tripwire? For an alarm?

I hoped nothing else. As Nash often warned his more redneck clients, injury-inducing and potentially lethal booby traps were illegal. You can defend your home, but a *Home Alone* mousetrap isn't self-defense in the eyes of the law. If an intruder was hurt or died, the home-owner went to jail. And would likely get sued.

It's the threat of a lawsuit that usually makes the client change their mind about buying a security system instead of creating their own.

At the back of the house, I hopped the fence and tiptoed across the perimeter. Someone had lined the cement slab running alongside the house with empty cans filled with coins and nails. A landmine field of noise. Christmas lights hung in tight rows in the back windows. Barri-cading the windows with lighting.

Their safety measures looked festive. In fact, the house had gone from Grinch cave to Whoville home in one evening.

Whether it would deter Jay or Krystal from a break-in, I wasn't sure. Maybe they'd already been arrested. It was the season of hope. Although finding "*Home Alone* meets Whoville" next door didn't give me much comfort.

Anyway, it looked like the visitors weren't welcomed at the artist's house.

I jogged toward Martha Mae's house. Hoarse shouting and pounding stopped me. I listened to the rising anger. A new voice. A woman's. But the strength of her fury didn't match the strength of her voice. Hurrying toward the corner of the house, I crouched, then poked my head around the corner.

A girl — or tiny woman, hard to tell by her size and the amount of clothing she had on — pounded and kicked Martha Mae's door.

Pulling back, I leaned my head against the house and stared at the moonless sky. Now what? New people kept popping up in my simple case to retrieve a bank-robbing, cop-kidnapping granddaughter (unless she'd become a nun). I held my face in my mittened hands and sighed. My breath warmed my face for a few seconds. Dropping my hands, my skin turned damp, cold, and miserable.

Just like my day. And now, night.

The light in the Christmas tree window grew brighter. The pounding stopped. Followed by the clicks and squeaks of a door unlocking and opening.

I peeked. The tiny woman entered the house. The woman who could be Krystal had let her in.

Sucktastic. Another body for the garden hole of doom.

I had lost my Christmas hope. Where was my Hallmark Channel angel when I needed one?

NINETEEN
CHERRY TUCKER

KRYS DIDN'T KNOW this wasn't my first time to be duct-taped. First time to share that experience with Pearl and my neighbor, though. Not that I enjoyed being duct-taped. In previous escapades, I'd been hogtied in various degrees by an assortment of nefarious characters. Criminals loved duct tape. And that was the sort of luck I ran. Maybe more due to my nature than luck, but that was neither here nor there.

The fact was, it took more than duct tape to get this artist down.

Not only had Pearl's ankles, wrists, and mouth been taped, she'd also been strapped to Martha Mae's toilet seat. Seeing me, Pearl's ruddy complexion had paled.

"Casey's safe," I'd said. "I know everything. The police are aware of the situation. It's all under control."

Pearl's eyes told me she knew a fibber when she saw one.

"Time for you to shut your mouth." Krys ripped off a piece of tape and slapped it over my mouth. "The police aren't aware of anything. I talked to them myself."

Lord, I thought. Jake Fells didn't know Pearl. Kind of surprising, since Pearl's mouth was bigger than mine. Why didn't Uncle Will send an older deputy over? One who actually knew citizens? And could spot a liar?

Mrs. Boyes lay in the bathtub — also taped — with an ugly welt around her neck and another on her forehead. Her skin was pasty and eyes closed. Unconscious. And if she didn't have a bad back now, she'd have one later, lying in a heap in a cold bathtub.

That sumbitch Santa. Strangled this sweet woman who couldn't bake worth a darn but gave out cookies and fruitcakes every Christmas all the same.

I thought I might explode with anger. Heat poured off me, making my skin sticky and hair slick.

Out of places to stash bodies in the master bath, Krys forced me to sit on the sink. Threw my coat and winter accessories in a corner. She taped my wrists before taping them to the underside of the sink faucet. Pulled off my boots to tape my ankles together. Unfortunately, found the pocketknife I'd slipped in my boot, too. Ran tape back and forth over my thighs until I was attached to the sink counter.

I'll tell you one thing, sitting in a sink basin is not comfortable in the least. But thank you, Lord, for giving me a skinny derriere despite my previous feelings on that subject.

"Try anything," said Krys, "And I'll shoot your grandma. You see the woman in the tub? That's what happens when you piss me off."

Pearl's eyes widened. She turned toward me, blinking rapidly.

I couldn't retort with the tape over my mouth, but I mentally flung a few well-chosen words at Krys. Waited until she closed the door and began working my wrists and ankles. All I needed was to jerk up and away. Or find a sharp corner to rub the tape against. However, I hadn't been taped to a faucet in my earlier duct tape experiences. Leaning back, I wiggled an elbow and succeeded in turning on the water, drenching the seat of my pants. Took another minute to knock the water off.

I was no longer hot.

Pearl snorted. Glad she still had a sense of humor. Still, I cut my eyes at her and gave her a good eye roll. She motioned with her chin at the cabinet behind me.

I scooted sideways as best I could, and after a series of misses, my right elbow bumped the bottom of the mirror. The magnet unlatched. I bent over my legs, my arms straining behind me. Leaned right and jerked up, smacking the mirror. Feeling like my arms might pull from their sockets, I flattened over my legs. The mirror swung open thirty degrees, brushing the top of my back. I nudged it farther with my right shoulder. Leaning sideways as far as possible, I pulled up behind the mirror.

I cranked my neck to see behind me. Rows of medication, ointments, powders, and lotions. I turned to see the other side. Barber scissors, nail files, manicure scissors, and other helpful items stood in a small plastic cup.

Jackpot.

I scooted back, then turned, knocking my shoulder into the shelf. Pill bottles rained over me. The plastic cup fell, spilling its contents on the sink, then rolled to the floor. Behind the open mirror, I couldn't see Pearl. I hoped she was mentally congratulating me on retrieving various cutting instruments.

Of course, I had no way of picking them up.

Round two.

I wiggled inside my wet jeans. The duct tape strap was stuck to my jeans, but I could move my thighs beneath them. Couldn't pull up my knees, though. I sucked in my stomach and backed into the faucet. Pinched my fingers. Twisted right and left. Working my fingers down the back of my pants, I pushed at the waistband. Water dripped down my back. Chills wracked my body, but I ignored them. Slowly I pulled down the jeans. Twisted and wriggled. For once the flu worked in my favor. I'd already lost weight. My jeans were loose, and my hips slipped free.

If Luke ever complained about my lack of booty, I'd use this as an example of a benefit.

Oh Lord, Luke.

The pit closed around me. Tears welled. Snot pooled in my nose. I sniffed it back.

Come on, Cherry. This is not a time to lose focus. Tuckers don't cry, we get even. Breathe. Remember Pearl and Mrs. Boyes are still here. Casey's next door with the lunatic nephew running around and the movie star PI is nowhere to be found.

My back scraped against the faucet. My fingers clawed at the denim. My shoulders hit the cabinet shelving. More bottles and tubes flew, showering the sink and floor. My hips lifted above the faucet. I had to lean back, using the cabinet to carry my weight. My thighs slid free, and a moment later, my feet climbed into the sink.

I twisted hard, trying to rip the tape on the faucet. Worked my wrists back and forth, loosening and rolling the tape. The cool air bit into my bare legs. Chills ran up my back, and sweat poured off my temples. Too intent to stop, I ignored the pain in my shoulders and arms. The rolled band of tape reached the apex of the faucet's curve and slid off in a series of jerks.

For a moment, I breathed in short puffs, then wiggled my hips through the circle of my arms. Brought them around, turned, and found the scissors. Poked them through the tape in my feet until I could rip them apart. Then scrambled out of the sink. And fell on the floor.

With my wrists still bound, I used my fingers to pull off the tape from my mouth.

Gasping, I looked up at Pearl. "How's that?"

Her eyebrows shot up, then lowered. She nodded toward her taped hands.

"I need you to hold the scissors as tight as you can, so I can rip the tape on my hands first."

Pearl shrugged.

I shoved the scissors between her fingers. She squeezed. I pushed my duct tape binds against the blades, sawing. She dropped the scissors. We tried again.

I didn't want to worry Pearl, but my energy level was in serious trouble. If I were a video game, it'd be flashing red. The inside of my head felt like an ocean breaking on a shore. Black dots danced before my eyes. The room spun.

The scissor blade pierced the tape. I ripped my wrists apart. Dropping to all fours, I ducked my head and panted. Above me, Pearl wiggled and grunted. Tried to kick me with her taped ankles.

"Just a tic," I said. "Give me a second or I'm going to lose all the Gatorade you made me drink."

Pearl stomped her feet. I cranked my head. She was staring at the door and grunting.

Someone was in the bedroom.

My wet pants were still taped to the sink. The cabinet mirror hung open. Miss Martha Mae's toiletries and medicines littered the floor.

Pants-less, I crawled across the floor. Rose to shaky knees and locked the bathroom door. Leaned my back against the door.

"One minute," I said to Pearl. And passed out.

TWENTY
MAIZIE ALBRIGHT

#DOYOUHEARWHATIHEAR
#YOUDON'TWANTTOHEARWHATIHEAR

SOON AFTER THE TINY, angry woman entered Martha Mae's home — If the day had gone differently, I might guess she to be an over-large elf. Her coat had a deer head silhouette painted on the back. Ornaments hung from his antlers. — Jay exited.

After trying Nash unsuccessfully, I hung up. My finger had pressed the numbers nine and one when the sound of a door closing sent shivers down my spine. After the last burst of noise, the eerie *snick* sounded foreboding. I snapped the phone shut and clutched it. From my squat against the side of the house, I peered around the corner.

Jay stood on the porch, pulling his pack of cigarettes from his coat pocket. His body faced the street but his head moved. Scanning the neighborhood. As he looked to his right, I ducked back.

Knowing where he likely headed — exactly where I crouched — I hauled butt toward the backyard.

Oh God, I thought. I changed my mind. All I want for Christmas is peace on earth and let it begin with me.

By keeping me alive.

In the garden, I crouched behind the fence. Martha Mae's Christmas fairy lights brightened the garden, darkening the area I needed to see. And creating a nice glow on my hiding spot. I ripped the lights off the fence. Pulled them into a pile until I reached the battery box and switched them off.

Where did Jay go?

My heart pounded. Don't worry about Jay. She-Who-Could-Be-Krystal was in the house with the angry elf and the grandmothers doing who knows what.

Call 9-1-1.

I pulled the phone from my pocket. Nearby, the loud crash of breaking glass broke the stillness. The screech of an alarm jerked me out of my shocked, frozen state.

The artist's house. She had trip-wired her bedroom window. And she was sick in bed. With a pregnant sister.

Oh, my God.

Yanking the string of lights off the ground, I ran for the house. The air conditioner blocked my ability to get close to the window. The window was broken. Pieces of shattered glass covered the unit. Under the glow of the Christmas lights, a man moved around the room. Jay. He flung the bedding aside. No sick artist.

Sick artist was the angry elf. But where was Casey? My stomach clenched. I glanced at my hand gripping the string of lights. Why did I bring lights? What was I going to do with this? Lasso him?

I sucked in frigid air. Held it to keep from screaming.

The overhead light blared on. Jay stood at the bedroom door. He rattled the knob, and another alarm shrieked. Leaping back, he stared at the door, then threw his body against it. A board that had been balanced above the lintel fell, raining jars and cans. Jay threw up his hands over his head. Paint splashed and dripped.

Jay was a multi-colored mess. And angry.

Shiztastic. Where was Casey?

"Open this door," he shouted. "Or I'm shooting the shit out of it. The police won't get here in time, so don't bother calling them again. That was your last mistake. You and your sister's nosiness was the first. You brought this on yourself by not minding your own business. Now I'm taking care of business."

Reaching into his jacket, he pulled out a pistol.

I screamed.

Jay spun, aiming the pistol at the window.

I fell to the ground.

A shot rang out. Followed by a second blast and the sound of broken glass.

TWENTY-ONE
CHERRY TUCKER

PEARL'S MUFFLED shouting woke me up. I blinked, noted my sprawl on the bathroom floor, and crawled to standing. Feeling like a bewildered prairie dog popped from his hole, I spun between the door to Pearl. Chose the door. I pressed my ear against the crack next to the jamb. The bedroom was quiet. I scuttled back to Pearl, ripped the tape off her mouth, then used the scissors to cut her free.

"Lord, I've never been so glad that Martha Mae has one of those cushioned toilet seats." Pearl stood and stretched, rubbing her back.

Not the first words I expected.

"We need to get Mrs. Boyes out of here," I said. "And you."

"Don't forget yourself," said Pearl. "You're not fit for saving anyone. You were laid out on that floor for five minutes."

"You want me to tape you up again?" I glared at Pearl, then softened. "Sorry. Are you all right?"

"My heart is still ticking, ain't it?" She glanced at Mrs. Boyes. "Don't know if I can say the same for Martha Mae. Lord, I've been praying she'll live. They just dumped here in the bathtub, can you believe it? What kind of folks dump old ladies in bathtubs?"

"Bank robbers. I saw the nephew strangle her." I touched her cheek. "She's still alive, Pearl."

"That girl said she did it."

"Doesn't matter who did it, Mrs. Boyes needs an ambulance. You think we should lift her?" I turned to look at Pearl.

She stared at the door. "That girl has a gun, Cherry. We need to stay put until the police arrive."

"They've already been here and left again. The streets aren't good for anything but hockey. There's no rescue coming."

Her knees gave way. She plopped on the toilet seat. The cushion hissed. "I've been locked in here all this time, and the sheriff's not coming for me?"

"They didn't have probable cause to search. Krys told Deputy Fells she was you. He didn't know the difference." I swallowed. "And he was in a hurry to get back to the manhunt."

"He should have known."

"I'd told you something fishy was going on, and you didn't believe me."

"You did no such thing. And you said Santa choked his reindeer, not bank robbers strangled poor Martha Mae."

"It doesn't matter, Pearl. I'm your rescue." I placed my hands on my hips, urging my weak body to appear tough.

A tear rolled down Pearl's cheek. "Well, if that doesn't just take the cake."

"Stay in here." I felt too sorry for Pearl to be offended. "Keep the door locked. Tend to Mrs. Boyes. Jam something between the door and the frame to keep Krys from opening it. If it's me, I'll say so."

"Maybe we need a secret word." Pearl sniffed. "If she can pretend to be me, that woman could pretend to be you."

"Okay." I patted Pearl's shoulder, then pulled on my boots and coat. "How about 'Merry Christmas?' I doubt a bank robber would think of such a thing."

I slowly opened the door, peering into the dark bedroom. Sidled out and closed the door. Behind me, I heard Pearl turning the lock. I needed a weapon. I glanced at my bare legs.

Pants would also be helpful.

Dresses and blouses filled her closet. I pulled open dresser drawers, yanking out clothes until I found something that resembled sweatpants. Four sizes too big. Yanked them on, stuffed them in my boots, and tied them with a strip of material I found in a basket on the floor.

A wave of dizziness hit me hard. I sank to the floor. Heard footsteps in the hall. I slid under Mrs. Boyes's bed.

Krys strode into the bedroom, eased up to the bathroom door, and listened.

For once in your life, please keep your mouth shut, Pearl.

Under the bed, dust bunnies threatened my nose. Krys wasn't moving from guard duty. I needed a distraction before she tried to open the door and find it locked. I didn't trust Pearl to stay quiet, the lock to hold, or Krys to not use her gun as a door opener.

I backed out from under the bed on the other side and crawled into the hallway. Tiptoed into the kitchen. Set the microwave to thirty seconds. Took ten seconds considering a heavy fruitcake versus Martha Mae's block of knives. I'd have a better chance of taking out Krys with a fruitcake lob to the head than using a knife in a gunfight. For safekeeping, I tossed the knife block into the garbage.

Twenty seconds. Dancing at the countdown, I looked left toward the garage door where I knew Martha Mae would have wicked gardening tools. Mrs. Boyes was a gardener. Kept me in tomatoes all summer. Glanced right and saw a shovel among all the debris on the screened-in porch.

Looked wicked enough to me. And with a longer reach than a carving knife. Less risky than a fruitcake.

The clock flashed ten. I scooted toward the porch, lugged open the sliding door, and hopped into the frigid night air. Grabbed the shovel. Scurried into the living room. Snatched the TV remote off the coffee table. Flattened against the wall next to the hall entrance.

The microwave beeped long and strong. Three times.

I gulped air. Three times.

A moment later, I heard Krys pattering down the hall. At her "What the hell," I smacked the TV remote, raised the volume, and tossed it. Gripped the shovel and swung it over my shoulder.

Across the living room, in matching blue headbands and rolled pants, Bing Crosby and Danny Kaye sang "Sisters."

Krys's "What the hell" rang out again. Footsteps rang in the kitchen.

My stomach tossed and churned. I tightened my grip and prayed for good aim.

Also, not to vomit.

A boot and the muzzle of her pistol appeared first. Taking a deep breath, I waited until she stepped into the room. Swung.

And a shot cracked the air just as Bing slapped Danny with his fan.

TWENTY-TWO
MAIZIE ALBRIGHT
#HARDCANDYCHRISTMAS

CLUTCHING MY HEART, I huddled on the ground next to the air conditioner unit. Across from me, Martha Mae's window had cracked, splintering into what looked like a giant snowflake. A center the size of a bullet hole. I looked up. Something blocked the artist's window. Rising slowly, I kept my back to the house and peeked. Jay stood with his back to the window. Pushed up against the broken frame.

What had happened? I'd heard two shots. Jay had aimed at me. My legs shook. I blinked past the spots dancing before my eyes.

Okay, don't think about Jay's gun. Think about the second shot. Because it hadn't sounded like the first. Muffled. But louder.

"I know where you're standing," yelled a voice from inside. "I've had tactical training and I ain't shooting with birdshot. These slugs will go through more than one wall. You think this hole is big? Think about what it'll do to a body. Get out of my house. Same way you came in."

Casey. Holy shizolis. The pregnant sister had blown a hole through the drywall with her sister's shotgun.

I had to stop the gun battle before someone was shot for real. A wall might slow a bullet, but it would still penetrate. She and her baby were at risk.

"Do it now," urged my inner Julia Pinkerton. "Save the woman and child while you still have the element of surprise. Her shotgun blast has him stunned. He's ready to climb out the window. In a second, he'll turn around."

All I had was a string of Christmas lights. I patted my pockets. And a candy cane.

Craptastic.

But if I wasn't so afraid of hurting someone, I'd be better armed.

One end of the candy cane had been sucked to a sharp point. Yanking off my mittens, I tested it against my thumb. No blood, but it made a small hole just the same. My (ruined) puffy jacket had kept it safe.

Time was of the essence, as they say. Julia Pinkerton had once stopped a would-be kidnapper with a homemade shiv made from a lipstick tube and a re-molded Jolly Rancher.

Not the time to remember Julia Pinkerton wasn't real. Or that the writers were sometimes lazy.

I sprung to my feet. Gripped the taped end of the candy cane in my fist. Flung the string of lights like a scarf around my neck. Climbed on the air conditioner, kicking off glass.

Grasping Jay's paint-covered collar with my left hand, I jabbed the pointed end of the candy cane into the side of his neck. Sliced across his skin. Then pressed the point in the softer flesh in the hollow of his jaw, beneath his ear.

Jay cursed. A jagged string of red dots crossed his neck. He clamped a hand over mine, letting go at the sound of the pump of the shotgun's slide.

"Hold it there, bucko," said Casey. "I see you through the hole. That first shot was a warning. I've got your chest sighted."

"I wouldn't move." Using my low, menacing Julia Pinkerton-on-the-prowl voice, I repeated the line from *Julia Pinkerton, Teen Detective* Season Eight, Episode Two. "Not unless you want to lose your carotid artery to my *sweet* blade."

I pressed harder, puncturing the skin. Hoped he didn't notice the peppermint scent. "Only takes two minutes to bleed out. Now, drop your weapon. Hands in the air."

"I'm going to kill you," said Jay. "Then I'm going to kill her."

"Casey, I've got Jay by the throat. But don't let that stop you." I studied the hardening rainbow colors on his hair and clothes. Drywall dust blew through the air. "I don't think you want to mess with these girls, Jay. They take home defense seriously."

"Drop your weapon, jackass," said Casey. "I've got the safety off. Maizie, y'all get out of the way. This shot will blow through him."

Jay cursed. A thunk sounded near his feet.

"He's unarmed, Maizie," yelled Casey. "I'm still covering you."

"Hands behind your back, Jay," I said. "Casey, if he tries anything, shoot first. I'm tying him up."

"This is not over," said Jay.

"Sit on the ledge," I growled.

White-knuckled with cold, I gripped the candy cane, matching the speed of my squat to Jay's sit. With my left hand, I yanked on the lights, pulling them off my neck. "Hands together. Cover me, Casey."

He strung an interesting litany of obscenities together.

Pocketing the candy cane, I blew on my hands and flexed my numb fingers. I wrapped the wired lighting around his wrists, yanked the wrists together, and wrapped them again. Pulling the string tight against his body, I wrapped his wrists to his torso. "If you move too much, the glass bulbs will break and cut your skin."

"I hope it cuts him up good," said Casey. "I'm coming in the bedroom."

In the distance, I heard a truck rumble.

"Casey," I hollered. "Someone's coming. Maybe the police."

The bedroom door banged open. "Man, Cherry stuck that doorstop in tight. What a mess. Paint and glass everywhere." Casey stomped into the bedroom, swinging the shotgun before her. "That's Nik. I called him a while ago. As a Slavic, he knows how to drive on ice. And he's got friends with a salt truck. Don't know how they got one, but they do. It's better not to know."

"You meet any Russians in prison, Jay?" I asked. "Her husband's Russian."

"Russian-ish. So are his friends." She aimed the gun barrel at Jay. "They don't play around. You better hope the police come before they learn you were going to shoot me."

"You got this, Casey?" I was a little worried about leaving Jay alone with her. For Jay's sake. Casey had the ferocious look of a mother bear protecting her cub. "I need to get to Martha Mae's. Find out what's going on over there."

"Yes, ma'am. You want his gun?" She'd squatted to scoop up the pistol and used the bed to climb back to her feet.

"Krystal had nothing to do with this," Jay spoke quickly, startling me. "It was all me."

"Are you confessing?" I pulled my phone from my pocket. "I want this recorded."

"Yep, I did it all. Krystal was just visiting her aunt."

Over Jay's head, I locked eyes with Casey. She shrugged. Leaned against the nightstand. Repositioned the gun.

"What exactly did you do?" I said. "For the record?"

"Drove the getaway car for the bank robbery. I can name everyone involved. Give a guess as to where they went after they split."

"You know where they took the cop?" said Casey sharply.

He hesitated. "No."

Casey pumped the shotgun's slide.

"I can give you all that information if you let Krystal go. She had nothing to do with this," said Jay. "I've done time. I know when I've lost. I'm willing to go back. Just let her go."

"What about Martha Mae Boyes? And Pearl?" I said. "What happened to them?"

"They're next door. I take full responsibility. Had them captive in the bathroom."

"You sumbitch," said Casey.

"I wasn't going to kill them. Just holding them until Krystal could get out of here. Same with you. We just needed to get gone first."

I looked at Casey. The police would want this information, but I didn't trust Jay. Why would he give up so easily? We might have double-teamed him, but he'd flipped from maniacal to melancholy.

Which reminded me of an episode of *Kung Fu Kate*, "Double-Crossed Deuces." I'd done that show at twelve, but still. The antagonist had been covering for someone. Like Jay might be doing for Krystal. But he must know Krystal would still be considered an accomplice.

"You're her father," I said. "You think you're helping Krystal."

His body tensed.

"Looks like she's past helping." Casey had picked up a pad of paper from the nightstand and flipped through the pages. "My sister drew everything she saw today. First picture shows Santa choking Mrs. Boyes. Except Santa's beard and hat had come off. It's a woman."

"That don't mean nothing," said Jay.

"You might not know this, but my sister is famous in these parts for her ability to quick sketch accurately. My uncle's hired her to sketch profiles at the sheriff's department. And she worked at Six Flags all during high school."

"What else is in that sketchbook?" I said. "That's evidence."

"You." Casey smirked. Tossing the sketchbook on the bed, she cradled the shotgun. "And this man showing me, you, and then Pearl the inside of Mrs. Boyes's house."

Oh boy, evidence of my breaking and entering. Oh well. There were more important considerations now.

"Do you have a phone on you, Jay?" I said. "Will Krystal answer if you call?"

At his nod, I reached into his coat pocket and retrieved the phone. He walked me through dialing Krystal's number.

"Well?" said Casey.

"She's not answering." I pocketed his phone.

"Dammit," said Jay. "Tell her I've given myself up. Immediately. Before you say anything else. Have her call me. I'll tell her. Before she does something she regrets."

"Casey, don't shoot him unless you absolutely have to. I'm going next door." I hopped off the air conditioner.

Then froze at the sound of a gunshot.

I whirled around, searching the artist's bedroom. But the sound hadn't come from this house. Casey had jumped to her feet and repositioned the shotgun. Jay had twisted to look out the window.

I leaned over the air conditioner. "Casey, can you get him into another room?"

She nodded.

"It's too late," said Jay morosely. "Damn girl."

"What's too late?" Scenes from every horror movie I'd ever known crossed my mind.

"Krystal crossed the line. There's no getting her back now."

"What are you talking about?"

"It's my fault. I couldn't protect Krystal when I was doing time. She managed to stay away from the law this long. Krystal's smart. But I told her to keep away from that woman, she'd lead her down the wrong road. Krys thinks she can play people, but I know better. That woman can talk her way in and out of situations better than Krys."

"What woman?" Please don't say, Celia Fowler, I thought. Please, don't let it be the grandma.

"Don't matter now," said Jay. "I tried to help her out of this situation. Willing to lay my life down for that girl. Go back to prison for my baby. But apples don't fall far from trees."

"Keep him talking, Casey. I've got to go next door to help." I glanced at Casey over his shoulder.

Her shoulders shook, but her dark eyes had shrunk into two slits, narrowed with rage.

"We need to know what's going on to help the police when they come."

"I heard that shot, same as you," she said. "And my sister doesn't have a gun. I know what's going on. You're going to get yourself killed, too."

"We don't know what happened." But as I ran, I prayed to my Hall-mark Channel angel. Please, please don't let anyone die.

TWENTY-THREE
MAIZIE ALBRIGHT

#GEEIWISHIWEREBACKINTHEARMY

NASH HADN'T TRAINED me in tactical defense situations. Despite what you see in the movies, private investigators aren't involved in shootouts. Nash hadn't bothered to train me much on anything. Except how to answer his phone, use his billing software, and to jiggle the office toilet handle when the water doesn't stop running.

Although I often discredited the writers on *Julia Pinkerton* and *Kung Fu Kate* for their unbelievable plots, my multitude of directors (TV production is a career meat grinder) had excelled at coaching me into making the unbelievable look believable. With the help of experts. Namely Detective Earl King, who showed me how to hold a gun properly and the real way officers clear a room.

Which was how I approached Martha Mae's house. Checking corners before proceeding. Running the wall. Scanning windows from the side.

I carefully climbed over the ice-coated porch rail and sidled to the front window. Repositioned to look again. Got a look from another angle. Hesitated. Then rang the doorbell and knocked.

An older woman in a sweatshirt decorated with goats answered. "Cherry told me not to let anyone in, but I figure if you're coming to kill us, you won't bother to ring the bell."

"Are you Pearl?" I said. "Are you all right?"

"My sciatica is acting up, thanks to sitting on a toilet all day, but other than that I'm fine." She stepped back, studying me. "You must be the nosy movie star."

"I'm Maizie Albright. Not a movie star, although I've done plenty of TV movies." I automatically stuck my hand out to shake hers. Luckily, I was used to improv. My adrenaline kick had subsided into a low hum and I turned myself over to another kind of instinct. Small talk with fans. "Now I'm a private investigator. Or at least training to be one. I hope. If it works out. Anyway, here to help."

"Can't say we need your help now unless you're driving an ambulance or a paddy wagon. Do you know where that man went?"

"Jay's been apprehended. Casey's got the shotgun on him. And help is on the way. I think."

She snorted. "Hope that baby doesn't throw her off balance. Guess you ought to come in. Colder than an Eskimo's outhouse out here."

I followed her inside. On the floor, a woman lay hogtied with what looked like lengths of fabric. She ducked her head up to study me.

"Are you Krystal Fowler?"

"Go to hell."

"Told us her name was Krys. I'm guessing her last name isn't Kringle." Pearl trotted to the couch, sat, and reached for the coffee cup on the coffee table.

White Christmas played on the TV. If it weren't for the hamstrung prisoner on the floor, it'd be a cozy scene.

"I'm watching her. I've got her gun right here. Shot it up the fireplace flue to show her I knew what I was doing." Pearl patted the pistol next to her thigh. "I didn't want to shoot up Martha Mae's house. It's a mess as it is."

"I'm going to kill you, old woman," said Krystal.

"You and what army? Try it, and I'll shoot you plain as day. I raise goats. I'm tougher than I look." Pearl's attention swiveled to the TV. She patted her chest and sniffled. "That Bing Crosby. Gets me every time."

Krystal's head thunked to the ground.

I'd entered a Christmas episode of *The Twilight Zone.*

"Aren't you worried she'll escape?" I said.

"Nah," said Pearl. "Too many knots. Plus, I have no compunction shooting someone who'd tied me to a toilet for hours on end. I'm stiffer than a corpse."

Okay, then. Take a note not to mess with Pearl.

"Where's Martha Mae Boyes?" I asked.

"On the bed. Took some work to get her there. She came to for a minute, but she's laid flat. That's why we need the ambulance. That girl choked her. I'm surprised Martha Mae didn't have a heart attack, but she's like me. Tough old bird."

"The artist?"

"Cherry? Passed out on the bedroom floor." Pearl shook her head, looking disgusted. "That's what happens when you overexert yourself with the flu. I warned her."

"Maybe you should check on them? I'll watch Krystal while you do."

"All right. I could use a break." Pearl rose, rubbing her lower back. She pointed toward the TV. "They're going to do that modern dance scene, anyway. Never cared for that number."

I waited until I heard the bedroom door close, then squatted next to their prisoner. "Krystal, what happened to the police officer? The one you took hostage?"

Her head flopped to the other side, facing the tree. "Probably dead."

My stomach lurched. "But where is he?"

She laughed. "Doesn't matter now."

Glancing up, I spotted the shovel leaning against the wall. Oh my God. The garden hole.

"Pearl, I've gotta go back out," I yelled. "Call for another ambulance."

TWENTY-FOUR

CHERRY TUCKER

I WOKE WITH A START, finding myself on the floor of a dark room. Leaping up, I lost my pants, tripped, and hit the floor again. I'd forgotten I had used my homemade belt to bind Krys's hands. After I repeatedly screamed "Merry Christmas" for what felt like forever, Pearl had bounded from the bathroom. I sent her to search for rope. Pearl brought me quilting strips and binding tape. Not my first choice in trussing material. But what was I going to do? Use a string of Christmas lights?

Snatching another strip of cloth from Martha Mae's basket, I tied the sweatpants around my waist and crept down the hall. *White Christmas* still played on the TV in the living room. I took it as a good sign and entered. Sighed with relief to see our prisoner still captive.

Pearl waved the gun.

I leaned over her. "Still unconscious? I walloped her pretty good."

"Naw," said Pearl. "Asleep. Told me my movie was boring."

"What kind of criminal falls asleep on the living room floor?"

"It's been a long day." Pearl patted the couch next to her. "Come watch *White Christmas* with me. You just missed that movie star gal. She was here earlier, then ran out. Came back unbelievably dirty."

"Why?"

"Dug up Martha Mae's garden. Strange night all around. But she was real excited about something she thinks is in the garage. Spied on those two earlier and overheard them talking in there. The movie star thought something important was in the trunk. She's gone back to get the keys from Martha Mae's nephew. She and Casey's got him tied up over at the house."

"He's not Martha Boyes's nephew," I said. "He's a bank robber. And he strangled Martha."

"The movie star said he didn't strangle Martha Mae."

"What does she know?"

"It's you who knows. You drew the girl strangling Martha Mae." Pearl pointed to a garbage bag under the tree. "And look in there. But don't touch it. It's evidence. Or so says Movie Star. She was all tore up about this gal being the one to strangle Martha and rob a bank. I think she hoped that man had done it all."

"Who wouldn't be tore up, but why does she care who did it?"

"Said it was the grandma's fault, but I didn't see any grandma threatening to kill us, did you?"

I shook my head. Maybe it was the flu. Maybe it was Pearl. But her explanation lacked something. Namely reason and logic. Hurrying over to the tree, I snatched an icicle ornament and used it to open the muddy bag and draw out the clothing inside.

"A Santa suit," I said.

"For a girl," said Pearl. "That nephew is too big. It's Krys's suit. You saw Krys strangling Martha Mae. The nephew is her father. He's a piece of work, mind you. But he didn't instigate any of this. He arrived to clean up the mess."

"Clean up the mess by terrorizing us." I pushed the Santa suit back into the bag.

"Oh, not just terrorize. The movie star said he meant to kill us. Get rid of the evidence, so Krys here wouldn't get caught. 'Course he probably meant to split her share of the bank's money. He's a felon, too."

"A felon for a father."

"And a bank robber for a grandfather, or so said the movie star. You can't pick your relatives." Pearl shook her head. "Speaking of relatives, your sister blew a hole in your bedroom wall."

"Did anybody think to call the sheriff about all this?"

"Of course, we did. Who do you think we are?"

Obviously not suffering from victim PTSD. Or maybe that came later. Right now, Pearl looked ready for chestnuts roasting on an open fire. Humming along to the movie.

"Casey said Nik called his foreign friends," said Pearl. "They're bringing a salt truck. You ever heard of such a thing?"

"I don't want to know how they got a hold of a salt truck, but we need it. Uncle Will can get here faster. Toss them in the—" I almost bit my tongue in my haste to change subjects. "Krys drove the getaway car. But Deputy Fells said the driver left when the bank's alarm went off. The bank robbers were given a van, but they never found Luke in the van or at the Winn Dixie."

Shaking her head, Pearl compressed her lips into a grim line.

"She could have been waiting to meet them." I leaned over Krys. "We searched her for weapons, but did we get her keys?"

"I told you that movie star went to get the man's keys. But the stuff from her pockets is on the kitchen table."

"If Movie Star is right, they must have driven separately." I ran toward the kitchen and saw the keys in a pile with a phone, lighter, and a small plastic ammo box. Holding my sweatpants in one hand, I grabbed the keys and darted through the door to the garage. Two vehicles. I pressed the key's unlock button.

One car flashed its lights.

I banged on the garage door opener to light the room and ran to the Toyota's trunk. Behind me, the door rumbled and lifted. I popped the trunk release and lifted the lid.

Tears welled in my eyes. Luke lay curled in the trunk, his head bent and limbs coiled to fit the space. He'd been gagged and bound with zip ties. Stripped of his coat, boots, and gear. A nasty cut marked his forehead. One eye had purpled. A bloody gash behind his ear revealed his takedown. Blue veins stood stark against his normally sun-browned skin, now turned white with cold.

They'd turned my tough, rugged officer into a human popsicle.

Anger stoked my fever. Tears blurred my eyes. I clawed my way toward the top of the pit, scrabbled against the long dark tunnel, and a howling sob tore from my chest.

"You've been here the entire time. Why didn't they tell me what happened to you? I would have kicked doors down to get to you." I reached to stroke a dusky curl off his forehead, then shrugged out of my coat to lay it over him. "You're so cold."

One gray eye opened slowly and blinked. He groaned through the gag. His big body trembled and shuddered, trying to fight the binds.

"Let me find something to cut you out of there." I scurried through the garage and returned with pruning clippers. A minute later, I helped him to uncurl, cringing at his sluggish, stiff movements. I climbed into the trunk to pull his trembling body against mine. I wanted to hurry him into the house, but Luke could barely move.

"Lord, you're colder than death. We need to get you in a bath or something."

"You're so warm. Scorching." He pressed against me, snuggling me into his arms. "I can think of a better way to heat up than a bath."

I pulled back. "Really? You've been stuck in a trunk for who knows how long. You probably have frostbite and a concussion. That's the first thing you think of?"

"I'll admit if I were leaning against the sheriff, that wouldn't be my first thought." He smiled weakly, but his eyes told a different story. "Where's Sheriff Thompson? Why isn't he here? Where am I? Did the team apprehend the bank heist gang?"

"I'm your rescuer. You are next door to my house. Long story. Your team consists of me, Pearl, Casey, and some movie star private detective."

"What?" He swayed.

I caught him before he tried to climb out of the trunk.

"The sheriff never should've let them go. Those bastards pistol-whipped me. I woke up in here, then couldn't stay awake in the cold. Tried to knock out the backlights but couldn't move. Felt like a human pretzel."

"Uncle Will knew they'd kill you otherwise." I pulled him against me. "It's not your fault."

"It shouldn't have happened." He fell silent, tensing against another onslaught of shaking. "Damn, I hate how weak I feel."

"Tell me about it. I've been saying that all day."

"In a minute. You have the flu. You should be in bed." He pulled my forehead to his lips. "Are you hot with fever or am I that cold? This isn't making sense. How did you end up here? Where is everyone?"

"Later." I caught him against my shoulder, feeling another tremor tear through him. "Right now, we're getting you in the house. Pearl's inside. She'll fix you up."

"Just a minute." He slipped his arms around me, pulling me against his chest.

Through his shirt, his chilled flesh cooled my hot cheek. I wrapped my arms around him, and his taut muscles shivered at my touch. My sister used to say we were like fire and ice. Tonight, it was a literal interpretation.

Luke rubbed his cheek against my hair. "Cherry, lying in that trunk, I thought I was going to die from exposure. I kept thinking about what it would do to you. I know how this time of year makes you feel." His chest rose and released slowly. "I'm sorry. I offered to be the hostage exchange. It's my job. I knew the risks. But..."

He swallowed hard. "Your Christmas was ruined. Again. Forgive me?"

I didn't want him to see my tears, but I drew away from his chest anyway. Placed my warm hands against his cold cheeks. And stared into his somber gray eyes.

"I don't know what you're talking about. I couldn't have asked for a better Christmas." I leaned in, using a kiss to heat his frosty lips. "Best Christmas ever."

TWENTY-FIVE
MAIZIE ALBRIGHT

THE CAVALRY ARRIVED in the guise of five large men with Eastern European accents. The smallest one — only six feet — ran up the porch steps, tripped over the lighting, and smacked his head on the wooden porch floor. The other four followed him inside the house, laughing and taking turns at head-splat sounds.

The banter stopped at the site of our prisoner.

While Nik dropped to his knees to press his face against his wife's belly, the others surrounded Jay, cracking their knuckles and uttering low, threatening phrases in a foreign language.

"He should be in police custody," I reminded them. "Anything that happens to him now is not self-defense. You could go to jail."

They ignored me.

"Or be sued."

Grumbling, they grabbed chairs from the kitchen. Circling Jay with their chairs, they continued the foreign threats. But half-heartedly. And while checking their phones.

"It's Pearl. Sheriff Thompson's on his way over," said Casey, one ear on the phone and a hand on her husband's waist. "Now that y'all are here, he wants you to drive that truck around town, so his deputies don't wreck their cars. He wants a clear path for the patrol cars and ambulances coming for Mrs. Boyes and Luke."

"How is the deputy?" I asked.

She hooted. "Sounds like Cherry's defrosting Luke."

"Smart man," said Nik.

"Not really. Luke's going to end up with the flu," said Casey. "And then we'll have two eating chicken soup instead of turkey on Christmas day."

"Turkey." Nik made a face. "We should have goose."

"Whoever heard of a goose for Christmas dinner? I'm going to make hot chocolate for everyone," said Casey. "But first I gotta tee-tee. This baby's dancing on my bladder like she's at a house party. Someone put those lights back on the tree. Cherry's got them strung up in the windows. I guess she was hoping to electrocute the bank robbers."

"He," said Nik. "It's boy. First born in my family is always the boys."

"Sorry to disappoint you, but I could tell by the way I held Daddy's shotgun that we're having a girl." Casey stuck her hands on her hips. "The girls in our family have excellent aim. Cody and Grandpa can't hit the side of a barn."

The Hallmark Channel always used "quirky" to describe small-town characters. Maybe "dangerous" was more appropriate.

The doorbell rang. The Russian-ish salt truck gang looked up from their phones.

"Police," I cried. "Finally."

"Not yet." Nik dropped his hands from Casey's hips. "A truck followed us from highway. It stopped next door. Let me check."

I moved behind him. "I've got a candy cane shiv if you need it."

Nik looked through the peephole, then cracked the door. "What you want?"

"Is Maizie Albright in there?"

Nash.

I clapped my hands, closed my eyes, and thanked my Hallmark Channel angel. "I'm here, Nash. Let him in."

Nik stepped aside, and Wyatt Nash walked through the door. His tall, strapping physique matched those of the salt truck gang, but before a round of alpha chest-beating began, he gave the group a deferential nod. His light blue eyes swept the room, noted Jay on the floor — still tied in Christmas lights — then rested on me. Placing a hand on my shoulder, he squeezed, then patted awkwardly.

This is what happens when you deny your feelings. Awkward patting.

As for me, I grinned like an idiot, indulging in the slight touch of the awkward pat.

"You look...like you've had a long day," said Nash. "I wish I'd been here to help."

I smiled, knowing my clothes and face were mud-splattered, paint stained my hands, and my chapped skin had turned red. But at least I smelled like candy canes.

After quick introductions and an even quicker assessment of the situation, he glanced at me. "Miss Albright, we need to talk."

"Y'all can use the guest bedroom for privacy," said Casey. "Mind the mess from the shotgun blast."

Nash's eyebrows lifted. Without remarking, he followed me to the bedroom. Seeing the blast hole, he crossed the room, examined the gash, then set an eyeball to it. Rising, he turned toward me. "Did you have anything to do with this hole?"

"That was Casey. The pregnant sister. She shot through the wall. But Jay shot at me first."

He took two steps to cross the room. Grabbing my shoulders, he lifted me slightly. Catching himself, he dropped his hands. "Maizie. Miss Albright."

"He was going to shoot Casey. I had to do something."

"And what did you do?" His cool blue eyes burned through me.

"Stabbed him with a candy cane and tied him up."

"With tree lights?"

"It was all I had."

"The police."

"Came, left, and did nothing."

"They had their hands full."

"We had bank robbers, too. And to think, Krystal's grandma is the one who sent us here." I chewed my thumbnail, fighting tears again. "Nash, Jay blames Mrs. Fowler for Krystal's crimes. Krystal drove the getaway car and willingly left a deputy to freeze to death in her trunk. Attacked her great-aunt to use her home as a safe house. Then tied up her, an elderly woman, and the neighbor girl sick with the flu, and left them in Martha Mae's bathroom."

"Are you sure it was Krystal and not Jim Riley who did all that?"

"He's not much better. Planned on helping her to get rid of the evidence. I don't think he wanted to kill anyone, but he would have to protect his daughter."

"Jim Riley specifically said Mrs. Fowler directed this?"

"He said he told Krystal to 'stay away from her.' And said she could talk her way in and out of situations better than Krystal. What kind of grandma encourages behavior like bank robbing?"

"Mrs. Fowler checks out. Krystal's mother, however, did not. There's good reason to believe she's one of the culprits who robbed the bank. Evidently, they split up after the sheriff arranged their escape. I hope they caught them."

"Not the grandmother?" I swallowed hard. "Celia's a good grandma? Her house was full of unwrapped products. I thought they were stolen."

"Just a home shopping nut." Nash grinned. "She'll probably want to bake you cookies. Once she gets over the fact that her granddaughter's a felon."

I squeezed my eyes shut, imagining myself bringing Christmas cookies to Mrs. Fowler. Cookies and gumdrops. Remi would like her, too. She could tell us stories about her bank-robbing husband and con-artist daughter and granddaughter.

Maybe I shouldn't share my adopted grandmother with Remi. She had Carol Lynn's mother, after all.

"You were right," I sighed. "Krystal wasn't a nun. I hoped she'd turn out differently. I didn't get Mrs. Fowler's granddaughter back to her."

"Aw, kid." Nash let out a big breath. "I don't like that about myself. It's better you see the good in people first before you suspect the bad. By the way, you did find the granddaughter. And saved several grand-mothers from her in the process."

"I kept trying to call you." Tears welled. I pinched the skin on my thumb, knowing good investigators don't cry. Particularly when they're no longer in danger. Except for my toes. Still numb. They were going to take a while to recover. "You said you'd always answer."

"I'm sorry, kid. Bad reception. I drove through the storm. But I'm here." He held out his arms and dropped them. Again. "I told you to just watch the house. Go to a motel."

"I couldn't." I sniffed. "Not knowing these people were in danger."

"That's why I had to come. And got here too late." He rubbed his jaw. Paced a small circle three times. Then stopped in front of me. "Dammit. Come here, Maizie."

I fell into his arms. Pressed my head against his shoulder. The leather felt cold and hard. Unzipped his bomber jacket and burrowed against his warm, firm chest. And cried.

Nash stroked my back. Ran his hands through my hair. Then caught my chin in his palm. Gently, he raised my face, meeting my gaze with his. "Please don't cry, Maizie. You're safe. They're safe. That's all that matters."

"Also, I'm finally warm," I whispered. "Thank you."

"Merry Christmas." Nash kissed the tip of my nose. "Let's get you home to Remi. In the morning, we'll follow the salt truck trail home. You've done enough here."

"Nash," I spoke drowsily. "What did you want to do tomorrow? On Christmas Eve?"

"This." Cupping my face between his two large palms, he brushed his lips against mine. "Merry Christmas, Maizie."

Christmas wishes do come true. Thank you, Hallmark Channel angels.

The End.

CONTINUE READING for **17.5 CARTRIDGES IN A PEAR TREE,** the next in the Maizie Albright Star Detective series.

ON A VIEW TO A CHILL

Writing a mystery from two points of view with two protagonists was a challenge I enjoyed. I like "upping the ante" when it comes to writing and this *Rashomon* approach gave me the kind of creative test I relish. I hope you enjoyed it as much as I did writing it!

This tale was originally written for an anthology I did with twelve other cozy mystery writers, THE 12 SLAYS OF CHRISTMAS. The anthology was enormously successful and made the *Wall Street Journal*'s bestselling ebook list December 14, 2017. But even better, the anthology was created to raise money for pets displaced in Hurricanes Harvey, Irma, and Maria. We raised a lot of money for local pet rescue organizations in Texas and Florida, plus gave money to the ASPCA.

If you haven't read Cherry Tucker previously, this book lands somewhere after book six. For Maizie, it's book four.

Continue on for Maizie Albright's "Between Cases" book 5, 17.5 Cartridges in a Pear Tree.

Happy Reading!
Larissa

17.5 CARTRIDGES IN A PEAR TREE

A MAIZIE ALBRIGHT STAR DETECTIVE "BETWEEN CASES" HOLIDAY NOVELLA

A Romantic Comedy Mystery Novel
Maizie Albright Star Detective
17.5 CARTIDGES IN A PEAR TREE
Wall Street Journal bestselling author
Larissa Reinhart

A NOTE TO MY READERS

I wasn't supposed to write this book. I was writing the next Maizie Albright, *18 Caliber*, when I took a break to write this one. But in September, I had an idea — and because my brain is a lot like Boomer Spayberry's Jack Russell terriers, bouncing and barking all over the dang place — I thought I could let myself have some fun. "Just write down some notes, for next year," I told myself. And found myself feverishly writing this story so I could give it to my readers before Christmas.

As you read *17-and-a-half* (that's how it sounds in my head), you might notice some resemblances to my favorite movie, *Raiders of the Lost Ark*. I've always been a Marion Ravenwood fan. She's the only Indy Jones heroine I liked, and I wanted to be Marion when I grew up. I even studied archaeology in college (then found out I'd have to learn dead languages, and I already had issues with the live ones, so I changed my mind). Let's get this straight. Maizie is no Marion. But they're both spunky, positive people in love with an adventurous, valiant, no-nonsense guy. And I believe, Maizie's learning how to become a Marion.

Maizie's on a Marion Ravenwood character arc, so to speak.

There are also *The Maltese Falcon* references. Maizie often examines her cases in a noir, Sam Spade-ish light (as well as a lot of other movies and TV shows) because she's an old movie buff, and of course, working as a private investigator, what wouldn't be more natural than Sam

Spade? Having a Ms. Wonderly show up to wreak some havoc in Maizie's new love life seemed like a given.

I hope you enjoy *17-and-one-half*. If you've read the other books, 17.5 occurs directly after A VIEW TO A CHILL (a week later). 18 CALIBER will happen directly after 17.5. After a hot summer and fall with 15-17, Black Pine Mountain is cooling off.

If you haven't read the other books, no worries. Maizie will catch you up. :)

Happy Reading & Happy Holidays!

Larissa

For fans of Sam Spade & Indiana Jones,
but particularly for those who wanted to be Marion Ravenwood.
Like me.

ONE

#NEWYEARNEWME

THIS NEW YEAR'S Eve in Black Pine, Georgia, was certainly different from my previous twenty-five. At least the ones I could remember. Prior to this year, Vicki — my ex-manager and still-mother — and I would have holidayed at whatever island she'd determined most exclusive and remote (yet still accessible to discerning paparazzi) and flown back in time to attend all the New Year's Eve parties she'd determined most exclusive and remote (yet also accessible to discerning paparazzi).

And I would do my best to celebrate stylishly, which for me was less about clothes and people and more about not passing out by midnight (From jet lag.) (Among other things).

This year I lived with my father's family. Thankfully. (And by judge's decree). Instead of lounging on white sand, I'd worked at Nash Security Solutions through most of the holidays. Maybe it's just me, but helping grandmas find lost granddaughters and serving subpoenas to deadbeat dads felt a much better way to spread Christmas joy than tipping cabana boys.

Plus, I had my ultimate cabana boy in Wyatt Nash, owner of Nash Security Solutions. Wyatt Nash had probably never carried a tray of bellinis in his life, but I think we were at the point in our relationship where he'd offer to rub SPF 80+ on my pale, ginger-cursed skin. Without charge.

I think.

You see, Wyatt Nash was above all, a Southern gentleman with a lot of rules about dating and working and how never the twain should meet. Unfortunately, he was still in the red after major medical expenses and a business that had been failing. His eyes might be on me, but his mind was always on the bottom line. Business wasn't forefront for me when my eyes were on him. With his imposing physique, square jaw and its wicked scar, large capable hands, and icy blue penetrating eyes, he looked more mercenary than gentlemanly. Plus he rarely smiled. But when he did?

Whoa, Nelly.

That smile made me want to cover myself in mistletoe with only my sea-glass green eyes and come-hither lips showing.

Actually, I might need to try that.

We were six months into a two-year agreement of Nash mentoring me until I could apply for my private investigation license. I'd pursued him professionally (and romantically) because I'd needed this opportunity (and was crazy about him) after my Hollywood crash and burn that landed me before a California judge who gave me the option of getting a new career in my father's North Georgia mountain town. A job that had nothing to do with the industry that had consumed me spiritually, emotionally, and financially.

Or, said the judge, I could go directly to jail and see how my idiocy played out before a jury.

I wasn't that much of an idiot. I'd been given the gift of leaving a life I wasn't sure I ever wanted but couldn't leave because of the whole my-mother-is-my-manager situation.

Parents can be tricky like that.

That trickiness continued because not only did Vicki follow me to Black Pine, she'd just bought a controlling interest in Nash's business for reasons I couldn't quite fathom and was more than a little afraid to ask. But then for the holidays, she'd flown to Fiji as usual, and I could pretend that my life was my own.

And so I did.

Even though it felt like someone else's life. Like I had chosen a role I'd intended to play and hadn't quite adopted the right character yet. Having lived in a Beverly Hills bubble most of my life, I was still learning "real world" living, as my Black Pine BFFs Tiffany and Rhonda called it.

Not that I'm complaining. My first Christmas living at Daddy's was pure homespun goodness, worthy of a Hallmark Channel B-roll. An eight-foot pine in the foyer of the DeerNose log cabin (more log than cabin at five thousand square feet). Two other Christmas trees in other parts of the house. Oodles of homemade cookies and treats baked by Daddy's wife, Carol Lynn, easily the best cook in Georgia. Church and carolers and family for dinner.

And Santa, of course. My half-sister was six and Remi had somehow managed to stay off his naughty list.

Evidently, the list had been made before she crawled into the chimney of Daddy's double-sided stone fireplace to set a trap. Which she claimed wasn't for Santa but for the Grinch.

The smell of bungee cords roasting by an open fire had driven us out of the house on Christmas Day.

"I was trying to protect y'all," Remi had said. "If it weren't for me, the Grinch would'a had the tree, the gifts, and the roast beast."

"You knew very well we were having turkey," Daddy had said. "Go to your room."

He'd snagged her slingshot before she'd darted away. A passel of Jack Russells had barked and bounced around her feet, following their Alpha to her den.

Remi's door slammed, and Daddy had turned to me. "God Almighty, that girl is going to put me in an early grave. And I thought you were the one who'd do that."

I couldn't tell if that was a compliment, so I'd kept my mouth shut.

THIS MEMORY (and many other similar memories of Remi pitting her wits against my father) came rushing back to me on New Year's Eve morning. Early, because Spayberrys were "up with the cock's crow and into bed at sundown" type of people.

Luckily, I was used to early call times on set, so no biggie. I'm a morning person. I love sunrises and breakfast and fresh starts and all that jazz.

But this morning, I was going to need an extra heavy dose of caffeine. My father had just finished telling me some terrible news. Remi's grandmother — Carol Lynn's mother — had fallen. Daddy and Carol Lynn were headed immediately for Brunswick — hours away —

for an indeterminable length of time. This was not the terrible news, although, of course, terrible for Carol Lynn's mother and father. She'd sprained her ankle, but as Daddy had said, she'd be "alright but laid up for a bit."

The terrible news was Daddy and Carol Lynn were putting me in charge of Remi until they returned from helping out her grandparents.

Remington Marie Spayberry was not anything like me as a little girl. Or any other little girl I'd ever met in my life, which, albeit, was mostly other actresses. She loved hunting and fishing. And ATVing. She didn't mind snakes or spiders or bugs. She loved building traps and walls and pits. She loved mud.

But the weirdest? She doesn't like food.

I just didn't get that.

I really wasn't sure what I was going to do with Remi. On my own. For an indeterminate amount of time. On New Year's Eve. I'd hoped my Southern gentleman would consider it a major date night, instead of spending the evening serving subpoenas, then dropping me off at my father's cabin (which we'd done almost every night this holiday season). Although on New Year's Eve, we'd really have the element of a subpoena surprise.

What was I even thinking?

"Of course. I'll take care of Remi," I told Daddy.

"She's a pistol." He stroked his almost-more-Santa-white-than-ginger beard. "But you know that."

I nodded. Boy, did I know.

"The dogs'll mind her, so don't worry about them. Just keep her busy, and she'll be fine."

Then he fled. To be honest, I think my six-foot-three, Paul Bunyanish father was a little scared of his spindly, six-year-old daughter. I was, too. Without an idea of how to entertain a six-year-old who was intent on taking out the Abominable Snow Monster with her bare hands, I took her with me to the office.

Where I found Nash with another woman.

TWO
#MALTEASE

AFTER BUYING Remi (and myself) a donut (or two) at the Dixie Kreme shop above which Nash Security Solutions was housed, I led her up the creaking wooden steps to the second floor and entered the dingy office. Dingy because it was in a historic building that let in more dirt than light. And because the Dixie Kreme building was owned by Lamar, whose idea of an update consisted of a fresh coat of paint every twenty years. Also because the office was run by Nash who regularly announced how much he hated change.

Which I guess meant keeping the dust.

I ushered Remi through the old-timey glass entry door, and she ran into the front room, spinning between the dented file cabinets, a lumpy couch, and Lamar's faded corduroy La-Z-Boy.

"I can't believe I'm finally here," she exclaimed like she'd just passed through the gates of Disney World.

Spotting the closed inner office door, I moved past her and knocked. "Are you decent, Nash?"

He slept in the office due to the ruinous state in which his divorce left his finances. I'd caught him a time or two in various states of dressing.

Not so bad for me, but today I had Remi to consider.

"Of course." His deep baritone had an odd lilt to it. Like he was trying to chuckle as he talked. Which was unnatural. Nash was many things but not a chuckler.

I opened the door. A beautiful woman wearing snug, winter white cashmere and bright red lipstick sat in the chair opposite his desk. She had alabaster skin and auburn hair like I did. As did Nash's ex-wife, Jolene. And the tattoo of Jessica Rabbit on his back.

Yep, Nash had a type and this woman fit the bill.

Naturally, I was suspicious.

Mostly due to my insecurities, of which there were many. My favorite ex-therapist, Renata, would have told me to focus on positive affirmations. I don't know what my new ex-therapist would say since he was currently in jail. Hopefully, he'd tell me how to stay out of jail, which would mean reining in my hot mess of feelings.

My mentor and sort-of boyfriend sat on the edge of the desk, facing this woman. He appeared more excited than guilty, which for Nash meant a brightening in his normally hooded eyes and a speedier pace to his drawl.

This signified a new case.

"Meet Ms. Wonderly," said Nash, waving his hand toward the woman. "She has a job for us. One I think you'll find real interesting."

Ms. Wonderly turned halfway in her chair and smiled beatifically. Her movement was smooth. Her chin raised and back straight. Quite the contortionist feat as her body still faced Nash. Her eyes skimmed over me then snapped forward once again, like a ballerina pirouetting.

I quirked an eyebrow, feeling my inner Julia Pinkerton kick in. Her character often comes to me in these situations. Partly because I played the teen detective for many years and partly because Julia was a lot cooler and more confident than me. "Ms. Wonderly? You're kidding."

"I assure you, I'm not," she said.

I circled her chair to sit on the other side of the desk, mirroring Nash. "I guess you're looking for a Maltese falcon?"

Her eyebrows quivered, and she shot me a questioning look. "No."

"Then you're looking for your sister. You suspect her boyfriend might have done her wrong. Except the sister isn't real. Because you're really hunting for the Maltese Falcon."

Ms. Wonderly looked from me to Nash. Nash nodded his head. She gave him a coy smile.

"I already went over this, Miss Albright. Ms. Wonderly's not familiar with the movie or the book. The name seems to be a coincidence."

"Oh, sorry. I love old movies." This was what I got for immediately going noir on her.

"Ms. Wonderly's had a hard time of it this holiday," continued Nash. "She was just telling me about her ogre of a boss. And she just lost her boyfriend."

"He died?"

She shook her head and sniffed, dabbing her eyes from a handkerchief she'd swiftly pulled from her bag. "He broke up with me on. On… Christmas Eve."

"Pretty jackassy," I said. "Sorry to hear it." Particularly because it meant she was single.

Rein it in, Maizie.

"It's an easy gig." Nash's voice had that excited edge to it again. "And they chose us because of you. She was sent here by her boss."

"What?" My cheeks sizzled from embarrassment. Now I really felt bad for judging Ms. Wonderly. "Someone heard about my work in investigations and was actually impressed?"

"Not exactly." Nash cleared his throat. "It's your previous employment that attracted their attention."

"Oh." My elation crashed. My previous employment attracted a lot of attention. Usually in a not-so-positive way. But negative attention also works when you're trying to stay in the media limelight. With the help of our PR advisor, Vicki spun my failures and humiliations to "our" advantage.

(Mostly her advantage since she was rich and I was broke after legal fees and college tuition.)

"What do they want?" I folded my arms over my chest. "An autograph in exchange for the job?"

"Nothing like that." Nash cleared his throat and tried on a smile. Which didn't fool me because I knew his real smile. His real smile could melt the polar ice caps. This smile was weird. And disturbing. Like he didn't know how to make himself fake smile, which for me, was as natural as real smiling. But I'd had a lot of practice. "You were in this movie, *Warhead Girl.*"

"Oh no." I shook my head. "I am not posing in that outfit again. A bandolier of bullets and not much else? Forget it."

"Really?" Nash cocked his head, seeming to contemplate me in a bandolier and not much else.

"It's not the bandolier we're interested in," said Ms. Wonderly.

"That's a relief. I don't think I could fit into that costume, even if I wanted to wear it." I looked at Nash. "Which I don't. Ever."

A crash from the waiting room snapped me out of it.

"Remi." I hopped from the edge of the desk and ran around Ms. Wonderly, who did that weird snap of her head while keeping her body facing forward. She didn't fidget the whole time she sat there.

Who didn't fidget?

But my concerns about Ms. Wonderly's unusual poise fled. The coffee table was on its side and Remi was upside down against it.

"Are you okay? What were you doing?" I patted her, seeking broken bones.

Remi shoved my hand away and sprung to her feet. "That chair is awesome. If you balance against the footrest and pull the handle, it'll shoot you right into the air. I almost made it onto the couch."

"That's Lamar's special chair. If you break it, he'll probably cry. Or make me buy a new one."

"Sorry." She didn't look very sorry. She was staring past me, watching Ms. Wonderly sashay from the office.

"Thank you, Mr. Nash. You've been so helpful." Ms. Wonderly clung to the hand he offered to shake. "Why don't you text me?"

"I'll be glad to, Ms. Wonderly." Inclining his head, Nash opened the office door for her. His eyes lingered on her stroll through the door, and he closed it behind her. Whistling, he ruffled Remi's hair, then flipped the coffee table upright. Probably unperturbed by the idea that she'd almost destroyed two pieces of furniture.

"How're you doing, kid?" he said to Remi.

"I have a new slingshot." She gazed at him with that sort of rapturous wonder saved for unicorns and boy bands.

"Santa knows his stuff. Look what I got." He strode to the filing cabinet and grabbed a dark brown, wool-felt fedora. Tucking it on his head, he tugged the brim and gave Remi his real smile.

I gazed at him with rapturous wonder. The hat was trés retro hot. The smile, even hotter.

The gunshot-like creak sounding from a footfall on the outside stair snapped me out of my euphoria. "What did Ms. Wonderly want with *Warhead Girl*?"

"There's some kind of necklace-thingy related to the movie." Nash's gaze skidded off my face and landed somewhere to the side of my head. "Just some movie junk they think you can help them locate."

I knew exactly what he was talking about. The death necklace.

"I better get Remi home." I grabbed Remi's hand and pulled her toward the door.

"Wait." Nash slipped in front of the door and placed a hand on my shoulder, skidding it toward my neck. He glanced at Remi and patted my shoulder. "It's worth a lot of money to her boss."

I shrugged off his hand and opened the door. "We need to go."

The stair creaked again. Before I could slip out, Nash moved to block me again.

"It's got a leather band with about twenty deer rifle cartridge shells hanging from it." Nash formed the shape with his hands. "You know the one I mean?"

"Yeah, I know it," I muttered. Moving around him, I glanced over the banister. Someone stood in the shadows between the donut shop and the outside doors.

"It's a worthless piece of junk that anyone can make but for some reason, they want the original," said Nash. "Are you going to give it to her?"

"I don't know where it is," I let my voice carry over the banister.

"Yes, you do," said Remi. "It's hang—"

"It's New Year's Eve," my voice rose over Remi's. "Remi and I are going to curl up by the fire. Do you want to join us for the countdown tonight? It'll be cozy."

Taking my hand, Nash led me from the banister. He gazed at me intently. Earnestly. Eagerly. "It could help get us out of debt. It would be on the books for *our* office, not Vicki's."

My heart twisted at the word "our." I wanted it to be our office. Nash hated working for Vicki even more than I did. Plus the word "our" always did a whammy on my heart. But I shook my head and pulled Remi out into the hall.

"See you later, Mr. Nash."

Below us, a door shut quietly.

THREE

#UNFANBELIEVABLE

WARHEAD GIRL HAD BEEN FILMED by a small studio, funded by foreign producers for a mostly international audience. Another career pivot role, chosen by my manager who tried to transition me from teen idol to adult star. The movie had lots of action and, like my wardrobe, not much else. Something my manager forgot to tell me.

Conveniently.

I'd sent Daddy the reviewers' cut DVD since he enjoyed action movies. Then given him the death necklace because he'd been fascinated with the director's choice of .444 Marlin cartridges. It was a way to stay connected to him during a difficult part of my career—and during those difficult years between teen and real adulthood.

"The .444 Marlin was introduced in 1964," Daddy had said when I'd presented the necklace. "Your Grandpa Spayberry had one. Cooler than custard back in the day. Pushed a 240-grain bullet to a muzzle velocity of 2,350 feet-per-second."

Which…whatever. But my middle name was Marlin, named after his favorite rifle at the time (written on the hospital birth certificate while my mother was hopped up on pain pills). That necklace remained special to him and me. When you were separated by a country due to your parents' divorce (and your mother's insistence that we live in LA for my career), fathers and daughters bonded over what they could.

Every Christmas that necklace hung on Daddy's tree along with all his other hunting decorations, which naturally, he collected as the

CEO and founder of DeerNose apparel company. (The apparel's specialty scent appealed to deer and hunters alike.) (For different reasons.)

An hour after leaving the office, I stood before the tree, studying the death necklace, when our gate alarm chimed.

Remi skidded into the large foyer, sliding on the granite in her tiny cowboy boots. "It's Mr. Nash. I buzzed him in." She climbed onto the hearth of the stone, double-sided fireplace that stood between the foyer and the living room. "You said we'd get cozy by the fire."

I rested my hands on my hips. "I hid the remote."

She stuck her hand in the bin holding the andirons and pulled out a small black box. "Found it." Pressing a button on the remote, a whump and click announced the gas igniting. Flames licked stacked logs in the grate.

"You pyromaniac," I yelled. "You're six. You can't start a fire."

She cocked her head. "But I just did."

"I meant, you shouldn't start fires." I coughed and ran to the fireplace, lifting her down. "And you forgot to open the flue."

She dashed away, and I heard her fumble with the door. The air frosted. I shivered inside the long shadow that fell past me. I pulled the lever for the flue and turned to face Nash. He stood in the doorway, with his fedora tugged down and the collar on his bomber jacket flipped up against the cold. Frigid air gusted past him and he stepped inside to shut the door.

"Hello, Miss Albright."

"Mr. Nash." Remi hopped up and down. "I made a fire."

He glanced down at her and ruffled her hair. "Good job, kid."

I pressed my lips into a hard line then blew air out of my nose. "Remi, go fix a plate of cookies or something. I think Mr. Nash's here to talk about business, not celebrate New Year's Eve."

I PURPOSEFULLY USHERED Nash past the Christmas tree and through the French doors on the other side of the fireplace that led to the living room. Carol Lynn had placed Remi's tree in here. I didn't have a tree yet, because I didn't have ornaments. Vicki had always hired a decorator for our holidays. This year, Remi had eschewed her baby ornaments for her My Little Pony collection. Carol Lynn had added popcorn and cranberry strings to disguise the fact that they hung from tiny nooses by their little necks.

Nash jerked to a halt in the middle of the room, squinted at the tree in the corner, and shook his head.

"You know where the necklace is. Does the studio still own it?" Nash took my hand, so I had to turn to face him. "Or do you? Why won't you give it to the client? This could do us a lot of good."

I dropped his hand. "I don't like to help collectors. If they find it on their own, it's their business, but I think people get a little too weird about movie props. They place all this symbolic importance on a piece of fiction. Speaking of Ms. Wonderly, the Maltese Falcon prop sold for more than four million."

Nash took a step back. "Four million dollars?"

"I mean, it's a free market, but as an actor it makes me feel kind of… icky."

"Icky?"

"I mean, it's all make-believe, right? But some fans get a little wrapped up in a world Hollywood created for entertainment value. The film business is a billion-dollar industry. And it feels kind of…exploitative or something."

"Do you feel exploited?" Nash ran a hand up my arm. "Or felt exploited?"

I shrugged. "As an actor, you know that it's part of the deal. You have to use every advantage you can to leverage your fame to get better and more roles. It's not that you mind being associated with a character. But some fans get a little nutty and forget that it's acting. And in a film like *Warhead Girl*? My character is a vigilante who blows up and kills as many people as possible. Bad guys, but still. I don't like the idea of someone using that necklace as some sort of symbol for…I don't know what. But it wouldn't be for hope, peace, and love."

I squeezed my eyebrows together. "At least, I wouldn't think so."

"I get it." The hand Nash had laid on my shoulder ran down my side and landed on my hip. He tugged me closer.

"Thank you." I wiggled until we were pressed together. I circled my arms around his shoulders. Gazing up into his cool blues, I felt my anxiety dissipate. "I knew you would understand."

The hands on my hips slid to my lower back. He angled his head so that his lips were within an inch of mine. "I'll take care of this. I wouldn't want you to be involved in something like that."

I brushed my lips against his, reveling in his solidity and the scent that was partially Acqua di Selva aftershave and mostly Nash.

He responded then pulled back. "Do you have the necklace?" His lips brushed mine again. "Just curious."

My brain was too busy enjoying the current physical sensations to answer. A hand caressed my back. His lips had moved to my throat. The other hand had moved to my nape. Fingers pushed into my hair. I knocked his hat off, ran my hand over his muscular neck, and pulled him closer.

"Maizie?" said Nash, his lips moving steadily down my neck. "The necklace is here?"

"Mmm." Remi had put Christmas music on the house speaker system. Mariah Carey hit a high note, and I felt a crescendo of pleasure as Nash's firm body fit against mine. His lips and scent and hands created an electric heat that combined with a blast of cold.

Until it just felt cold. Really cold.

Shivering, I pulled away to figure out where the icy blast came from. In a Disney princess dress and cowboy boots, Remi stood before the open patio door. Snow blew in around her feet. Six hundred barking Jack Russell terriers — or maybe just six — hurtled through the doorway.

I gasped, released my stranglehold on Nash's shoulders, and turned around fully. "Remi, what are you doing?"

"Getting the smoky smell out. Letting the Jacks in." She scrunched her nose. "What are *you* doing?"

"Keeping Miss Albright warm," said Nash quickly. He reached to pat one of the dogs that bounced around our legs. "I thought it smelled like smoke."

"I forgot about the flue, but I won't next time." She eyed Nash and jerked her chin. "It looked like you were biting Maizie's neck."

"Nash is not a vampire," I said, imagining Remi's next project. "Anyway, it's none of your business, and you shouldn't be sneaking in on me like that."

"Y'all shouldn't be kissing in my living room. I'm going to tell Daddy."

I flushed. "Daddy knows that Mr. Nash and I are dating."

"He shouldn't be dating you in our living room." Remi stamped her boot. "You're supposed to be watching me."

She was right. Here I was all wrapped up in Nash and not even paying attention to my baby sister. "I'm sorry. We were just talking about—"

"I'll leave you now." Nash picked up his hat and winked at Remi. "I'm sorry, too. Don't get your sister in too much trouble. And you stay out of trouble, too."

He ruffled Remi's hair, pulled the patio door shut, then strode toward the foyer. I watched, running my thoughts through our conversation about the death necklace. I jerked from my reverie and sped toward the entryway, passing Nash, to halt in front of the tree. In the living room, the dogs barked and yipped then stopped. Remi had quieted them to listen.

"You didn't have to see me out." Nash zipped his leather bomber jacket.

I pushed my lips into a smile. "What will you tell Ms. Wonderly?"

"I'll think of something." He pulled open the big wooden door and turned, tugging his fedora brim. "Take good care of Remi."

The door closed and I spun around to study the tree. The possible symbol for vigilante violence hung between a silver deer and a tin crappie. It was safe. Hopefully Nash hadn't spotted it.

I trusted this man with my heart, but for some reason, I didn't trust him with this necklace.

FOUR

#YOU'REASCHARMINGASANEEL

REMI SLID through the French doors, then tiptoed toward the tree, shimmied under my arm, and leaned against me.

"What are you looking at?" She cocked her head, studying the tree.

"I love Christmas trees," I said. "Some people might think it's weird to have a tree full of hunting ornaments, but it reminds me of Daddy, so I like it."

"That's why we each get a tree," said Remi. "But mine's not weird."

I held back my thoughts on her ornament-hanging methods. "Your mom's kitchen tree is super cute with all the metal cookie cutters hanging on it."

"She usually hangs cookies on it, but they got eaten this year." Remi patted me. "It's okay. Next year, you'll know better."

A piece of wood popped in the fire, and above us, the doorbell chimed a heavy gong. I shrieked and Remi jumped, landing on my foot. Wincing, I freed my foot from beneath her boot heel.

"It's Mr. Nash?" she said.

"Maybe." But I had a feeling he was in a hurry to return to the office to learn more about the client who wanted my bullet necklace. I checked the monitor by the door. A group of three men stood on the porch.

"That's not Nash. How'd they get to the front door? The gates should be closed." I immediately regretted my words.

"The alarms." Remi's voice pitched to a high whine. "You didn't turn them on and now the Grinch is here. He must've heard about my trap."

"It's not the Grinch." But I had turned the alarm on. I peered at the dark system panel.

"Oh, good," said Remi.

I spun around, too late. Remi had already opened the door. It creaked, swinging wide, and an eddy of snow blew in on an icy gust. A middle-aged man in a wool trilby and trench coat crossed the threshold. Two men had flanked him, and as he moved forward, they filled the doorway behind him.

Involuntarily, I slid backward and pushed Remi behind me, holding her with my left arm. I hesitated, glancing at where the open door rested against the wall. It felt impolite to walk over to grasp the handle, particularly with Remi now clinging to my waist.

"Good day, Miss Albright." The man had an odd accent I couldn't place. "I'm a big fan."

"Thank you, but I don't—"

Moving forward, he held out a gloved hand for me to shake. "I'm Rudolph Gentz. I am sorry to show up on New Year's Eve, but I need your help."

"He's not Rudolph. It's the Grinch," whispered Remi, peeking around my back. "His skin is green."

Beneath the gray herringbone trilby, his chalky white complexion almost looked green. His pallor made a startling contrast to his dark eyes. Despite his pastiness, he was tall and solidly built. But it wasn't his size that dominated. The air seemed to vibrate around him. His presence seemed to fill the room.

I gripped Remi's arm. "What do you want, Mr. Gentz?"

"May I?" Not waiting for my reply, Gentz strode into the foyer to warm himself by the fire. His cohorts followed, shutting the door behind them. Facing the fireplace, he said, "It's so chilly outside. But the sun should be out soon."

Shocked by his presumptuousness, I floundered for words.

"Is your father home, Miss Albright?" said Gentz, slowly pulling off his gloves. He shoved them in his pocket and turned from the fireplace.

"No, come back later," said Remi.

"She means he'll be back later." I pressed Remi closer. "Did you need to talk to my dad? Are you a business associate?"

"I hope to do business with him. I want to purchase something from him, at a very good price."

"Today? It's New Year's Eve. Kind of a holiday?"

"It can't wait. My employer wants it very badly. Before the clock strikes twelve, so to speak. So he sent me all the way to Georgia to see if I could retrieve this special gift. He just learned you might have it. As it's still morning, I think it shouldn't be a problem getting it to him in time."

Remi popped her head from behind my back. "Why didn't he get it for Christmas? Is it because his heart is two sizes too small?"

Gentz forced a raspy heh-heh-heh chuckle. "Very cute, this one."

"What is this thing your employer wants?" I dreaded the answer. Was he also working for Ms. Wonderly's ogre of a boss?

"The same thing Mr. Wyatt Nash's client wants. Surely, you suspected there'd be other interested parties." Gentz smiled, showing his teeth. He could do the fake smile, unlike Nash, although Gentz's was creepier. "I understand you gave it to your father a long time ago. Perhaps you know where he keeps it?"

What was going on with that necklace? It was just eighteen long, brass bullets, each tied to the woven leather cord. Heavy as Hades when you wore it paired with a bandolier of bullets and a rocket launcher on a frigid soundstage that was mostly green screen.

To be honest, although I'd told Nash all that stuff about not wanting the necklace to become a symbol of vigilante violence, I'd mostly wanted to keep it as that special father-daughter gift it was meant to be.

This was what happened when I tried to sound intelligent instead of honest.

"Why now?"

"The fifth anniversary of *Warhead Girl* is New Year's Day. It also marks the year the story was set. The writer thought a cataclysmic event would happen tomorrow."

"You know your movie facts," I said. "But you have some trivia confused. The comic it was based on was written about fifty years ago. The screenwriter kept the original date, even though it didn't make much sense that within five years, a country called Nuke would begin a global war."

Gentz chortled his disturbing heh-heh-heh giggle. "Yes, the Supreme Commander. My favorite character."

Weirdo. The Supreme Commander was a fanatical evil dictator. "I meant why are you looking for the necklace today? Why not a year, or a month ago, or even yesterday?"

"Perhaps you aren't aware that in recent entertainment news, another studio announced they are making the sequel. Someone told reporters this sweet story about you giving your father the necklace."

"I no longer pay attention to that sort of gossip. Usually, it's not true." I lifted my chin.

"That's unfortunate. Your father still has the bullet necklace, though?"

"I knew it. He's here for the decorations. I've got to save the roast beast," screamed Remi, ripping away from my hold. She charged down the hallway.

"Remi," I called, then stopped. Hopefully, she'd lock herself in her room and I'd calm her down later.

Gentz nodded at the two men. They'd remained so quiet I'd almost forgotten them. Henchmen. They were too skulky and lurky in their winter trench coats to be business associates.

The shorter of the two men — *Igor, if there ever was one* — jerked his head. The taller — *Must be Oddjob* — followed him down the hall to the back of the house. The same direction in which Remi had just proceeded.

"Hey, what are you doing?"

"We're retrieving your sister for you. For her safety." Before I could make sense of his words, Gentz grabbed my arm and plucked my phone from my back pocket. "Now go get the necklace."

FIVE

#IGORIT

I DIDN'T BOTHER FIGHTING him for my phone but ran after Remi. As much as I didn't want to leave Gentz alone in the foyer with the deer cartridge necklace hanging in the tree, I feared for Remi. Not only for her safety but with that new slingshot, she could do a lot of damage.

To the house. People. Dogs. Maybe to herself.

Remi had dashed down the hall that opened into the kitchen. Through the kitchen, another hall led to a wing of bedrooms. A cacophony of barking dogs grew louder, and I knew she had opened whatever door had barred the Jacks from an earlier escape. It made it hard to hear where anyone else had gone. Five ebullient Jack Russell terriers bounded past me toward the foyer. I skirted the long pine table and benches. A lone Jack stood on top of the table, helping herself to a plate of cookies.

"Get down, Teeny," I hollered, running past. The little white and brown spotted dog looked up, leaped off the table, and followed me toward the bedroom wing. "Remi, where are you?"

In the hall, the doors stood open. I took the first right into the master bedroom. The taller of Gentz's henchmen, the one I dubbed Oddjob, rifled through Daddy's closet. He glanced behind his shoulder, spotting me, but returned to pawing through my father's things.

"Hey," I screamed. "Get out of there."

The little dog growled. Like a windup toy released, Teeny sprang forward, leaping at the man. Oddjob kicked, but the dog hopped over his outstretched leg, barking.

Panic gnawed my stomach. I ran for the wall near the bed where a panel for the alarm system had been installed. I tapped in the code. The panel remained dim. I punched in the code again.

"No. No. No." Hells. They had somehow disabled the alarm. Okay, new plan.

Oddjob cursed and Teeny growled. I glanced behind me. The man had a metal lockbox under one arm and tried to shake off the Jack Russell with the other. She bared her teeth and snarled, then leaped to bite the man's inner thigh. Oddjob howled and dropped the box to pry Teeny off his leg.

"Good girl," I yelled, running for the door. "Police are on their way."

It was a lie, but I had to find Remi. I took a quick turn through the remaining bedrooms, calling for her, then charged back through the kitchen hall. I skidded to a stop in the wide foyer.

The shorter henchman, Igor, held Remi around her middle. She kicked and flayed her arms. Next to the fireplace, the French doors to the living room had been shut. Behind the doors, five Jack Russells barked and sprang at them, crashing against the glass.

"Put her down," I screamed.

Standing before the double doors, Gentz held a small canister in his hands. "Miss Albright, we found your sister for you. You need to call off your dogs. They're quite loud."

"Remi, are you okay?" I rushed toward her.

"I recommend you stay where you are." Gentz waved the canister. "It's just pepper spray, but it would be quite horrible for such a small child to experience. She's very unruly."

"I'll get you, Grinch," said Remi, wiggling in Igor's arms. "Just you wait."

"Put her down," I pleaded. "She's not going to do anything."

Oddjob jogged into the foyer, carrying the metal box.

"Why are you doing this?"

"We only want the necklace," said Gentz. "It's very simple."

I closed my eyes briefly. It was just a stupid movie prop. But why were they going to these lengths to get it? "It's not in that box. Put Remi down, and I'll tell you where it is."

Gentz nodded at Igor. The henchman released his hold on Remi, who dropped to the ground, then rolled, pulling something from her boot.

"You're not stealing our trees," she cried and pulled back the elastic band on her slingshot. A rock zinged through the air, past Gentz, and smacked the glass on the French door. A crack appeared. Then began to splinter into a spiraling web.

"Remi," I gasped.

The air seemed to still. The dogs stopped barking. Like us, they watched the widening crack. Teeny bounded from the hall, yipping. Ten human eyes and ten dog eyes noted her trajectory.

"No." I vaulted forward to catch her. She bounced over my arms and smacked into the French door. The glass shattered. Bellowing Jack Russells hurdled through the window frame. Teeny jumped into the living room, shaking off glass.

Remi spun and fired her slingshot at the men.

"Stop," I yelled.

"Grab her," hollered Gentz.

Barking dogs bounded about the foyer like a load of spilled bouncy balls. Remi jumped onto the fireplace hearth, aiming her slingshot at the men. Gentz whipped his hat off, swinging it in front of his face as missile-like pebbles zinged through the air.

I reached for Remi, but Igor knocked me aside. She lifted a log from the firewood rack and swung at him. Igor ripped it from Remi's hand. I sprang from the floor and stepped on a dog's tail. The Jack howled, darted forward, and bit the man's ankle. I bowled into Igor with my shoulder, knocking him away from Remi, and snatched the wood. The Jack Russell jumped and caught the man's hand in his teeth.

"Call off the dogs," yelled Gentz.

"Call off *your* dogs," I hollered and seized Remi around her waist. I hoisted her onto my hip and threw the wood into the fireplace. The log crashed into the burning wood, knocking the stack loose. Burning logs and embers rolled out of the fireplace and crashed onto the granite floor.

"For shizz's sake," I cried.

With Remi flopping against my hip, I kicked at the logs. Remi pushed off my shoulder and jumped to the ground. I let her go and grabbed the fireplace tongs. "Get out of here, Remi."

Behind me, the dogs grew louder. Something crashed and a dog yelped. I turned, swinging a smoldering log clenched in the tongs. The tree tipped precariously. Remi had darted beneath it and was trying to hold it up.

"Remi, get out of there," I yelled.

"Grab her," said Gentz.

Oddjob kicked at the snarling dogs who tore at his pant legs. The dogs bared their teeth and lunged. Igor limped toward the tree, dragging a dog clamped to his calf. Teeny lay at Gentz's feet, whimpering. He aimed his pepper spray at another Jack who barked and hopped around his feet.

I swung the log at Igor. The wood crumbled in the tong's grip. Burning embers flurried. Charred bits flew. Pieces of burning log fell to the stone and the henchman hot-footed over them. Losing his balance, he fell into the tree.

"I can't hold it," yelled Remi.

The tree crashed onto the floor, landing on the burning log. Remi popped out and ran down the hall. Three dogs took off after her. The tree smoked and crackled. The man shrieked and crawled out from under the tree. The remaining two dogs yipped and bounded over the broken glass into the living room.

I gazed, horrified, at the tree stand. Lying on its side. No water puddled from it. The tree was as dry as a week-old turkey.

Gentz grabbed the man's hand, pulled him to his feet, and leaned over the smoking tree. A flame shot up and he reared back.

"We forgot to water the tree," I cried. I glanced around for something to put out the fire and was yanked back. Oddjob gripped my elbow. He threw his arm around me, pinning me.

"Where is the necklace," screamed Gentz. "Tell us now."

The tree popped and sizzled. Another flame licked up, consuming a wooden rainbow bass ornament.

"It's on the tree," I cried. "We use it as a decoration, you—"

He slapped me. "Idiot."

My eyes burned hotter than the cheek he'd just slapped. "Take it and get out."

"Let her go."

We glanced from the burning tree to the doorway where a large figure stood. Teeny yipped, sprang from her prone position, and ran to the figure, barking. Sniffed his leg. And rubbed against him.

Nash stepped into the foyer. His blue eyes burned beneath the brim of his hat. One hand unzipped his coat, and another reached inside. "I'm armed. Touch her again and you're dead."

I kicked backward, whacking Oddjob's shin with the heel of my boot. His arms loosened. I shimmied from his grasp and ran to Nash. He gripped his .38 Special in both hands. Jerking his chin, he motioned me to get behind him.

"They want the necklace, too," I said.

Unruffled, Gentz held up his hands. His men put up their hands and moved toward their boss.

"I assure you that's all we want. Then we'll leave and not return," said Gentz.

"Where's Remi?" Nash's eyes didn't leave the three men.

"She ran toward the kitchen."

"Call the police," Nash's voice remained steady. "Your security system is dead."

The tree snapped and crackled. Another flame licked out. Ornaments tinkled and dropped to the granite, clattering in a sad symphony.

"I've got to get something for the fire." My throat constricted and not just from smoke filling the room. "They took my phone."

"My inside pocket," said Nash. "Then get a fire extinguisher."

I patted his jacket, reached inside, and pulled out his phone. "What's your password?"

Nash sighed. "Your birthday."

A flame shot from my heart to heat my cheeks. Much like the one consuming our tree.

Gentz snapped his fingers. The two men sprinted at Nash. I shrieked. Nash shoved me behind him. A shot rang out. I backed toward the open doorway, dialing 9-1-1. Ducking, Gentz ran toward the tree. He yanked on an object caught on a limb. Flames ate the top of the tree, lapping toward his hand. Oddjob wrestled with Nash for his gun. Igor circled them, his hands out.

"Nash, behind you," I shouted.

Nash had brought a gun to a pepper spray fight and could be killed for his efforts. I had nothing to help but a wheelhouse of action movie training. Stage kung fu was better than nothing. I shoved the phone into my pocket and jumped toward Igor. Landing on one foot, I shot out the other leg. Missed Igor. And fell into Oddjob. He collapsed against

Gentz. Gentz stumbled and the necklace, pinched between his two fingers, whipped around. The bullets swung up, smacking his hand and wrist. The bullets sizzled against his skin. He howled, dropped the necklace, and dashed out the door. Oddjob followed, scrambling to help his boss.

"Maizie, watch out," cried Nash.

I wheeled around. Grasping the pistol, Nash pulled back, staggering from Igor. I dropped into a squat and swept a leg beneath the man's feet. Igor tripped backward out the door and fell into Gentz, who'd plunged his burned hand into the snow.

I sprang to slam the door shut and turn the lock. Behind me, I heard a thunderous whoosh. I spun from the door. Surrounded by white smoke, Remi lay on her back, the kitchen fire extinguisher clutched in one hand. I dashed toward her, jumped the tree stand, and caught her up in my arms. "Remi, you scared me."

"Just knocked me over, is all. That stuff is stronger than it looks," she muttered into my chest.

"That's not what I meant—never mind." I squeezed her against me. Dogs surrounded us, whining and licking. I heard the door open and shut and glanced over my shoulder.

"They're gone." Nash grasped the bullet necklace in a gloved hand. "But they didn't get this. They'll be back."

"YOU CAME BACK." I carried Remi to where Nash examined the death necklace. We'd watch the men leave on the security monitors but were still unable to reset the alarms or close the gate. I'd found my phone and Gentz's gloves on the entry table and finished my call to the police.

Nash tipped his hat back, and I could better see the worry in his eyes. "Something didn't sit right with me. I passed their Mercedes on the way to the office. I got to thinking how strange it was for a car like that to be out in this area of Black Pine. Boomer owns all the property on this end of town, so unless they were headed here or the DeerNose factory there was no reason for anyone to be out this way."

"Thank you." I rose on my toes to give him a quick kiss on his cheek. "I don't know what would have happened if you hadn't shown up."

"I was fixing to spray those men with the fire 'stinguisher," said Remi. "Shoot them straight out the door."

"That was quick thinking," said Nash. "But I'm glad you used it on the tree instead."

We turned to examine the tree, looking shriveled under a blanket of white puffy goo. Like someone had gone crazy with the fake snow.

"That Grinch rooned our tree," muttered Remi.

"Ruined, but we can save some of the ornaments," I said. "I need to clean up. There's glass everywhere. I don't want you or the Jacks to get hurt."

The dogs had returned to sniff around the tree then our legs. The noxious chemical scent mixed with the smoke and burnt pine. I handed Remi to Nash and bent to examine Teeny. "Poor Teeny got a mouthful of bad guy and pepper-sprayed. Her eyes are still red. That's jacked up."

"He's a mean one, that Grinch." Remi nodded vigorously.

"We'll take her to the vet. With the alarm system not working, y'all can't stay here." With one arm, Nash had clamped Remi against him — with her swinging like a rag doll — and used his other to hold the hot necklace away from her. "I'll drop you somewhere, too. Take the kid." He jiggled his arm and Remi bounced against him.

Ignoring his request, I picked up Gentz's leather glove and snatched the necklace from him. "Drop us? Where are you going?"

"To find out who those men were and why they want the necklace."

"You're not going anywhere without me. This all because of the stupid movie I did."

"Me, too," said Remi. "I want in on this action."

"No," Nash and I spoke in unison.

"Y'all are always having fun without me." Still dangling from Nash's arm, she pointed at me. "Anyways, Maizie's supposed to be watchin' me."

"It's too dangerous," I said. "Look at what those men did. They pepper-sprayed Teeny and would have done the same to you. Daddy's house was almost burned down."

"The house burning down was mostly your fault." Remi pursed her lips. "I tried to save the tree, and you knocked that man into it."

"Forget it. I'm putting you both in a hotel," said Nash.

"What about the Jacks?" Remi wiggled around to climb Nash like a lumberjack up a stout oak. Grasping his shoulder with one hand, she pushed his hat back and narrowed her eyes. Her little brows rose. "The dogs would go bonkers in a hotel. Just like me. We'll get kicked out. On New Year's Eve. The Grinch'll find us, and that'll be *your* fault."

"Listen, kid. I'll figure out something." Nash hoisted Remi off his trunk, letting her dangle in mid-air. "But you're both staying out of this."

Remi glanced back at me and I nodded, confirming Remi would most definitely stay out of this hot fan-war mess. But I gave Nash my best *Julia Pinkerton, Teen Detective* "that's what you think" look.

I wasn't spending New Year's Eve without him. Or that necklace.

SIX
#WARHEADGIRLPOWER

"GOODNESS," said Rhonda, my Black Pine BFF. Her full lips pursed between round cheeks. "So many little dogs."

Our other bestie, Tiffany, squatted next to her. Since my move to Black Pine, Rhonda and Tiffany had become the grits and bacon to my sunny-side-up eggs. Their advice — also salty and meaty — kept me grounded, much like the bathroom scale after a hearty breakfast. Plus, they kept me somewhat stylish — a vanity holdover from my years of forced spa'ing— due to the fact they were hair and nail estheticians.

Tiffany eyeballed the five Jack Russells, who — for once in their lives — sat quietly with only a quick sniff or scratch to show they were more than little brown and white statues. Getting the dogs into Nash's truck had been as easy as squeezing into a pair of Spanx three sizes too small. They kept popping out before we could close the door. That they were still and behaved now was nothing short of a New Year's miracle.

"They're cute as the dickens," said Tiffany.

"Teeny had to go to the doctor," said Remi.

"There's more?"

"This here's Mighty, Jerry, Sorrel, Scratch, and Angela. She's the mother. Sorrel's Mighty and Teeny's daddy. Scratch might be Jerry's uncle. We tend to forget because we always have a lot of 'em," explained Remi. "Seems like new puppies just pop out of the woodwork. Daddy says a stork brings 'em, but I've seen them come out of Angela. It's a messy business like none other."

"Thanks for taking them in on New Year's Eve," I said to Tiffany, hoping to move Remi away from the details of puppy birth. "It's a huge ask from me, I know."

"It's no big thing." Tiffany stood. Her blue-tipped bob swung, framing her pointed features. "Me and Rhonda always celebrate starting early. We watch movies all day, then the countdown. Ever since Shithead—oops, um…" She squinted at Remi. "My ex-husband found New Year's Eve an excellent night to rob…I mean, unlawfully gain commerce from convenience stores."

"Cool." Remi's eyes had widened and sparked in a way that made me nervous.

"You got an important case or something?" Rhonda wore leopard print fleece and held a frothy blended drink in one hand. It seemed they really planned on staying in all day. "Seems like a shame on New Year's Eve. I thought tonight you'd be getting jiggy— On a date with Mr. Nash."

"Some weirdo is after a deer cartridge necklace I had given to Daddy. It's from a movie I did."

"*Warhead Girl*?" said Rhonda. "They've been talking about the fifth anniversary. There's this dude who's nutty for that movie. He's even dressing like the guy in the movie for all his political parades and stuff."

"I don't know that movie," said Tiffany. "But is that the dude who claims to have missiles pointing all over the place? He's a nut job."

"Maybe not that nut job," said Rhonda. "It's hard to tell which one."

I bit my lip. "Is he calling himself the Supreme Commander?"

Rhonda's emphatic yes had her braids bouncing on her back. "That nut job. That's the one."

"That's the name of the bad guy from the movie. In the comic book, he put a bounty on the necklace, but only if *Warhead Girl*'s head was still attached."

"Ew," said Rhonda.

I hurried a look at Remi, but she wasn't paying attention to our conversation. She had corralled the dogs around the TV and was flipping through stations with Tiffany's remote control.

"The producer made them change it in the script because the ratings were already over-the-top for violence. In the movie, the Supreme Commander just wanted the necklace. He thought it would give him special powers, not realizing the power of *Warhead Girl* came from within herself."

"Girl power." Rhonda nodded.

"More like uncontrollable rage at the system, but since *Warhead Girl* was a girl, I guess that works, too." I grimaced. "The character, Belinda Jenkins was just a regular girl living in a totalitarian regime who saw her parents run over by a tank and her boyfriend falsely arrested and murdered. When she put on the necklace and bandolier of bullets, she became Warhead Girl. Although I thought the rocket launcher made the difference."

"Miss Albright." Nash appeared in the doorway, holding his phone in his hand. "Ms. Wonderly wants to meet me. Maybe she'll have information about Gentz and why he's also after the necklace."

The dogs sat around the TV, staring at the screen like the 101 Dalmatian pups.

"Where's Remi?" I said.

"Maybe she needed to use the facilities," said Rhonda, sipping her drink. "Don't worry. We'll take good care of her."

"I'm more worried about you. I took away the slingshot, but she's pretty good at engineering devices. Don't leave any tools laying around. Including scissors, rubber bands, and paper clips. Maybe put up the silverware, too."

"Or you could stay here and watch her," said Nash.

"Oh, no. You're not going without me." I didn't trust Ms. Wonderly much more than I did Gentz. We didn't know why she or her supposed boss wanted the necklace, either. I glanced down at my Think Rolyn black puffer jacket hiding the necklace. The bullets hung heavy around my neck. Literally and figuratively.

"I'm all set for kids. I got plenty of candy canes and candy kisses," said Tiffany. "Sour Patch Kids Christmas candies. Coke. And I made Rice Krispy treats that look like champagne bottles. We'll take good care of her."

"You didn't tell me you had Sour Patch Kids," squealed Rhonda.

"That's a lot of sugar—"

"Miss Albright, I'm leaving," said Nash.

"Remi," I called out. "I'll be back in a little bit. We're just going to check on something really boring."

Which I truly hoped was the case.

. . .

"OUR CLIENT WANTS to meet me at Black Pine Winter Market," said Nash, opening the truck's passenger door for me. He glanced at his watch. "I said I'd be there by one thirty."

I faced him, not ready to step into the truck. "You keep saying *our* client. Is that to placate me?"

"Does it?" He used that weird smile again.

"No." I folded my arms. "We told her no, so why does Ms. Wonderly want to meet again? We don't know why she wants the necklace either."

"Maybe she hopes we'll change our minds." He dropped the smile. "I'm hoping to find out why Gentz wants the necklace. That might reveal why her boss wants it, too. She won't tell me anything over the phone."

Winter white and red lipstick made a better impression in person, I thought, but said, "You don't find that suspicious?"

He shrugged. "We need to hurry. I don't want to miss her. The police are looking for Gentz, but that's going to take some time."

"If I had just given him the necklace, none of that would've happened." My bottom lip bumped out.

Nash brushed his thumb against my lip. "You told me you'd never give it up to someone like him. All that stuff about a symbol for vigilante violence." He paused, studying me. "Maybe you should give me the necklace."

I placed a hand over my chest. "No way."

"You don't trust me?" Nash reared back.

"I didn't say that. Can you trust Ms. Wonderly? Maybe she's into thug life, too. She could bring her own minions."

"Let's find out." He smiled, but this time with a lazy grin. A small dimple popped into view and the intensity of his eyes appeared more determined than steely.

Within me, I bundled hope that he had my best intentions at heart.

The weight of the bullets around my neck felt a bit lighter. But I still wasn't taking them off.

SEVEN

#DISTRUSTMUCH

GENTZ HAD BEEN RIGHT about the day warming with the sun. That's winter in Georgia. Sunshine brought shoppers to Black Pine's Winter Market. An outdoor market set up on the edge of Black Pine Lake, the small shops and stalls did a brisk business. The market was always lively on New Year's Eve. By sunset, the ground along the lake, already cleared of snow, would be covered with blankets for those who were stalwart enough to brave the cold for the midnight fireworks show.

Children ran the grounds while adults strolled along the paths, enjoying the decorations and holiday tunes playing from the bandstand. Fire pits for toasting marshmallows (conveniently sold at s'more stands) were scattered along the lake edge. The scent of pine smoke mixed with the smell of fried dough and chocolate from stalls selling churros, cocoa, and fudge.

Throughout the summer months, the outdoor artisan shops and cafes attracted tourists. Shops also rented kayaks, fishing boats, and fiberglass paddle boats shaped like swans. The Winter Market was meant for tourists, but locals loved it as well. Every year the Christmas yacht flotilla brought locals together for a mega-holiday party, where at least one drunk had to be rescued from drowning by the Black Pine Marine Police boat.

I loved the Winter Market. Daddy and I used to go every year during my monthly visit. The bullets around my chest also reminded me of past holidays. Visits with Daddy had been droplets of reality in the bubble of my Hollywood life. Black Pine mountain and lake had given me a visual escape. Daddy had provided an emotional escape.

And now someone was intent on taking one of the best gifts I had given him during that time of separation? It didn't make sense.

Particularly because of the ridiculous nature of that gift.

Nash and I strolled the path teeming with tourists and townies. We walked between stalls dotting the rise above the lake. He had his eye out for Ms. Wonderly. I had my eye out for the Dixie Kreme Donut stand. Not hard to find because of the long line wrapped around it.

"Is Lamar working?" I said.

"Probably," said Nash. "He wouldn't want his employees working on New Year's Eve. He's closed tomorrow."

"We should say hello."

Nash smirked. "And maybe get you a donut?"

"I'm all about supporting small businesses."

"Lamar's in a good spot. He'll have noticed anything unusual at the market."

Also, because Lamar was a retired cop who had often helped Nash on his cases. He had a keen eye and a keener mind, often using his shop and local network to gather information that might otherwise seem disconnected. Lamar's practical, unerring sense of judgment went beyond adherence to the law. As a cop, he often saw justice underserved and found people like Nash could help the public in ways the law couldn't.

After Lamar took over his father's donut business (like a lot of cops, Lamar had a good sense of humor), Nash rented the office above the Dixie Kreme shop and opened Nash Security Solutions. Lamar had known Nash most of his life, but they were both tight-lipped about the early years. Lamar didn't tell other people's stories, and Nash took strong and silent to an extreme. Whereas years of therapy (and years of interviews and other marketing events) had me spilling details of my life ad nauseam, Nash didn't believe his past worth discussing.

Which might be why I didn't quite trust him not to betray my wishes about the necklace. I had begun to realize there was a lot in Nash's past I didn't know.

"These crowds are ridic," I muttered.

"Didn't use to be so bad before the movie people moved in," said

Nash, curling his lip. "What'd they think? They'll see a movie star in this mob?"

"Good luck with that. Celebrities know better than to hang out in crowded markets. Most have gone home for the holidays, like everyone else."

"I need to get to a spot where Ms. Wonderly can find me," said Nash. "There are fewer people down by the lake. I'll grab a bench."

"It's all very 007, isn't it? A mysterious client who wants you to steal my Christmas gift to my father. A mysterious client who might be a crazy dictator?"

"You don't believe that, do you?" said Nash.

"Not really. They would have just kidnapped me and been done with it. Like in the seventies, when Kim Jong-il kidnapped that actress and director to force them to make movies." I shook my head. "Something else is going on here."

Nash stared at me for a long pause. "I meant, you don't believe that I would steal your gift to your father."

"Oh." I gave him a half-shrug. "That, too."

"Right." Nash's gaze darted through the throng. "See if Lamar's heard anything. I'll catch up with you after I speak to Ms. Wonderly."

"You don't want me there, do you?" My frayed nerves sagged under the weight of disappointment.

"You're a little emotional about the necklace. I want to be able to focus on getting Ms. Wonderly to talk." Nash laid a hand on my shoulder. "Don't take it personal."

"Whatever," I said, resorting to a favorite comeback from my eponymous character, Julia Pinkerton. Who was, after all, a teen detective. Even though I was twenty-five and should use more adult responses.

I waited in line at the Dixie Kreme Donut stall while Nash located an empty bench on the lake path. I lost sight of him when crowds passed between us. Which happened fairly often. The donut line crept and my attempts to move forward were halted by snarling adults intent on getting their caffeine and sugar fix.

Rising on my toes, I tried to see through the crowd to the lake. Nash's brown fedora popped into view, but I couldn't see if anyone had joined him.

"Hey, Maizie," said a voice as smooth and deep as hot buttered rum. Similar to Morgan Freeman's. Total ASMR to my ears.

I turned from my Nash-watch to the open window in the wooden stall decorated with pine boughs. Inside an older African American man in a ski cap, scarf, and thick quilted coat leaned on the counter. He handed me a cup of coffee. "I thought you were watching little Remi while Boomer and Carol Lynn were in Brunswick."

"Something came up." I glanced around, nervous to speak about the death necklace in public. "We had unexpected…and unwanted visitors. Remi and the dogs are with friends while Nash and I try to figure out what's going on."

"I heard." He leveled me with a look. "Did quite the job on Boomer's cabin, too. The police aren't interested in pursuing the suspect?"

"They have an APB out on their vehicle and descriptions. But—"

"A lot of work with a limited force. It's that time of year. Car accidents, fires, and domestic disturbances take top billing." His brows rose, and he gave me a half-smile. "You know why the culprits wanted what they wanted?"

I shook my head. "It seems so crazy. Two groups interested in the same thing. And after all this time…"

"That would make me wonder, why now? Did the interest of one party spur on the involvement of the other?"

"That's a good point, Lamar."

"Possibly one reacting to the other." He handed me a sugar packet for my coffee, smiling at the next customer but still speaking to me. "Like a bidding war."

A bidding war over a movie prop? They sold bullet necklaces at Comic-Con. "Maybe Nash will learn something." I looked down the hill but the crowd milling before the shopping arcade blocked my view. "I should go."

"I've got a donut for you. Just a minute." Lamar moved to the back of the stall. Returning he passed me a pumpkin spice. "As soon as I sell out here, I'm on my way to my sister's house in Atlanta. I'll wish you a Happy New Year's now." He leaned forward. "Be careful, Maizie."

"Thanks, Lamar." I waved the donut at him, moved away, and stopped at a barista table to set down my coffee. Inside the donut's napkin was a receipt. I took a bite of the donut and glanced at the slip where Lamar had written, "Manganoid" and "50K."

I knew Manganoid as an indie studio that mainly did sci-fi and superhero movies. Was Ms. Wonderly working for the production studio and fifty thousand the amount they were willing to pay for it? Why would a studio pay that much money for a prop they could make?

But the real burning question was the amount of the finder's fee that Nash would have gotten from fifty thousand dollars.

My stomach soured. I tossed the coffee, already feeling jittery. Even the donut tasted like paste. Well, not quite paste. More like airy pumpkin spice with a light crunch. A holiday food miracle. But hard to enjoy during all the possible betrayal happening with the man I thought I loved.

Still loved. I sniffled. But I had been in love before. Depending on the costar. I played the screwed-over ingenue more times than I wanted to count. In real life. Betrayal was as much a part of dating for me as dinner and a movie. Was Nash just another costar crush, and I now faced the ugly reality of who he was? Someone who'd take a hefty kickback from gaining a symbolic movie prop from the woman he allegedly loved?

Although he had not told me he loved me, had he? At least not with words…

My chest hurt from this revelation. I needed to speak to Lamar, to see if he was warning me about Nash's motives or just reporting facts. I did have a bad habit of jumping to conclusions. But I didn't want to stand in line again and Lamar seemed in a hurry to leave. Maybe it was better to confront Nash with the evidence.

I shoved the receipt into my pocket. A gust of wind blew over the lake and I shivered, hunching my shoulders inside my puffy coat. Black Pine Mountain loomed across the lake. An icy mist surrounded the peaks, making the mountain appear slightly sinister and foreboding. Smoke from the fire pits whipped through the crowd. I waved it away, coughing. The chatter of people around me and shouting of children grew louder.

Ahead of me, a couple argued. Still blinking the smoke from my eyes, I spied an elf leaning against the side of a stall, sipping off a flask. I felt his eyes on me. As I passed, he slipped from between the stalls to walk behind me.

The crowds pressed in and suddenly the Winter Market didn't seem so festive.

At a wide space between stalls, I rose on my toes, trying to see over shoppers' heads to the park bench where I'd last spotted Nash. I couldn't see his dark brown fedora.

My heart galloped. Had he gone somewhere with Ms. Wonderly? Sold me out like a holiday s'more?

A family passed and the mother's purse whacked me, jostling me off my toes. I tripped. A hand jerked me back before I fell into a group of teenagers.

"Hey," I cried and clutched the front of my coat, ready to protect the necklace.

"Gotcha." Nash's hat rode low, hiding his features, and he'd pulled up his jacket collar. Tucking my arm through his, he moved us through the crowded market. He lowered his voice. "Anything from Lamar?"

"He'd heard about the trouble at the cabin. That's all." I didn't want to confront him in this crowd. Somewhere private where I could watch his face. And possibly cry if my suspicions rang true. "Did you see your client?"

Nash kept his eyes on the crowd in front of us and spoke in a low murmur. "A kid came up to me. Handed me a note that told me to watch out for Gentz. It also said I should turn up with the merchandise at the office by five this evening."

"A kid?"

"Just a messenger. She didn't show for some reason." Nash glanced at me. "What's the matter?"

"Can't you call Ms. Wonderly? To tell her you don't have the necklace?"

"Sure." He slid his arm out from mine and circled it around my waist. A non-Nash thing to do in public. Normally I would enjoy the PDA. Today I found it extra suspicious but decided to play along. "Let's get out of here. I'll take you back to your friend's house and then I'll head to the office."

"Back to Tiffany's?" I stopped walking. "But we don't know anything."

"The police know about Gentz. He doesn't know your friends, so y'all are safe. And after five, Gentz will leave."

"Why?"

"Because Ms. Wonderly will have the necklace."

EIGHT

"WHAT?" I cried. Sliding out from his arm, I turned to face him. Despite the frosty air blowing from the lake, my face felt hot. "You're not serious."

Nash shoved his hands in his pockets. "Doesn't it seem like the best option? Let them handle Gentz." His eyes flit from mine to skim the crowd. "I don't like the thought of it at the cabin where someone else can turn up and threaten you."

"You don't know anything about Ms. Wonderly's boss." I folded my arms. "How much are they paying you?"

"Let's talk about this in the truck." Nash glanced over his shoulder.

A man carrying a large package shouldered his way between us, followed by his family. I stepped back to let them pass and spotted a small figure in a pink, puffy camouflage coat ducking between stalls. My stomach burbled heat into my chest. I wanted to vomit and faint at the same time.

Remi had a camo puffy coat.

Spinning away from Nash, I ran toward the alley between stalls. Pulling out my phone, I dialed Tiffany.

"Is Remi there?" I panted.

"We're fixing her a plate right now," said Tiffany. "Stop it, Rhon—"

A clatter hurt my ear. I darted out of the alley and found a café filled with families drinking cocoa and hot mulled wine. "Hello?"

"Hey Maizie," said Rhonda. "Whatcha doing?"

I didn't want to accuse my BFFs of being negligent, however, I knew Remi all too well. "Do you see Remi, Rhonda? Like right now. With your eyes?"

"Hang on. We're in the kitchen. She was watching TV with the dogs."

My phone was yanked from my hand. I felt something hard press against my back. I flicked a glance over my shoulder. An elf stared down, his eyes menacing. The object in my back pressed harder, and I sucked in a breath.

"Is that a gun?" I squeaked.

"Come with me. Nothing funny."

He yanked on my arm and we spun toward a stall. Pushing me inside, he locked the door and released the shutter. It banged shut. The stall was filled with wreaths, smelling of wet pine, like woods on a snowy evening. But without the pleasant solitude, thanks to the elf with the gun.

"Who are you?" My voice trembled. "Besides Santa's helper, I mean."

The elf stood before the door. One hand held my phone and the other, the flask he'd been sipping from earlier. No gun, but he did have pockets. Bright green on a background of red and white stripes. Very festive, considering.

"How much is he willing to pay?" The elf shoved the flask into a pocket.

"Who?"

"HG."

"I don't know HG." I edged toward the stall window. "And I'm not sure what you're talking about."

"Don't give me that, lady. Look, we'll pay more. Think of it as a late Christmas gift."

"Lady?" The elf wasn't from around here. If he was, he'd say "girl," "hon'," or "miss" in his menacing tone devoid of accent. Or "ma'am," if he felt more polite. "You're not a Black Pine elf. Who do you work for?"

"You said it yourself," the elf sneered, "Santa."

I pressed my weight onto my left foot and slid it forward a few inches. "Santa would never hire an elf with bad manners."

"Guess you never saw *Bad Santa*."

This dude was an actor and doing a terrible job of improvisation. And I was fairly certain he'd stuck the flask in my back, pretending it was a gun. Probably stolen from a movie clip. If he really wanted to play the part well, he should've used the bale of wreath wire to tie me up, then torture me for the information I didn't have.

Hello, Maizie. A little disturbing your mind had gone there.

However, the elf did have my phone. And that was an issue because I needed to apologize for hanging up on my babysitters.

But first, who in the hellsbah was HG?

"Listen, Elf," I said, adopting *Warhead Girl*'s gruff, snarly voice. "You tell me what I want to know, and I'll let you out of this beautifully scented wreath stall without harm."

"Oh, yeah?" His eyes narrowed, and he pushed his jingly cap back to a rakish angle. The elf was getting into his tough-guy character. Evidently, he needed an improv partner to spark his creativity. "You and what army?"

This guy was terrible.

"My army of four." A line from *Kung Fu Kate*. Which I had starred in as a preteen. But lines from a kid show seemed to be on par with this guy's level of craft.

I raised two fists, planted my left foot, and delivered a roundhouse kick with my right. This time it connected. My foot slammed into the elf's chest and my phone popped out of his hand. I scooped up the phone while he leaned over, retching.

"You tell your boss that I'm not selling," I growled. "And that's what you get for taking nips in a family-friendly environment."

I scrambled around him and shoved through the door. Stumbling out into the crowd, I felt another hand grip me and yank me to my feet. I screamed and looked up.

Nash.

"Come on," he said. "Gentz is here."

NINE

#TROUBLEINPUMPKINSPICE

WE PUSHED THROUGH THE CROWD, glancing over our shoulders.

"Nash," I said. "An elf shoved me into a shop, demanding to know what HG is willing to pay for the necklace. Who is HG?"

"I've got no clue." Nash sucked in a breath. "I think I see Gentz."

We ducked around the side of a cocoa stall and hid behind the line of customers.

"An elf grabbed you?" said Nash. "Like an elf, elf?"

"Never mind that." I pulled out my phone. "I need to call the girls. I thought I saw Remi."

Nash mopped his brow. "How can—"

"It's Remi. Who knows?" The phone clicked as Rhonda answered. "Sorry about earlier. An elf—never mind. Is Remi there? I thought I saw her here."

"You hung up on us for an elf?" said Rhonda.

"Technically, he hung up on you. Is Remi there?"

"That's okay then. For what we're doing for you, girl…"

"I know, I know. The dogs alone."

"Anyway," said Rhonda. "You had us worried, so we checked on her and she's asleep."

"Asleep?"

"In Tiffany's bed. Poor kid, all that earlier excitement must have worn her out. All curled up under the covers."

I'd not known Remi to willingly sleep at any time of the day or night, but Rhonda could be right. It wasn't every day she was attacked in her own home. I released a long breath. "Thank goodness. Things are getting weirder by the minute here."

"Your dogs are getting weirder by the minute. Do you know how high they can jump?"

"Jack Russells are very bouncy dogs." My eyes narrowed, spotting one of Gentz's minions. Oddjob. Nash pulled off his hat, laid a hand on my arm, and we shrank against the cocoa stand. "I'll check in later. We've got the bad guys in our sights."

"Oh," breathed Rhonda. "Your life is so exciting. But I'm eating Sour Patch Christmas candy in my comfies and watching *Bridget Jones's Diary*, so things are good here, too. I love me some Colin Firth."

"Excellent." I snapped my phone shut. An advantage of not being able to afford a smartphone. Touching a home button doesn't have the same endorphin release as a clamshell click.

"Do you think they followed us?" I whispered.

"Or they found out I was meeting our client." Nash's eyes trailed the henchman's movement.

Oddjob had his hands tucked inside his trench coat's pockets. Like he was hiding something rather than warming his fingers.

"You think he's packing?" I said. "Carrying heat?"

Nash looked at me. "What character are you doing?"

I sighed. "The elf's. He really needs to work on his craft."

"It's hard to say, but I'd think he'd more likely carry in a shoulder or belt holster than in a pocket. Maybe his hands are cold."

"That makes sense."

The henchman moved in a slow circle, searching the crowds. As he pivoted toward us, we ducked to hide behind the cocoa line. A little girl pulled on her mother's arm and pointed at us.

Looking at the girl, I smiled and placed a finger to my lips. "We're hiding," I whispered to her then leaned toward Nash. "Do you think this HG could be Ms. Wonderly's boss?"

"Possibly," said Nash. "Or a third party. She sent a kid with the message, not an elf."

Gentz's man moved on. We slid to the edge of the cocoa stall and peeked behind it.

"Let's get out of here." Nash pulled on my hand, and I yanked it back.

"Just a minute. Before I go anywhere with you, I need to know your intentions."

"My intentions?" Nash gaped. "You want to do this now? We've got a shot to get out of here before Gentz sees us."

"What percentage are you getting for the necklace?"

"Maizie, I told you—"

"You didn't tell me anything. Look at this." I reached into my pocket to pull out the receipt. Nothing. Rummaged deeper. Checked the other pocket. "It's not here. Someone stole it."

"Stole what?"

"The receipt Lamar gave me."

"For a donut?" Nash gave an exasperated sigh. "We need to go. Now."

"No, it was information for me."

"You said Lamar didn't know anything."

"I lied." I curled my lip. "Manganoid's paying fifty thousand. How much are they paying you?"

"You're kidding?" Nash's eyes narrowed. "You'd think I'd let some… whatever that is, buy me off? The whole thing is stupid. It's a piece of junk any idiot can make with a box of four-forty-fours."

"Stupid to you, but not to my father. I didn't bring home art projects as a kid. All I could offer him were review copies and headshots." Tears welled in my eyes. "This was one of the few pieces of movie property he found remotely interesting. It hung on his tree. That makes it special."

"Okay, I'm sorry," he hissed. "Can we go now?"

I blinked back the tears. "How can I trust you?"

"Because it's me?" His face pinched. "What are you saying?"

"I'm worried you might just be another costar, ready to sell me out for a better offer." I whirled away, stalking past the cocoa line.

And barreled right into Gentz.

TEN

#PORTANOTTY

"MISS ALBRIGHT, so good to see you again," said Gentz in his heavy accent. Grabbing my hand, he slid it through his elbow. "We need to talk."

"Don't even try me," I shouted, yanking my arm free. "Nash. It's Gentz."

"You won't scream. I have this." He pressed something hard against my side.

I glanced down and gasped. His hand was wrapped in a bandage, and he didn't hold a flask. Nor did it look like a prop gun. Gentz was not Hollywooding. "Isn't that a little extreme?"

"The last time we encountered you, you sicced a pack of wild dogs on me and set a tree on fire."

"They're not really a pack," I said shakily. Who was I kidding? The Jacks were one step from *The Call of the Wild*. "And you'd invaded our house. Hello? Self-defense?"

Oddjob wrapped his beefy arm around my waist. My puffy jacket squeezed out on either side of his arm, like a split can of biscuit dough. My scarf rose, almost covering my eyes. The men heaved, lifting me, dragging my feet above the ground. Cutting through the crowd, they sped toward the parking lot.

The number one rule in escaping an abduction is never to get in a car with anyone. Number two was never to panic. Keep a cool head. I couldn't remember number three, but I imagine it was to run. I couldn't run. I also couldn't see with my coat and scarf pushed above my chin.

So I panicked.

I squealed, kicked, and thrashed, trying to yank out of their grasp while they exclaimed loudly about my inability to hold my mulled wine.

"Don't tussle so," said Gentz. "You are making it very difficult to carry you."

"Kind of the point," I shouted. My heel caught Oddjob's knee. He grunted and tightened his grip on my waist.

"Really, Miss Albright," said Gentz. "Calm down. We're just taking you somewhere to talk."

Above my scarf, a group bobbed in view. People waiting in line at the churro stand.

"Help me," I called through layers of down and wool. A nearby speaker churned out holiday favorites and drowned out my words.

I struggled harder, trying to catch their attention. My scarf slipped. The entire line leaned against the stall, waiting on churros. Eyes down. Focused on their phones. A lone toddler looked up and caught my squint. Then refocused on the screen his mother held.

I craned my neck above my coat, trying to find Nash. He'd been right behind me. Igor wasn't around either.

Shiztastic. Nash had been waylaid by Igor, while I was stuck with Gentz and Oddjob.

Unless Nash had gotten annoyed enough not to follow me and had no idea that I was a kidnap victim.

"Quick," said Gentz. "In here. We'll get her later."

I swung my legs out. Before I could jerk back to attack their knees, Gentz dropped my arm and yanked open the door of a porta-potty. Oddjob tossed me inside.

My hands flew forward to prevent me from falling into the dark hold. My palms thudded against the back wall. The door slammed. I rammed the door, but something lodged it shut. Inside the rank box, I banged on the door and walls, screaming to be let out. The beeping sound of a large truck backing up covered my screams.

Above me, a chain rattled. Something heavy thwacked the walls. The truck made a grinding sound, and the box shifted.

"The hey?" I braced myself against the door. And felt the ground fall from my feet. Without my feet ever leaving the ground. Which must be how a dog experiences an elevator.

"Let me out," I shouted and pounded on the door. "I'm inside."

The box tilted and swayed. My stomach flipped, and I breathed through my mouth in tiny, rapid sips. Of foul-smelling air. Lightly scented with some kind of lavender spritz.

I was claustrophobic. Stuck in a portable toilet that hung in mid-air. Even worse than my nightmare where I was stuck in a tiny aquarium filled with baby sharks. I couldn't breathe in either one. But the aquarium probably smelled better.

Pressing my face against the crack of light rimming the doorway, I sucked in fresh air. I clawed at the door, not caring how high I was suspended. I kicked the door, managing to widen the crack at the bottom. But whatever wrapped the box held the door shut. Necessary in porta-potty transportation, but a defeat if you're stuck inside while it's swinging above Black Pine Lake.

Failing all other options, I sank to the sticky porta-potty floor and squatted by the door. Despair won out over disgust and gave in to tears.

Gears ground and a motor roared. The box reeled, sloshing me and the rest of the porta's contents. Feeling sick, I pressed my hands and feet against the doorframe and prayed nothing would spill from either place. The elevator feeling reappeared, but this time we descended. Quickly. Too quickly. I sucked in air with tiny sips, telling myself that as porta-potty deaths went, crashing was better than death by suffocation.

Didn't help.

The stall slammed into the ground. I fell over, landing on my side of the sticky floor. The porta stayed upright. The ground beneath it felt solid. I pushed to my feet. And yanked off a piece of toilet paper stuck to my puffy coat.

Later I would need a ten-thousand-hour shower and possibly all the hot water in Black Pine to do so, but for now, I needed to get out of this damn stank house of a coffin and find my sister before Gentz found her first.

ELEVEN

#NOTONUTBALLS

I STAYED WEDGED against the door, ready to pop out. With the sound of chains hitting the ground, I flew out of the door. Tripped on a rising contraption and fell on a metal floor. The steel felt like ice against my face. But clean ice.

At least, cleaner than my most recent floor experience.

Rolling onto my back, I gulped crisp, wood-scented air, and watched a bracketed lift swing overhead. Surrounded by porta-potties, I lay on the bed of a truck with an attached crane. Gathering my senses, I heard shouts and calls from the crane operator and another man moving the portable toilets.

Gentz must have thrown me inside, knowing the stall was about to get lifted. Was he hoping to transport me to a dump station where he would interrogate me?

The truck bed was already crowded with portable toilets. Before one crashed on me, I hopped up. Slipping between the plastic booths, I made my way to the side facing the lake, away from the parking lot. Grabbing the edge of the truck bed, I swung to the ground and crept around the truck. A black Mercedes was parked at the edge of the lot. Igor leaned next to it, speaking to someone through the window.

Probably Gentz. I pressed my lips together and tasted toilet filth. While I spat on the ground — while trying not to puke — shouting caught my ear. Angry shouting. Glancing up, I saw another porta-potty flying overhead. For a moment, I gazed in wonderment, imagining myself inside. The shouts I heard jolted me from my reverie.

I recognized that voice. Nash. Screaming at the crane operator. Something about a woman inside…

Nash had the wrong porta-potty.

Or the wrong woman.

Jumping to my feet, I sprinted toward the voices. And halted. A tiny figure in a camo puffy coat snuck between cars toward the Mercedes.

Remi. I knew she'd never take a nap without threats or handcuffing. What in the hellsbah was she doing? It looked like she was going to approach—

I bolted toward the parking lot, calling Remi's name. The girl in the parking lot halted, then slipped behind a truck. Igor's bent form shot up from his window lean. He dashed around the Mercedes. The front passenger door opened, and Oddjob dislodged himself from the car. Both hurried toward me. I slowed my run, my gaze on the parking lot, searching for Remi.

"Remi," I yelled. "Find Nash."

She'd disappeared. I blew out a breath and glanced behind me, looking for Nash. Surely he'd heard me. I gasped. A crowd had gathered. The suspended porta-potty swung wildly over the lake. Inside the cab of the truck, two men fought. The crane moved erratically, shaking the toilet like a dog on a stuffed toy.

"Nash?" I called. "I'm—"

A hand landed on my arm, whipping me around. "Gentz wants a word with you."

I shrieked, then forced myself to act cool. I didn't need Remi leaping out to save me. Taking a breath, I assumed my *Warhead Girl* character and gained courage. "Back off."

My eyes scoured the parking lot as I walked toward the Mercedes. I wanted Gentz to leave before he saw Remi. If he thought I wouldn't talk, he might try Remi. He probably thought he'd more easily gain the information from her.

He didn't know Remi.

Reaching the car, I jerked open the rear passenger door. Inside, Gentz leaned toward me. "Miss Albright, I'm surprised to see you. We planned to pick you up at the next pit stop." He chuckled. "I thought you'd be otherwise occupied."

Even the real bad guys use bad-guy humor. The Hollywood writers I knew would've enjoyed that line.

Instead of resorting to Julia Pinkerton's snark or Warhead Girl's anger, I collapsed on the seat next to him. "Let's go."

"Go where?" Gentz sniffed then grimaced. "We couldn't find the necklace at your father's cabin. My team checked carefully."

I shuddered at the thought of Gentz's men searching my father's home. I was glad we had quickly moved the dogs and Remi to Tiffany's. Except Remi had somehow escaped.

"I'll tell you where it is." I peered over his shoulder into the parking lot. Spotted something dart between cars. We needed to get away before Remi tried to come with me. "But not here."

"Fine." He snapped his fingers and Igor started the car. "We'll go to our hotel. I'm glad you're seeing reason. You'll be rewarded, of course."

"I don't care about that," I mumbled, focused on the parking lot.

"My client pays very well. But that's your decision." Gentz shrugged, pulled out his phone, and turned away from me.

I hoped Remi had heard me about finding Nash. She thought this was an adventure. These men were dangerous. They didn't care about the destruction of the cabin or the risks to our lives, let alone the fact that this stupid necklace was special to my family. They were just doing a job. Hired guns.

I knew contract killers, heavies, cleaners, or what-have-yous were a real thing. But I thought they'd take their work more seriously. Like stick with organized crime, spy rings, and whatnot. Not work for nut jobs who wanted show biz memorabilia.

I hated the thought of a wacko with a necklace representing vigilante girl power. There were enough screwballs on Youtube and the like, inciting more lunatics to violence. The psycho would probably piece clips from the movie into his nutball act. And I'd be forever associated with his fanatic cuckoo ways. That could possibly harm other people.

The nutjob association was enough motivation to keep the necklace out of this maniac's hands. I was no longer a star, able to use my Hollywood pedestal (and my own minions) to keep the crazies away from the necklace. I was out in the real world. Apprenticing as a private investigator. Trying to be one of the good guys.

There was no way I would give up this necklace.

But first Remi's safety. I'd let Gentz think I was willing to deal. That his threats had worked. Then...

A loud splash and a long scream halted my thoughts. I turned in the seat toward the rear window. Although still positioned over the lake, the crane no longer held the porta-potty. A man leaped from the cab and ran to the edge of the lake.

Nash.

He must have thought I was still in the porta-potty. Horrified, I watched his hat sail off. Then his coat.

Holy shiz. I shoved my hand in my coat pocket, searching for my phone. Scrabbling through my pockets, I realized it must have fallen out inside the porta-potty. I punched the window button.

"Unlock my window," I cried. "I need to—"

"It's too cold for that," said Gentz.

"Nash thinks I'm in the lake." I turned to Gentz. "He's going to jump in. It's freezing. Just let me yell—"

"He won't hear you, Miss Albright," said Gentz. "It's too late. Besides, we have an appointment to make."

"Nash could get pneumonia," I pleaded. "Turn around. Please. He'll do anything to save me. He might drown."

Gentz gave me a long look. He tapped the driver's shoulder with his bandaged hand. "Brian, did you hear that?"

"Thank you." I clasped my hands together. "It'll only take a few minutes. Then we can go wherever you want and deal with the—"

"That means the police and emergency vehicles will be here soon. Step on it, Brian."

TWELVE
#THEDON'TCOMEINN

BRIAN — Although I still thought of him as Igor — sped through downtown Black Pine toward the outskirts of town. Slowing, the Mercedes' headlights swept over a dirty snowdrift beneath a neon sign advertising the Dukem Inn. We pulled into the motor lodge. The motel had been painted white and made to look like an alpine lodge with faux brown shutters around each room's windows. Under strings of Christmas lights, the white appeared mustard yellow. Tired fake flowers peeked from snow-covered window boxes. Next to the outdoor pool, an old purple Christmas tree listed against the chain-link fence.

A restaurant and bar with the same name shared a parking lot with the motel. Also Alpine-y, mustardy, and more than slightly cheesy. It could have been cute if someone had bothered with the upkeep.

"The Dukem Inn? Why aren't you staying at Black Pine Resort?" I said to Gentz, then mentally kicked myself. Of all the stupid questions.

"You don't approve of our accommodations?" Gentz smirked. "When not on assignment, I'm sure I'd prefer Black Pine Resort. Maybe next time I visit."

I flopped against my seat.

Gentz chuckled with his throaty rasp. "You hope there won't be a next time. I see. Well, this meeting will determine that. Give JJ the necklace and we'll leave."

"Is that your boss?"

Gentz shook his head. "My director is extraordinarily busy. JJ is one of his assistants. The department is appropriations, I believe."

Again, with the dry chuckle. Gentz needed a throat lozenge. Or morals.

"And don't think you can appeal to JJ with stories of mistreatment or mishandling," continued Gentz. "JJ believes in our leader's mission. And is paid extremely well for services rendered."

Great. Really looking forward to meeting this JJ.

Brian parked the car before a room at the end of the motel. Far from the front desk, restaurant, and sad Christmas tree. By the dark windows lining this end of the long building, I didn't have much hope of anyone hearing us. By the look of the motel, I didn't have much hope of anyone caring.

Heaving a sigh, I followed Gentz and the minions to the motel door. He knocked, used an actual key — didn't know those still existed — and pushed open the door. Before my mind could register all the plaid in the room — wallpaper, bedspreads, curtains — I noticed the woman sitting at a table. A youngish woman, probably in her thirties. With balayage hair pulled back in a loose braid and deliberately messy bun. Wearing couture. I was sure of it. With her long legs and athletic build, she could pass off any ready-to-wear. But with the side ties, puffy sleeves, and bohemian vibe, it spoke of a designer I followed.

"OMG, MaisonCléo," I murmured, not able to help myself.

The woman smirked.

I cleared my throat. "You're JJ?"

"You sound surprised," she said, her voice slightly tinged with SoCal upspeak. A Southern Californian.

Great. She must work in the industry, too. Which meant so did her boss. Did Gentz and JJ work for Manganoid?

Behind me, Gentz gave orders to the trench coat brothers. The wind whipped inside, and the door banged.

"Have a seat, Maizie." She wrinkled her nose. "Or do you want to change first? Mr. Gentz told me where you've been."

I clamped my lips together. Why was I allowing myself to get distracted by fashion? I was on a mission. She might look like an Instagram model, but JJ was no better than Gentz. Or her crazy-pants boss.

"I'm good." I found it easier to lie using Julia Pinkerton's character. As myself, I wasn't believable. "Let's get this deal done."

"Are you sure?" JJ wrinkled her nose. "'cause like, I find it kind of hard to concentrate. You reek."

She moved to a closet, flicked through some hangers, and pulled out a white silk dress. Off-the-shoulder with a flared ruffle gathered at the yoke. Lying it over her arm, she approached me. "I didn't bring much with me. How about this?"

"So inappropriate for winter weather here," I murmured. Found myself stroking the silk and yanked my hand back. "Bevza. In Black Pine. Ridic."

"You know your fashion." She handed me the dress, bent down, and dangled a pair of square-toed, white silk mules. "I even have the kicks."

"It's beautiful." A knot formed in my throat. Partially due to my recent lack of accessible fashion. Partially due to the thought of Nash swimming in an icy lake for the partner, he wouldn't find in a submerged toilet.

Maybe placating JJ would help. I shrugged. "Fine."

"Why don't you shower while you're at it." JJ hitched a thumb toward the bathroom.

She was one smug baddie.

"I just want to get this done. My partner could be drowning at this very minute." And I didn't know if Remi had found him or was now captain of a pirate ship. You could never tell with Remi. "I've got more important considerations than the state of my ensemble."

"I'd be worried about all the germs after your toilet adventure, but whatevs. However, know this, you're not going anywhere in a hurry. Not until we have the necklace and it's been authenticated." JJ crossed her arms. "Then we'll see. So might as well get comfortable. It'll be a long afternoon."

My spirits plummeted. But not my stench. "Fine." I stalked to the bathroom.

THIRTEEN

#NOSLEIGHBELLSJUSTSCHNITZEL

I APPRECIATED the hot shower and the Bumble and Bumble products. However, the dress barely fit me — I was built more for bearing children than athletics — and it left me freezing. JJ had taken my coat, clothes, and shoes, leaving me dressed for wintering in St. Tropez, not Black Pine.

Hugging my bare arms, I shlepped out of the bathroom.

"Better. I can't believe how awful you smelled." JJ waved at the table where she sat. "Gentz brought us lunch. The restaurant has decent food."

Food? What was this? Some kind of temptation in the wilderness of Black Pine?

Shivering, I stopped before the table, eyeing the plates of bratwurst, potato salad, pretzels, and schnitzel. Not your usual Black Pine fare, but I suppose it went with the Alpine theme.

I got it. JJ and Gentz were good-copping/bad-copping me. Weakening me so I would give up the death necklace. They certainly figured out how to break me. Couture, hot showers, and a carb fest.

"I'm not hungry." My stomach growled. "I had a donut at Winter Market."

"Chill already. I told you, you're not going anywhere. You might as well eat." JJ waved at the food. "I saw you don't have the necklace on you. While we eat, you can tell me where to find it."

I'd taken the death necklace into the shower with me, figuring JJ would search my stuff. The dress was more than form-fitting so I couldn't hide it on me. Smart on her part. After showering, I used the noise of the hairdryer to cover the sound of me hiding it in the tank of the toilet.

That necklace had been through a lot in one day.

I sank onto a chair, rubbing my arms and pressing my legs together for warmth. Heat blasted noisily from the wall unit. JJ took the chair across from me and began filling her plate.

"Eat," she said. "It's not poisoned."

Okay, I hadn't considered that. Now I had *The Princess Bride* battle of wits scene going through my head. *Focus, Maizie.* Instead of worrying about locaine powder, I needed to figure out how to escape. Without my coat and Gentz's men outside the door.

If I could escape, I could tell the police exactly where they were staying. No need to give up the necklace to these lunatics. Then we'd be down to one less crazy, as we still had Ms. Wonderly and an elf to worry about.

"The food does look good," I murmured. I picked up my fork in my right, and with my left hand, dropped my napkin over the remaining cutlery.

"It's delicious." JJ chewed and cut another piece of bratwurst with her steak knife. "I rarely get the chance to eat like this in California."

"LA?" I said.

"Born and raised, but I live in Silicon Valley now." She delved into another brat.

Silicon Valley? Okay, maybe she didn't work for the movies. Why would someone in Silicon Valley want the *Warhead Girl* necklace, though?

I watched her eat, wondering if I could interrogate her without being too obvious. With the hot air blowing, the room began to feel cozy. Perfect for napping. My plan began to form. If she was going to act like it was totally normal to eat German food in a dumpy hotel on New Year's Eve day while three heavies stood outside the door, I could, too.

"Can you turn up the heat?" My teeth chattered, and I rubbed my arms. "I'm too cold to eat."

JJ moved to the unit below the window and poked buttons.

"How's the potato salad?" I said pushing the bowl toward her. "The pretzels look great. Is that beer mustard?"

"Mmm," said JJ. "And there's Black Forest cake for dessert. I love German food."

I picked up my fork and stabbed a bratwurst. Held it aloft. Took a bite. My teeth pierced the crispy skin, savory juice filled my mouth. Holy Schmolies. I set the brat down and grabbed a pretzel.

"There are at least two parties interested in the necklace." I tore off another hunk of pretzel. "I was attacked by an elf at the festival. He wanted to know how much HG would pay. Is HG your boss?"

"An elf?" JJ chuckled and scooped schnitzel onto her plate. "HG will pay whatever it takes if that's what you're asking. He's got more money than God."

I didn't believe God needed money, but whatever. "What does he do?"

"Silicon tech mostly. He's funded a lot of well-known apps, sold them for even more. The same with exotic real estate. Rinse and repeat. But his real love is an operating system he's developed. It's going to make history. He thinks it will save the world."

"Save the world from what? How?"

"By my contract, I'm not allowed to get into the details. But it's going to change the internet. For the better, too."

"Save the world with the internet? Like a faster, more polite version of Ask Jeeves?"

"You wouldn't understand." JJ tore off a pretzel end and dipped it in mustard. "Why don't you have another bratwurst? Or are you ready for cake?

These people were mental. I sighed and accepted the cake she placed before me.

"So, the *Warhead Girl* necklace," she paused to finish chewing. "We'll pay more than anyone else."

"It's not for sale." I folded my arms. "It was a gift to my father. Besides, it's a movie prop. The movie wasn't even that good."

She quirked a brow. "It's become a cult classic. In certain circles."

I rolled my eyes. "I had a body double for—"

"Not because of that. It's the dystopian themes. You know, David and Goliath."

"I don't think David and Goliath are dystop—"

"It doesn't matter," she snapped. "HG wants it and—" JJ took a breath, composing herself. She laid her fork down. "It's important to him."

"It's important to my dad, too."

"This is 'bigger picture' than some movie prop you once gave to your dad out of guilt."

"How did you know it was out of guilt—never mind. You can get a copy on eBay, for heaven's sake."

"Those are not the real McCoy." JJ cleared her throat and tried smiling. Not very convincingly.

It was a day for weird smiles. Maybe Remi was right about the Grinch.

"HG is…kind of an intense guy. You know the type. Doesn't sleep because of all the awesome ideas keeping him awake. Plus he needs to do business with Asia in real time. When he's focused on an idea, nothing will stop him." JJ paused, forked a piece of cake, and looked at me. "Listen, it doesn't matter what he believes. HG wants the real thing, and he'll get the real thing. He told me 'at any cost.' So I'm going with it."

"That's insane."

"And it's important he has it by the end of the day. He's been looking for it for five years. And now it's within his grasp, like literally."

Only literally if he used JJ's toilet, but now was not the time to quibble over semantics.

She smiled and pushed back from the table. "I'm so full. I'll go for a run tomorrow morning to work off the cake."

I hated JJ. And not just because she could eat whatever she wanted. She didn't care her boss was a delusional genius nutball.

A ruthless delusional genius nutball.

"You must be sleepy," I said, yawning. "All that food, and it's so cozy in here now. I'm not even cold anymore."

"Yeah." JJ patted her stomach. "What I wouldn't give to curl up and watch Netflix. Am I right?"

"So right." I narrowed my eyes and slipped the knife from under my napkin. Flipping it around, I gripped the handle and hid the point against the underside of my arm. "I'm going to use the bathroom. Be right back."

JJ yawned. "You're not sleepy?"

"Sure." I yawned in response, backing toward the bathroom. "Be back in a minute."

"We haven't finished our discussion about the necklace." JJ pouted.

"I'll tell you in a minute. I've really got to go." I laid a hand on the bathroom knob. "Just rest your eyes, and I'll be out in a second."

"I won't fall asleep." JJ rose from the table and approached me. "If that's what you're hoping."

"What?" I stammered. "I mean, what do you mean?"

"You kept pushing food? And cranking the heat? Nice ploy, but it's not like I'm going to fall asleep and forget why you're here. I've got an awesome metabolism. I can eat my weight in brats and not get sleepy." She smiled. "But you will."

"You're wrong." I glared at her. "I've been conditioned by years of craft food grazing during long waits for sound and lighting checks. As an actress, I'm trained to be alert and ready for the camera at all times."

"Uh, Maizie, sorry to be the one to break the news. Your body shape tells a different story."

"There's nothing wrong with my body shape," I snapped. "It's called Rubenesque, and it's making a comeback."

She snorted. "Yeah, right."

I whipped out the steak knife. "Okay. I'm done playing. It's time for me to go. I said I'm not selling." I grabbed her arm — actually only muscle over bone, no body fat, dammit — yanked it behind her back, and flattened her against me. I whipped the knifepoint to her throat.

"You don't need to resort to this." She played it cool, but I could feel her heart hammering through her thin body.

"I think I do. It's been a long day and you're not listening to me." Holding the knife against her throat, I walked her to the door. I hated leaving the necklace, but they didn't know it was in the room. Nash and I would have to come back later.

If he hadn't drowned or been hospitalized for pneumonia.

The door flew open. Gentz and Igor — I mean, Brian — stalked inside the room, slamming the door behind them.

"Miss Albright, whatever are you doing?" Gentz sighed and pulled his gun from his pocket. "Brian."

Brian strode to me, sliced his hand down, chopping the joint between my neck and shoulder. My arm instantly numbed, and I dropped the knife. JJ backed away, rolling her eyes.

"As if," she said. "She doesn't have the necklace on her. See what you can do. I'm going to bounce. Best not to witness your action."

He nodded, turned to the closet, and pulled out a hanger. Metal, not wooden.

"What are you going to do with that?" I backed away and slammed into Brian.

"Ah, Miss Albright." Gentz smiled. "You should know how much I enjoy my job before we proceed."

FOURTEEN

#THEGERMANINQUISITION

GENTZ HANDED BRIAN THE HANGER, then slipped off his coat. "It's so warm in here. We should all be comfortable before we begin."

Brian returned the hanger to him, and Gentz slipped his coat on it, then turned to hang the trench coat in the closet. I let out a long breath. Brian shoved me into the chair by the table, then yanked my arms behind my back.

"What do you think you're doing?"

"Getting comfortable, Miss Albright." Gentz handed Brian a bundle of plastic loops. "Proceed, Brian."

Making quick work, Brian zip-tied my ankles to the chair legs and my hands behind the chair. I wiggled, hoping for slack, but Brian yanked the end of the zip-ties, tightening them.

"This is so illegal," I said. "Your boss is in a lot of trouble. I know who he is now, and I am so reporting him. He's dunzo. You better think about that before you do anything else."

"Why do you think JJ left? She knows nothing. But she could report you for holding a knife to her throat. That's assault, isn't it, Miss Albright? Perhaps even attempted murder?"

"So not cool. I was kidnapped. Again, self-defense."

"You entered the car on your own and told me to 'go.' JJ fed you, cleaned you, and gave you clothes. She thought you were her guest. I think you're quite lacking a suitable defense." Gentz tilted his head to each side, popping his neck. "Let's proceed."

I swallowed. Squirmed. Felt the plastic cut into my wrists and stopped squirming.

"Where is the necklace, Miss Albright?"

"I'm not selling."

"Ah, Miss Albright, you misunderstand. Buying the necklace was JJ's job. As she wasn't successful, now it's my turn." He grabbed my face with the bandaged hand and jerked my head, forcing me to stare into his cold, dark eyes. "I don't purchase, I just obtain."

Gentz squeezed, hurting my jaw. He waved at Brian. "Give me the knife she dropped."

"At the office," I blurted. Which was difficult to say with my mouth squeezed like we were playing chubby-baby. "In a safe."

"Your private investigation office?" He nodded to Brian.

Brian stepped to the door, opened it, and spoke to Oddjob standing outside.

"And who can open this safe, Miss Albright?"

Gentz released my mouth. I worked my sore jaw. "Me."

"What about your employer, Mr. Nash?"

"He's not my employer anymore. Not really. Like just a mentor? My ex-manager bought his ex-wife's shares of the company because he lost—"

I stopped myself from rambling and focused on finding another character. Preferably one who was tougher than my real self. A lot tougher. Even if I'd given a lie, it hadn't taken more than a face squeeze to get me to talk. *Warhead Girl* wouldn't have blabbed. My eyes narrowed, and I sneered. "Do you really want the details? Anyway, I can open the safe. You already sent Nash into the lake. He's either dead or in the hospital."

Hopefully not, but I didn't think this was a good place to cry.

Lifting my chin, I glared at Gentz. "Let's go, bro. Take me to the office." The office also had an emergency call button. And we kept weapons in the safe. Which I really hoped I wouldn't have to use.

"Where in the office is this safe?" Gentz didn't seem particularly intimidated. Or in a hurry.

"The inner office. Against the back wall. You need a thumbprint to unlock it. We don't mess around."

"A moment, Miss Albright."

He took his time putting on his coat, then moved outside. Brian followed. The door banged behind them. A few minutes passed. My arms ached from their backward pull but when I tried to scoot in the chair, the ties cut into my ankles. Brian had done too good of a job.

"Hey," I yelled. "Are we going to the office or not?"

A weighted silence.

"I have to use the bathroom," I called out. "JJ, are you around?"

Had they left for the office? Maybe they were going to lift the whole safe. Or cut it open with a blow torch or something.

Hells. I should've thought. I was a terrible kidnap victim. They'd get our weapons, Nash's important papers, and the petty cash. Plus the bag of Christmas Snickers I hid inside to keep myself from eating them. They would return, do whatever torture Gentz specialized in, and I'd have to tell them the stupid necklace had been in the toilet the whole time.

A scuffling sounded outside the door. I sat forward, felt the pain in my armpits, and relaxed in the chair.

"Hello?"

Something thumped against the door. Then banged repeatedly. Smashed into the window. And thudded on the floor. A key turned in the lock. The door slammed open, and a wild-eyed Nash looked around the room.

"Maizie." Nash ran to me, knelt, and cupped my face between his large palms. "Oh, Maizie. I thought I'd lost you." He kissed me gently, then roughly until I cried out in pain.

"Did they hurt you?" He ran his hands over my shoulders.

"No, the zip ties are cutting into my skin. And my arms feel like they're going to pull out of the sockets. But kiss me anyway."

He obliged.

"What happened out there?"

"I knocked out the smaller guy with a fire extinguisher." Nash glanced behind him. "I should probably bring him inside and tie him up before he wakes. Where did the others go?"

"The office." I told him about my plan. "But they're going to bring the safe to me or break it open and find out I was lying. Gentz was smarter than I thought not to take me to the office."

"That means they'll be back soon." He kissed me again, then stroked my cheek. "I'd never sell you out. Not for fifty thousand or fifty million. That's all I could think about when they shoved you in that toilet, and I saw it fall into the lake."

"That's the most romantic thing anybody's ever said to me." I sighed. "I knew you would come. Unless you were dead. And I'm so glad you're not. How did you find me?"

"Remi. She got to me in time before I jumped into the lake. Told me you left in a car with Gentz. She heard him talking to one of the two stooges about the Dukem Inn. That kid's a good little spy." Nash shoved his hand in his pocket and pulled out a knife. "Don't worry. I took her back to Tiffany's before I came here."

"I hope they tie her up because that's what it's going to take to keep her—" I stopped because Nash had put his knife back in his pocket. "What are you doing? You've got to cut me loose."

"They're coming back. We could trap them."

"No, cut me loose. Don't do this, Nash. My arms are killing me and I'm going to have burns on my wrists and ankles as it is."

He shook his head. "Right. What am I thinking?"

I relaxed. "No idea, but you—"

"Ms. Wonderly is supposed to meet us at the office." He bent over to cut the tie on my ankle. "We've got to get there before Gentz finds her. I'm going to need your help."

FIFTEEN

#ACRISISOFVIOLENCE

STILL STINGING over Nash's obsession with saving Ms. Wonderly over cutting me free, I climbed into his truck without thanking him for opening the door for me.

He studied me before closing the passenger door. "What are you wearing, anyway? You're going to freeze to death."

"I didn't—"

"Here." He shrugged out of his bomber jacket.

I slipped the coat over the cartridge necklace I had retrieved from the toilet tank. "JJ made me wear this. She's the assistant to HG, some tech billionaire who's crazier than—" I couldn't imagine anyone crazier than someone who thought a movie prop would save the world. "Really crazy. She said he gave orders to get the necklace at any cost. "

"That's the dumbest thing I've ever heard." Nash bundled me into the truck seat. "Your legs are going to get cold. And how do you keep the shoes on?"

"Let's focus on getting to the office before Ms. Wonderly does." He was right, though. I could kill for a pair of sweatpants and sneakers. Not literally. I wasn't as crazy as HG. "Do you think they'll do something to her?"

"I don't know." Nash started the truck and pulled out of the Dukem Inn. "Hopefully they don't know each other."

"I still don't get wants Manganoid wants with an old stage prop."

Nash cut me a look and accelerated. "I have no idea what

Manganoid is nor where Lamar got the information. We could be looking at three groups after the same item. And in that case—"

"We don't know who we might find at the office at five."

FROM THE DOORWAY of the Black Pine Gazette, Nash and I slunk in the early evening shadows. He hugged his flannel arms against the cold. Bundled in his bomber jacket, I pressed my bare legs together, trying to warm my gooseflesh. Across the street, the Dixie Kreme Donut's neon red "Hot and Fresh" sign had been turned off. Visible by security lighting, the shop on the first floor of the old brick building was empty. Emergency lighting dimly lit the half-moon window above the door to the second-floor stairway. The office itself was dark. However, through the upper-story windows, a tiny light flashed and bobbed.

"Can you tell if it's more than one person?" I squinted at the window. "Looks like it's just one to me. Ms. Wonderly?"

"If the note said to meet her here, why would she break in? You know Gentz was headed here. That makes more sense."

I had a lot of questions about Ms. Wonderly — namely, how did she win Nash over in such a short amount of time — but he did have a point. "So where's Gentz's Mercedes?"

"Unless Gentz dropped off one of the two stooges, this might be someone else. But how'd they get inside?" Nash grunted. "That really chaps my hide. We're a flippin' security solutions office. What if it gets out that someone overrode our locks?"

"The building is super old." I placed a comforting hand on his arm. "And we don't know who we're dealing with. It could be anyone."

"That doesn't console me, Miss Albright. Maybe the whole thing is a ruse by a competitor to prove we can't even keep a dumb movie prop safe."

"I don't think we have any competitors that savvy," I whispered. "And you're the only PI in town."

"Everyone's putting in those doorbell camera gizmos now." Nash scowled. "If your mother and Jolene don't put me out of business, those will."

"Jolene closed her shop when Vicki bought Jolene's shares in your business. It can't be them."

"Still doesn't help with the doorbell gizmos."

"If we can't do security solutions, there's always cheating husbands. And cheating wives. And subpoenas. You know how much you like serving subpoenas."

He flashed me a tight smile. "Thanks."

"You're welcome." My grin faltered. "So where's your client?"

"Our client."

"It could be Ms. Wonderly sneaking around your office, checking things out before we're due to arrive." I wouldn't put it past her. But I didn't say this aloud. My heart still pounded from the "our client" bit.

Nash heaved a sigh and stepped out of the shadow of the *Black Pine Gazette*. "There's only one way to find out."

I placed my hand on his arm again. This time not so much in consolation as in fear. "What if it's not Wonderly? Shouldn't we wait for the police?"

"It's New Year's Eve. Mowry's sending a deputy, but it's going to take a while, and I don't want to lose the bastard who's rummaging around my business." He narrowed his eyes, then glanced at me. "Our business."

"What if they're armed?"

"I've got my .38," said Nash. "And Lamar keeps a shotgun in his office. I've got a key to the Dixie Kreme. We'll grab the shotgun, then wait for the intruder to come out of the office. Catch him on the landing by surprise."

"What if he shoots us first?"

Nash grabbed my hand. "Generally speaking, when you open a door to a sawed-off double barrel, you tend *not* to shoot first. You'll be great."

"I'll be great?" I stopped, digging my mules into the sidewalk as best I could. "Come again?"

"Lamar uses the double-barrel for cowboy action competitions, but it makes an effective deterrent if there's any trouble at the shop."

"Cowboy action competitions whatsit?"

"Hobby. He's pretty good, too." Nash smirked. "Never mind that. You're going to stand in front of the office door and point the shotgun at whoever comes out. I'll hide behind the door and jump them. It's a great plan."

"Except for the part where I'm standing in front of the office with a shotgun. You know I don't like guns."

"You grew up with guns. Your dad is the founder and CEO of a hunting apparel company. You own a .38, too." He grinned, flexing his dimple. "Just like me."

"Except mine is pink and was a sixteenth birthday present that I hoped was a car. Daddy's cabin might have an arsenal, but I didn't grow up in the land of hunting. I grew up in the land of car jackings. I don't like guns."

"Alright, I'll stand in front of the door. You jump the guy who's broken into our office. I'll hold the gun on him while you tie him up. Then we'll call the police."

I glanced at him. Nash had his serious face on. One where the scar stood out against his chin and his dimple hid somewhere in his taut cheeks. His muscular frame had tensed, waiting. Nash would let me do it, too. Tackle a man probably bigger than me, then expect me to hold him down and attempt to tie him up. *Kung Fu Kate*, *Warhead Girl*, and *Julia Pinkerton* never had to deal with real-life issues of size and strength.

If only I knew that it was Wonderly in our office. The idea of jumping Ms. Wonderly gave me some sort of visceral pleasure I didn't know existed within me.

However, the thought of someone other than Ms. Wonderly gave me another sort of feeling. One with which I was more familiar. Fear.

"Fine, I'll hold the shotgun."

"You don't have to use it. Just hold it. Lamar's only got birdshot for the thing, anyway." Nash kissed the top of my head. "Thank you. I was really looking forward to tackling this guy."

"There's a lot more violence in my life now," I said sadly.

Nash lifted an eyebrow. "Says the one who played a character called Warhead Girl."

SIXTEEN

#COWBOYACTION

ON THE SECOND-FLOOR LANDING, I stood before the old wooden door with "Nash Security Solutions" stenciled on the glass. In the past six months, I had a lot of memories — mostly good — associated with this door. Particularly my first impression, when I found Nash only half-dressed. I learned to always knock first. I also learned a man could have a six-pack and ripped pecs without taking supplements.

However, this was the first time I stood on the landing holding a shotgun. Waiting on whoever burgled our office. Nash stood poised against the wall where he would jump out and tackle the intruder. Hopefully without getting either one of us shot. It was a situation that required a lot of faith. And hope.

I needed more of both in my life.

On the other side of the door, a loud thump accompanied an arc of light flashing from the door to the ceiling. Nash threw me a look as if to say, "get ready," then turned his attention back to the door.

Standing in a clingy satin gown, matching mules, and a bomber jacket six sizes too big, I was far from ready. My arms shook from holding the shotgun aloft — why hadn't I lowered it until this point? — and my knees trembled as a chilly draft blew up my bare legs. The door thudded. I flinched, and Nash tensed. He cocked his head, then frowned. He held up a finger.

My arms ached, but I lifted the shotgun to eye level and widened my stance. Prayed that I wouldn't actually have to shoot anyone.

Then said that prayer again.

Three more thumps and a muffled groan. The door swung open. A man dressed in a black hoodie and dark pants dashed out. Nash jumped out. The door crashed against the wall.

"Stop right there." I pulled back the safety, wishing it was the kind of shotgun that had the pump for the sound effect. Not even glancing at the shotgun, the man dodged Nash's tackle. Barreling into me, he knocked the gun aside. My finger slipped. The gun fired. He bounced off me and half-fell down the stairs. Snow showered the landing.

I stared at the ceiling, now littered with holes.

Nash rushed over, took the gun, and pulled me into his side. "Are you okay?"

"I'm okay."

"Which one was that?"

"Oddjob."

Nash brushed plaster dust off my shoulders. "Go in and see what damage he's done. I'm following him."

I glanced at the ceiling. "I did some damage."

"Birdshot. We'll patch it later." He handed over the shotgun, slipped around me, and ran down the stairs.

Shaking plaster off my hair, I walked into the office. And stopped. On the floor, next to Lamar's corduroy recliner, lay the elf. This time dressed in jeans and a parka. But even without the striped tights and jaunty hat, I'd recognized his lanky build and wannabe actor features. Falling to my knees, I scanned him for injuries.

His forehead had a cut that wasn't bleeding too badly. But he lay on his side, and I was afraid to move him to check for injuries.

"Elf," I said. "Elf? Are you okay?"

He didn't respond. Biting my lip, I laid my fingers against his neck. Warm, but I couldn't feel a pulse. I tried his wrist. My hands were cold and shaking. I couldn't feel my own pulse. His parka was zipped closed. My hand shook pulling on the zipper. I laid a hand on his sweater.

Was he breathing or not? Why was it so hard to tell?

Come on, Maizie. Think. CPR? What if he had a neck injury?

No, ambulance first.

"I'll be back in a minute." I hopped up and dashed into the office. Grabbed the receiver of the desk phone. Dialed 9-1-1, explained my emergency, then hung up (at their protest) and called Nash.

"Couldn't catch him," said Nash. "I'm on my way back. Can you tell if he took anything?"

"I don't know," my voice trembled. "I think the elf is dead."

"It sounds like you said—"

"I did."

"I'll be right there. You need me to call—"

"Already done. Hurry." I turned toward the desk.

"Maizie?" Nash's voice sounded strained and gruff. Also, panting because he'd been running. "I just want to say…"

"Yes?"

The front door creaked.

"Nash, the EMTs must be here—" I dropped the phone and dashed into the front room. The door stood open. "Hello? He's right here—"

The elf was gone.

SEVENTEEN
#NOTGUDINOFF

FROM THE STOOP of the Dixie Kreme shop, I spotted the elf jumping into an old VW bug. I also spotted Nash sprinting up the street. Sirens blared in the background. They sounded seconds away.

"The elf," I shouted at Nash, pointing at the Volkswagen. "He's not dead."

Nash jerked to a stop. "What?"

The elf glanced up, sighted me, then Nash. The little car's engine started.

Nash's startled expression turned flinty, and he pivoted toward the Volkswagen. "Come on."

Lights flashed on the street. An ambulance flew around the corner, siren blasting. A Black Pine police car followed. The bug backed out, and the ambulance pulled up, blocking the VW. Hurtling down the sidewalk, Nash vaulted the curb and threw himself against the driver's door of the yellow bug. Jerking the door open, he grabbed the elf.

I rushed down the steps to join Nash.

"Park it," bellowed Nash. "I'm hauling you out either way."

The police car pulled in next to the Volkswagen. Getting out of his car, the deputy waved to the ambulance crew to stay in the truck.

"Who are you?" Nash slammed the elf against the little, yellow bug.

"Wyatt Nash, let go of that man," said the police officer.

Nash glanced behind him, then smiled. "We're the ones who called you,

Sam. This bozo nabbed Miss Albright at the Winter Market, pretending he had a gun on her. Then he broke into my office. He let Miss Albright think he was dead, for Cripe's sake. Then dashed out when she wasn't looking."

"She kicked me in the gut at the market, and I was attacked here," protested the elf. "If anyone has room to complain, it's me."

Sam looked at me.

"It's all true," I said. "I think he got knocked out by the other guy. My hands were too cold to feel his pulse. But it did freak me out, which is why I called emergency services."

"Other guy?" said Sam. "Who's that?"

"Oddjob." I shrugged. "But that's just what I call him. He works for a scary man called Gentz. Gentz works for a rich tech dude named HG. And that's as far as we've gotten with names."

"We're about to get a little farther." Nash tightened his grip on the elf's coat and shoved him against the car.

"Hey," said the elf. "You're just going to let this knucklehead hold on to me? My feet aren't even touching the ground."

"Would you rather I hold you there?" said Sam. "Your feet will touch the ground, but your hands will be behind your back."

The elf glared at us. "I hate this place."

"What's your name, son?" said Sam.

"Gordon Gudinoff."

I blew out a snort. "No, it's not. That's your stage name. What's your real name?"

"It is so." Gordon the elf directed his scowl at me. "How'd you know I was an actor?"

"Takes one to know one, I guess." I folded my arms. "Who are you working for? And why do they want my *Warhead Girl* necklace?"

"Were you in that movie?" said Sam. "I loved that movie."

"Sam, get that look off your face," growled Nash. "Miss Albright is no longer an actress. She's a professional investigator."

"Almost," I said. "Two years of training until my license. Anyway, back to you, Gordon. Talk."

"How'd you get in my office?" said Nash. "And who's the other guy?"

Sam pulled out a little notebook.

"Am I under arrest?" said Gordon.

"I haven't decided," said Sam. "Tell us what you were doing in that office, and how you got in. And the stuff Miss Albright asked."

"Not without a lawyer," said Gordon.

"Sam," said Nash. "How about you take a little walk upstairs? Check out the scene of the crime."

"There was no crime," said Gordon. "Unless you count the guy who knocked me out. I wasn't pretending to be dead. He attacked me, and I must've hit my head. And now this guy is attacking me. I should sue all of you."

"I'm going to check out the office," said Sam. "The EMTs will be with you shortly, Gordon. Mr. Nash will escort you to the ambulance as soon as y'all are done talking."

"This isn't legal," squealed Gordon. "I know my rights."

"Miss Albright, would you like to go upstairs with me? You can show me where you found Mr. Gudinoff." Sam shoved his notebook into his pocket. "I have some questions about *Warhead Girl* for you, too. How old were you when you did that movie?"

"Nineteen or twenty," I said.

"Oh good." Sam expelled a breath. "So, how did they keep that bandolier in place—"

"Sam, Miss Albright is going to stay right here." Nash's jaw tightened. "She wants to talk to Gordon."

Sam glanced at Nash. "Okey-doke. Be right back."

"Hey," yelled Gordon. "What kind of Keystone Cops run this place?"

"Listen, Gordon," I said. "Mr. Nash will set you down. But he's upset about what you did to me earlier today and really upset about you breaking and entering Nash Security Solutions."

"It wasn't breaking and entering. I had a key and a code. I was given permission."

"The hell you were." Nash shook him. "That's my office. I didn't give you diddly."

"Stop." Gordon held his hands up. "Look, the person who hired me gave it to me. They said they owned the place and after I get the necklace from you, I should wait inside for the buyer. I should've turned the lights on, but I went in early because it's friggin' cold out here. Aren't you freezing, dude? You're not even wearing a coat."

"I'm not cold now." Nash flashed his teeth in a wolfish smile.

"Nash." Sam appeared on the stoop. "Who shot your ceiling?"

"I did, Sam," I called. "By accident."

Nash shook his head. He released Gordon, then held up a hand before Gordon could step away. Turning to me, Nash lowered his voice. "Maizie, we need to get going. Before a certain party realizes you're missing."

I nodded, and Nash called up to Sam. "Mr. Gudinoff is all yours. Miss Albright and I will make our statements at the station in a bit. Tell anyone else on duty to check out the Dukem Inn on Highway 76. The people we reported breaking into Boomer Spayberry's cabin and attacking Miss Albright and her sister are staying there."

"Room 129," I said. "Rudolph Gentz, two other men, and a woman named JJ something."

"By the way, I found this on the floor by the recliner." Sam held up something pinched between his fingers. It glittered in the light shining above the stoop. "It's a key. Fits the door to your office."

I squinted, then walked over to the stoop and took it from him. "Shiztastic."

"What's wrong?" said Nash.

My lips pressed together in a firm line. "The keyring is Louis Vuitton. Vicki gave Gordon the key."

EIGHTEEN

#HALLMARKMOVIEDREAMS

"WHERE ARE WE GOING?" I'd insisted on returning Nash's coat which offended his Southern gentlemanly sensibilities.

But I had my own sensibilities — mainly guilt and stubbornness — and had taken one of his giant sweatshirts and a pair of sweatpants from the bottom drawer of the file cabinet. Wrapped in fleece and Nash's scent, it was almost as good as the bomber jacket. A pity I couldn't borrow a pair of shoes, because the rolled sweatpants, Nash's gym socks, and white satin mules just didn't "do," as Vicki would say.

Also because my toes were numb with cold.

"We're going back to Boomer's cabin," said Nash, his voice gruff with worry and Southern gentleman irritation. "Gentz said they'd already searched it, so it seems like the ideal place to hide the damn necklace. We also need to regroup and get a plan. I want to call Ms. Wonderly and find out why she didn't show."

It still bothered me that he thought that was her name. Not for a minute, did I believe in that sort of coincidence. Wonderly hadn't even been Wonderly's name in *The Maltese Falcon*.

Probably I was jealous. More than probably.

"Going to the cabin makes sense. We can also do research there," I said, taking the figurative high road. "For example, I'd like to know how HG, Manganoid, and Vicki could be related."

"Knowing Vicki, she arranged this whole debacle just to drive me nuts," muttered Nash.

"Vicki is in Fiji with Giulio. How could she have given Gordon the key to your office?"

"I'm sure they have a post office in Fiji."

"It's so cute you think Vicki would use the post office." I patted his leg. "But really, she's been gone for two weeks. How could she be involved?"

"The more important question is why. What would she want with a movie prop? She was your manager when that movie was made. Why now?"

I chewed on my thumbnail, got a mouthful of fleece, and gave up. "To keep HG from getting it? But why would she care if some tech guy wants it? I think she'd be flattered a zillionaire would like the movie that much."

"Gordon said he was waiting for the buyer. Maybe HG was the buyer."

"Then why go to all the trouble to force me to give up the necklace? They went to the office to steal the safe."

"Why pay for something they could get for free?" countered Nash.

I sighed. "None of this makes any sense. And if Gordon's working for Vicki and Gentz is working for HG, who is Wonderly working for? Manganoid?"

"The whole thing is ridiculous." Nash looked over at me. "Gentz is dangerous. I want to get you and your sister out of town until the police can find these guys."

"What about you?"

"They don't care about me."

"What about the necklace?"

He kept his eyes on the road. "I won't let anything happen to it."

Unless Ms. Wonderly got her mitts on him. I didn't trust her one bit. But did I trust Nash?

AT THE CABIN, we moved from room to room, checking for signs of Gentz or his men. They hadn't disturbed much, most of the damage remained in the foyer. Nash hauled the tree outside while I swept up the glass. Daddy's Christmas tree had been ruined, but the rest of the house had withstood HG's men.

I handed Nash my laptop, then went to my room and changed.

From satin and fleece to denim and thermal. A Jil Sander oversized sweater paired with my R13 skinny jeans and Sartore fur-lined ankle boots.

Take that JJ and your impractical-for-Black-Pine ensembles. One can still rock winter and be warm.

I hurried into the kitchen where Nash sat at our massive pine table with my laptop. In the short time I'd lived in Black Pine, Daddy's cabin had gone from "theirs" to "ours" in my mind, just like Nash's office. They'd both begun to feel like home. Was this a sign I'd become more Black Pine and less Hollywood?

Since moving back, Remi had become a real sister, not just my father's other family. Carol Lynn didn't pretend to be my mother, but we were friends. And although Daddy and I were still trying to resolve our relationship as an adult child and father, I cherished this chance to live with him and feel like a family again.

I wiped my eyes and sniffed. My first real New Year's in Black Pine hadn't been the Hallmark movie of my dreams, but it had certainly been memorable. I glanced at Nash, who frowned at my laptop and typed with two fingers. Felt a rush of warmth for his part in this holiday. Even if it had been by inviting Ms. Wonderly into the mess.

Would Nash become a part of this family, too? I clasped my hands together, imagining next Christmas with Nash sitting at this table with Daddy's family — I mean, my family — sharing our Christmas turkey and roast beast.

Nash looked up. "There you are. I texted Ms, Wonderly. I should talk to her. Find out why she didn't show at the Winter Market and Gordon the elf did instead. I'd made a big mistake assuming she'd sent that note."

As Nash's lips formed Ms. W's name, I felt mine thin. I quickly licked them and tossed away my silly family-around-the-table fantasies. "What did you learn about HG and Manganoid?"

"Manganoid is the studio trying to do a *Warhead Girl* reboot. They mentioned you." Nash leaned back, studying me. "There are a lot of photos of you in that outfit."

"Probably stills from the movie." I felt my face grow warm. "If Vicki's involved, this is the reason. She handled the original contract and had some production rights. When the movie flopped, she dismissed it, but as it grew to cult status, she probably started looking for ways to make her money back."

Nash peered at the screen. "This doesn't look like a film still. You're surrounded by teenage boys and adults dressed for Halloween."

The flames licking my cheeks heated my neck and ears. "I had to do Comic-Cons for a few years. Dressed like *Warhead Girl.*"

"You went out like that in public?" His eyes traveled from the screen and back to me.

I bit my lip and glanced away.

Nash cleared his throat. "Anyway, some tech company tried to stop the second movie from being made."

"That must be HG. But why would he halt production if he loves *Warhead Girl?*"

"The story said he thought it would ruin the integrity of the first movie."

I laughed. "I told you fans could get crazy."

"He offered fifty million to buy the rights."

"Holy shmizzles." I stared at Nash. "That must have been what Lamar meant. Fifty million is a lot different than fifty thousand."

"The man is more than crazy. Do you know HG built an underwater resort? You can rent a room that's basically an inverse aquarium. Costs about a hundred thousand a night, but they're booked for the next twenty years."

I shuddered. "I think I had a nightmare about that once."

"By the way, your friends called me." Nash waved the phone. "They've been trying to reach you."

"Thanks." I grabbed the phone from his hand, slid onto the bench, and dialed Rhonda's number. "Probably checking in about Remi. Let's hope they're sitting on her."

"Where've you been?" said Rhonda.

"My phone is currently in a portable toilet. I'm back at the cabin now."

"Oh," purred Rhonda. "With Mr. Nash? Are you getting cozy for New Year's Eve?"

"I wouldn't say cozy. We're still working on the case. But everything's fine. Tell Remi I'm at the cabin, and it's all good."

I didn't want to freak them out by telling Rhonda about the hostage showdown in the Dukem Inn. Or worse, let it slip to Remi who might feel she had to save me. She already saw me get into a car with Gentz. Nash had reassured her I was fine when he dropped Remi off at Tiffany's.

Nash glanced over his shoulder. "Did you hear that?"

"What?" I held my hand over the receiver.

"Sounded like something, maybe in the garage. I'll check it out." Nash pushed off the bench and strode across the kitchen to the garage door.

"How's Remi?" I hopped up from the bench. Poised to run, I kept my eyes on the door Nash had left open.

"Just fine." Rhonda paused. "The thing is, we locked her in the bedroom. With food, drinks, and a tv. We were worried about her getting out again after that sleeping-in-the-bed trick. We also shoved a table in front of the door. This was a harder babysitting assignment than I thought…"

"No, that's fine," I said absently, my attention on the door to the garage. "As long as she's safe."

Nash returned from the garage and shrugged. I released the breath I hadn't realized I held and sat down.

"But there're the dogs…" continued Rhonda.

"I'm sorry about the Jacks. They have a lot of energy."

"We put them in the room with Remi, I hope that's okay. They behave so much better with her. Haven't heard a peep from any of them for a while, so I think it was the right thing to do…"

The phone clattered. "Girl," said Tiffany. "Those dogs ate all our Rice Krispy treats. And they got in the fridge and ate my Swiss Colony cheese and sausage sampler. It was in the damn deli drawer."

"Wow," I said. "I knew the Jacks were smart, but I didn't—"

"Wait," said Tiffany. "Rhonda looks guilty."

"I didn't know you were saving that," Rhonda called from the background. "But I needed something other than Sour Patch Kids."

"I put out a veggie tray," said Tiffany. "That should've balanced out all that candy."

"The dogs ate that," yelled Rhonda. "Who knew they loved broccoli so much?"

Nash's phone beeped. "Hang on." I glanced at the screen and read the text, "Meet me at my room. Alone." My chest tightened. Why was she always trying to meet him alone? And how did he know her hotel room?

I placed a hand over the phone's receiver and crossed my fingers over the screen. "Nash, Wonderly wants us to meet her at her hotel room."

"Good." Nash snapped the computer shut. "We should get out of here, anyway. Gentz will be looking for you."

"I've got to go," I said to Tiffany. "The dogs will listen to Remi. But it sounds like you've got it under control. I can't thank you enough. It's imperative that Remi keeps away from me. At least until...the police arrest some people."

NINETEEN
#WONDERLIED

I DIDN'T ASK when Nash had learned Ms. Wonderly stayed at the newly built Black Pine Lodge in room 112. She'd told him. Sometime. But I gathered at an earlier time. Which, for a client, was totally normal. I guess.

The Lodge had a similar alpine vibe to the Dukem Inn, except the wooden beams and plaster were real, not concrete. The views from the balconies were Black Pine lake and mountain, not a parking lot. The rooms opened to an indoor courtyard, featuring a large fountain and a Christmas tree that was not purple and leaning against a pool fence. The beautifully decorated tree stood fifteen-plus feet high, next to a massive stone fireplace.

"This is a little different than the Dukem Inn." We stood in the glass vestibule, taking note of our surroundings. A vent blew hot air on my boots and caused my hair to flutter in staticky strands. "JJ and Gentz should have checked other places. Although Black Pine Lodge does look booked up."

"The Dukem is appropriate for criminals hiding from the law. Ms. Wonderly is not a sociopath." Nash pursed his lips and moved forward, so the doors slid open and we were assaulted with "YMCA."

The song. Not the club.

"Looks like they're having a rocking New Year's party," I said, instead of a snide remark about the wonderful Ms. Wonderly. In my book, "not a sociopath" shouldn't top a list of positive qualities.

However, I didn't think Nash heard me over the sounds of the party, which was just as well.

Jealousy didn't make for thoughtful observations.

Nash strode without hesitation to room 112. Or at least, that's how it looked to me. Upon knocking, the door cracked open, then widened.

"You're not alone. But that's okay, I guess," said Ms. Wonderly in her breathy, Marilyn Monroe-ish voice. She wore a cropped white hoodie and matching leggings. Without a hint of muffin top, I was sorry to see.

"Glad to hear it," I said, striding inside.

The room had a king-size bed, sofa, and flat screen. No plaid or German food in sight, but there was a fruit basket. I checked it for a card and not seeing one, turned back to Ms. Wonderly. "Frankly, I'm surprised to see you here. You have a habit of not showing when you said you're going to be somewhere. At the Winter Market, you sent a kid with a message to meet us at the office at five, and then you didn't even show there."

"A man approached me and told me to stop asking about the necklace. So I got scared and I didn't go to the Winter Market." She looked at Nash and, I swear, fluttered her lashes. "I didn't know about the office."

"Thanks a lot for bailing." I placed my hands on my hips. "And if we'd been earlier, that might have been us lying on the floor."

"Lying on the floor?" she squeaked.

"Sit down, Ms. Wonderly. You look pale," said Nash. "Miss Albright, I think I should explain."

"You've got to help me." Wonderly pulled Nash down on the bed next to her. Even though she had a perfectly good sofa. "If they killed someone, they'll be after me next."

"No one was killed, Ms. Wonderly." Nash's voice gentled, "Don't worry."

"They were knocked unconscious, though," I said. "That's pretty bad. His head was bleeding."

"Miss Albright," said Nash. "Maybe tone it down a notch."

"I'm so frightened. What if someone tries to kill me?" Wonderly leaned toward Nash. "What am I going to do? Can you protect me?"

"You've got to be kidding me." I threw my hands up. "I'm the one who has the necklace. Why would anyone kill you?"

"Miss Albright," hissed Nash. "Let me handle this."

I waved a hand at Wonderly. "She didn't even show up at the office. She sent someone else to get killed."

Wonderly teared up. "I didn't—"

From inside Nash's jacket, the metallic tones of his cell phone sang. Jerking his phone from his pocket, he glanced at it. His jaw tightened, making the scar on his chin whiten. He rose from the bed and sauntered to the bathroom, speaking in hushed tones.

"Who's your boss? Why the big mystery-o act? You couldn't come up with anything better than Wonderly? You're no Mary Astor, by the way. You're not even a good Bebe Daniels," I said. "Let me tell you something, you might have this big galoot fooled, but not me. You either work for HG, Manganoid, or Vicki. By the way, Ms. Wonderly gets arrested at the end. You're on my list, lady."

"I don't know my employer." Fat tears cascaded down Wonderly's face splashing on her winter white leggings. Hells, she even cried prettily. "I'm really scared. I didn't think it was going to be like this at all."

Two could play at this game. I found my inner noir snark to better face her femme fatale, passive-aggressive vulnerability. "You better tell us. Or it's lights out for you, too."

"Lights out, Miss Albright?" Nash stood behind me.

I spun around, feeling my cheeks warm. "Who was on the phone?"

"Mowry." His jaw worked. "Ms. Wonderly…"

"I'm calling the police," sobbed Wonderly.

"Mowry is the police," I said. "They're looking for Gentz, as we speak. The man who held me hostage."

"Hostage?" She gasped and sprang from the bed.

"Don't worry. They'll find him." Nash held his hands out. "We know where they're staying."

"They're probably long gone from there," I said. "They're not stupid."

"Miss Albright," said Nash in a choked voice.

"My agent didn't say this was going to be dangerous," cried Wonderly. "I thought it was a weird audition, but they said I'd get a bonus if I could convince you to give me the necklace. I needed that money, but this is crazy."

"Now Ms. Wonderly," said Nash. "Calm down. I won't let anything happen to you."

"How can you? Hostages and attacks?" She bounded past us. "I'm not sticking around."

"But we need to know who—" The door slammed before I could finish.

"Dammit," said Nash, shoving past me to chase after Wonderly. He jerked the door open, and a scream ripped through the buzz of the party. "Sumbitch."

I raced after Nash who'd pushed through the throng of people standing before the fountain. A man had hopped in and was helping Ms. Wonderly stand. Her white workout clothes had shrunk around her. Without a fat roll in sight. She looked like Phoebe Cates in *Fast Times at Ridgemont High*, slicked-back hair, red lipstick, and all. The crowd cheered as she stepped out of the fountain.

She simpered, then caught sight of us and screamed.

The people facing her turned to look at us. Nash and I backed away.

"She's probably safe enough here," muttered Nash. "I'll call Mowry and tell him to send someone over to sit with her."

"Oh," I groaned. "I feel terrible. An audition. No wonder she was acting so weird in the office. She thought there was a camera. Rookies never turn their backs on the camera."

"What are you talking about?" said Nash. "What camera? We wouldn't invade our client's privacy like that."

Poor guy, I felt sorry for him, too. "She's an actress. I told you Wonderly's a character. Actually, the femme fatale pretended to be Wonderly in *The Maltese Falcon* to get Spade to take on the case, then he learned she was an actual femme fatale. Our Wonderly thought she was being filmed."

"What?" Nash closed his eyes. "Shit. Vicki."

"I'm sure. She probably hired Gordon and Wonderly. Wonderly was for you and Gordon for me."

"Why?"

"Well," I drew out the word. "She probably knew you had a type. The helpless female victim. And for me, she probably knew Gordon would scare me into giving up the death necklace. Although if she knew what a bad actor Gordon was, she wouldn't have hired him. He must have auditioned well."

"I meant, why would Vicki want the necklace?" growled Nash. "And why do you think my type is helpless females?"

Inside his jacket, the phone rang again. He glanced at the phone, shoved it at me, and stalked toward the front doors.

"Hello?" Pulling the phone to my ear, I watched Nash stomp into the vestibule. My stomach churned and bubbled up to grip my heart.

Feeling guilty, I turned my back on the doors and looked for Ms. Wonderly. Someone had given her a towel and a glass of champagne. She didn't look in a hurry to change or dry off.

The man who rescued her also didn't look to be in a hurry for her to change or dry off.

"Why won't you pick up?" said Rhonda.

"It's Nash's phone and we've been a little busy—"

"Put your case on hold for a minute. The dogs—"

"The dogs are a pain I know, but—"

"No, it's your sister," said Rhonda. "When we went to check on her, the dogs got excited, jumped against the door, and kept pushing it closed. When Remi wouldn't answer, we went outside, around to the back of the house. The screen from the bedroom window was on the ground."

"What are you saying, Rhonda?" My breath hitched.

"Remi's gone again. We don't know for how long. Or if someone took her."

TWENTY
#ODDJOBED

I ALMOST DROPPED the phone but gathered myself to reassure Rhonda that we'd find Remi. Taking shallow breaths, I ran toward the front door. Under the lodge's overhang, I scanned the parking lot for Nash's truck. The Silverado had been parked in front. Or at least, I thought it had. But there was a Lexus filling that space.

He wouldn't have left me. Nash wasn't one to storm off in a pique. Anyway, I had his phone. I jogged into the parking lot and spun around, fighting tears. This was panic. I couldn't afford to panic. I'd forgotten where he parked because all I could think about was Remi.

Remi was missing. Remi had run away to save me. Or she'd been kidnapped.

Ujjayi breaths, Maizie. I'd pass out with all this hyperventilating and that wouldn't help anyone. But now was also not the time for yoga.

Taking a deep cleansing breath, I turned and walked through the sliding doors, back into the lobby. "The Macarena" boomed from giant speakers. Cheers and whistles emerged from above the music. On a table, Ms. Wonderly danced with her rescuer while a hotel employee waved at them to get down.

All's well that ended well, for Ms. W, I supposed.

But not so well for my sister. Or me.

I needed Nash pronto. He'd help me find Remi. I stared at the phone in my hand, looked up, and shrieked. Gentz smiled at me and took the phone. He handed it to Oddjob, who stood behind him.

"Hello, Miss Albright," said Gentz. "We're out of time. I've come to fetch you."

My mouth opened and closed. I darted a look at the front desk. Empty. Of course. The desk clerk was too busy trying to get Ms. Wonderly from dancing on tables. Behind me, the party raged, too loud and crazy for anyone to notice us.

"You're quite easy to track," continued Gentz. "Kind of sad for a private investigator's apprentice, isn't it?"

"I'm still learning?"

"I think you'll want to come with us. I have a little extra work for you. All this dilly-dallying on your part has forced us to change our plans." Gentz waved at the parking lot.

My heart sank. Remi. They'd taken her. Where was Nash? The police were on their way to watch Ms. Wonderly. If I could stall, the police could take down Gentz and his men.

"Fire," I screamed. "Help, fire."

The party drowned out my words.

"Really," sighed Gentz. "You're constantly forcing our hand. It's tiresome."

Oddjob grabbed my arm and tugged me toward the vestibule. I tried to plant my feet, but my boots glided across the tiles. The doors whisked open. Heat blew up from grates and my hair whirled around my face. I continued to scream, but now the doors had sealed my fate.

Quite literally it seemed. They did a good job of keeping out the cold air.

"There's no camera in the vestibule," Gentz glanced behind him. "Grant, if you would…"

Grant. Oddjob's name was Grant? That wasn't very henchman-like. I glanced over my shoulder. Grant held a black leather strap. Above my head. Then slammed it against my head.

And I stopped thinking about Grant at all.

TWENTY-ONE
#ALTEREGOISM

A JOSTLING and shaking roused me, and for a moment I thought I was back in California, woken by an earthquake. I cracked my eyelids. It was dark and my head ached.

Had I gone to a party?

Lights flashed, and I widened my eyes. I wasn't in California at all. I was in Black Pine, traveling in a car. And my head hurt. I stiffened, then jerked from my slump against the seat. Turning from the window, I found Gentz sitting next to me.

"Good evening," said Gentz.

The whole arch-villain-pleasantries-made-to-sound-sinister-thing had grown super stale. But I wasn't going to tell Gentz. He'd probably enjoy it. He had Remi, after all.

At least, I thought he did.

I pinched the base of my thumb to stop my tears. Assistant private investigators shouldn't cry. They needed to keep a cool head. Even if it was aching due to a kiboshing. I sought my inner Julia Pinkerton. The snarky teenage detective never cried. Except in Season Two Episode Nine, when her dog died saving a group of high school students in a flood. Julia was hard, but she wasn't a robot.

"Where are we going?" I snarled. "Back to the Dukem? You really missed out on a great party by not staying at Black Pine Lodge."

He rasped his dry chuckle. "No, when we discovered you'd left the Dukem Inn, we thought it best to leave. Poor Brian had to be rescued from his shackles. I'm sure his head is still aching from that fire extinguisher."

Gentz tsked, and I glared at him. "Maybe we should've used a billy club like Grant did on my head?"

"Anyway," Gentz waved his hand. "We've set up in a new location. We're going home."

"By the rules of my probation, I'm not allowed to leave Georgia. And if you cross state boundaries, the FBI will be after you, too, not just local police."

"So kind of you to worry about me. Don't worry. I have very good legal counsel." Gentz smiled.

The man smiled entirely too much.

"Here we are," he said.

I glanced out the window and realized we weren't headed to California — or wherever Gentz lived. Transylvania, possibly? — but sped through the gates and up the drive to the cabin. My home. Near the front door, a van had been parked. At our approach, JJ slid out and walked to the car.

"Escape is futile," said Gentz. "You've seen what we're capable of."

I wanted to roll my eyes at his phrasing, but he really had a point.

JJ opened my door. "Maizie, thanks for joining us."

"Are you for real?" I clambered out, rubbing the back of my head. "Why am I constantly being thanked for things you're forcing me to do?"

"It's called politeness?" Millennial sarcasm laced her voice. "We're running really late. Come on."

"Where's my sister?"

"Not my department."

Grant opened the passenger door. I hurried past him to follow JJ inside. In the foyer, the French doors stood open and in the living room, Brian set up computer equipment on our console table. Equipment boxes stood open and the furniture had been moved. Thick cords trailed from the living room, through the foyer, and out the front door.

"What's going on?" I said. "What are you doing to the cabin?"

Grant shoved me after JJ, who hurried past the living room and into the back hall that led to Daddy's study. Book and gun cases lined the wood-paneled walls. Daddy's desk was a mess of paperwork, samples, and camo-print cloth swatches. Nothing looked out of place. That I could tell.

"Where's Remi?"

"We're out of time," said JJ. "The necklace, Maizie."

The door to the study opened. Gentz shoved Remi through the door and shook her slingshot at us. She stumbled, righted herself, and tossed him an angry glance over her shoulder.

I bounded across the room and caught her against me. "Remi, did they hurt you?"

"No. Big bullies." She hugged me and tried to push away, but I hung on.

Snapping the slingshot in half, Gentz threw it on the floor. "JJ, you're not focused. Miss Albright should be ready by now." Gentz folded his arms, then turned to me. "The death necklace?"

"You're squeezing too tight, Maizie," said Remi's muffled voice against my chest.

"How dare you take my sister. You're facing serious prison time." I grappled Remi, ignored her squirming, and kept my eyes on Gentz.

"Your sister found us." Gentz smirked. "Had her own list of demands. Unfortunately, we weren't able to meet them."

"I'll get you, Grinch," Remi's tinny voice rose, high but fierce. "I'm gonna make your heart grow two sizes."

"My heart is already the right size, missy," shouted Gentz. Collecting himself, he turned to face the cabinets. "Your father has quite the gun collection, too. Where does he keep the keys?"

"On hisself," said Remi. "He took them to Brunswick. Nobody's allowed to touch them over his dead body. Even then, he says he'll haunt me."

Gentz strolled to the desk and grabbed a wooden duck decoy.

"Daddy ain't going to like this," whispered Remi. "That's antique. We're not allowed to play with it."

Walking to a cabinet filled with rifles, Gentz bounded forward, smashing the duck against the glass. The duck bounced off, and he tripped backward, falling against a leather settee. "What is this cabinet made of?"

"Steel?" I said.

"Bulletproof glass, too," said Remi. "You can't shoot it, neither."

"Whatever. I've got my own gun. I'm not going to steal your father's.

I'm not a thief." He yanked a pistol from his belt holster. "See? Get the necklace. Now."

Shaking, I walked to a gun cabinet, opened a drawer beneath the locked glass, and pulled out a box of shotgun cartridges. "Here."

"Hidden in plain sight. How wonderful." Opening the box, his breath shuddered ecstatically, and I felt myself flinch.

"Put away your weapon." I pulled Remi against my side. She backed against my hip, folding her arms, her angry eyes on Gentz.

He holstered his gun but turned his attention to JJ. "Warhead Girl needs to dress. The Supreme Commander's waiting for her."

"Wait, what?" I clasped Remi against me.

"And JJ. Have Brian do something with the child."

"You didn't say it would be like this." JJ crossed the room to touch Gentz's arm. "That's a little girl."

Gentz's brow furrowed. "Do you want to accompany the child, JJ?"

"No," she whispered.

"Then shut up and do your job," he screamed and shuttered his features. "Excuse me. I'm sorry to lose my temper."

She shuddered.

"Haven't I treated you very well? I realize I have my eccentricities, but you've not minded in the past. You've been at my side all along. You've met sultans and CEOs. Celebrities and the best programmers. Do I not pay enough?"

"It's not the money…" she murmured.

"I think it's the money," whispered Remi. "She looks 'xpensive."

Remi was right, but my thoughts had crashed on a different shore. "Holy shiz, you're HG. Gentz is a…what? Alter ego? This isn't the *Maltese Falcon*. It's *Batman*."

"*Spiderman*'s better," said Remi.

"Shut up," screamed Gentz-HG. He beamed at JJ, then frowned and studied his gauze-wrapped hand. "You're not just an employee to me, JJ. But I'm wondering if you can really handle the job. I promised you a seat in the first rocket, maybe I was rash."

"No, no. I really want to go to Mars—"

"Brian, you can escort JJ."

She opened her mouth to protest but held up her hands before Brian could touch her. "Fine. I'll check on the satellite broadcast."

HG watched them leave. "Damn it. JJ was supposed to help Miss Albright dress."

"Maizie's already dressed," said Remi. "She knows how."

Ignoring us, HG leaned into the hall. "Grant? Bring in the costume."

"Costume?" I said. "You have the death necklace. You can let us go now."

"I had another idea for the necklace." HG smiled, an echo of Gentz's smirk but more cunning. "You've caused me quite a delay today, but now you can help me."

I said a little prayer that he didn't plan to cut off my head like the Supreme Commander wanted in the *Warhead Girl* graphic novel. But I didn't feel very hopeful.

"Warhead Girl and the new Supreme Commander will appear tonight. A marketing blitz," said HG. "Originally, I hadn't planned on Warhead Girl, but now that we have all the authentic pieces, why not? At midnight tonight, I'd planned for the world to meet the Supreme Commander with Warhead Girls' trophies. Instead, the Supreme Commander will have Warhead Girl as a trophy."

"I don't get it," whispered Remi.

I fingered my neck and squeezed her against me.

HG walked to the door. "Grant? Where are you?"

"Remi," I whisper. "We need to get out of here. How did you get to the cabin?"

"The back of Nash's truck. I've been riding in it the whole time. You never found me. Daddy and Momma never let me ride in the bed. It's so much fun. A little cold, though."

I moaned. "Wait. Nash's truck is here?"

A deep baritone called from the hallway. "Gentz? I'll give you the necklace. Let Maizie go, and you can have it."

HG laughed, and I internally groaned.

"Mr. Nash doesn't realize how late he's arrived at this party." HG pursed his lips. "Brian had best do a better job securing him this time."

"Give me the stupid costume," I said. "I'll do whatever you want, just don't hurt them.

TWENTY-TWO
#I'MREADYFORMYCLOSEUP

AT TIMES, I'd thought my Hollywood life was stranger than fiction. I'd spent past New Year's Eves partying with rock stars, models, and athletes. I'd met Dick Clark and Ryan Seacrest. I'd counted down the seconds to midnight from the back of an elephant. I'd been on a stage in Times Square and found myself kissing a boy band at midnight.

All six members.

I'd sang "Auld Lang Syne" on the stage of the Hollywood Bowl with Ozzy Osborne, Janet Jackson, and the cast of *Glee*.

Nothing topped strange like this New Year's Eve. But then, my past had brought me here. It would have to be my past that would get us out of this predicament. I wasn't going to rely on Nash to save me. I would save him and Remi, even if it killed me.

Which I really hoped it didn't.

I had a plan. A plan based on a movie. But at least it was a better movie than the really stupid movie that had gotten me into this mess.

Dressed as Warhead Girl, I peeked around the corner to the living room. A camera faced a portable green screen. JJ sat at the console table, typing into a computer. In the video monitor next to her, the backdrop on the green screen appeared to look like a mountainous desert. The setting from the final scene in *Warhead Girl*, where I faced the Supreme Commander. Before the screen, a wooden pole had been mounted. More for heretics than strippers. This was the wooden stake meant for ending

Warhead Girl in a fiery death, an Easter egg tribute to Joan of Arc, from whom the graphic novelist had derived *Warhead Girl*. Loosely.

Very loosely. But I could work with loosely.

Regardless, I took heart that HG was basing the scene on the film and not the graphic novel. I'd rather burn at the stake than face an executioner's block. My chances felt greater. Plus Warhead Girl had escaped the burning by catching her guard's head between her thighs when he bent to light the fire. That might take some work without the help of wires and a stunt double, but I had a greater incentive.

I'd take the heat for Remi and Nash. Literally.

Out of synch with the setting was a table set before the screen. On the table lay a black box, decorated with a big gold bow and lit up with green, yellow, and red lights. Like a Christmas gift that the world maybe didn't want.

But who knew? For a better internet, maybe they didn't care if an ex-actress and the people she loved most in the world were being held hostage for a PR stunt.

Speaking of my people, where were they?

My heart fluttered. Sidling forward, I spotted the decorative holiday pillows tossed on the floor in a pile before Remi's My Little Pony tree. The loveseat had been pushed from the fireplace across the room, on the other side of the green screen, near the patio door.

Brian and his gun stood next to the sofa. Tied back-to-back, Remi and Nash sat on the loveseat. Awkwardly.

Looking more excited than scared, Remi jerked her little body back and forth, trying to see the proceedings. Cursing to himself, Nash's shoulders shifted, his arms clamped to his side, pinned by Remi's body tied to his. His fingers fumbled trying to reach the knots tied to his wrists.

Before I could rush to them, Grant placed a large hand on my bare shoulder and held me back. "Where do you want her?" said Grant.

HG turned from checking the camera angle to face me. He wore the Supreme Commander's white and gold uniform. And he'd taken off the bandage on his hand.

"Excellent." HG's eyes moved over me. "Although I don't remember the costume fitting exactly like that."

"When I last wore it, I was nineteen," I snapped.

At my voice, Nash glanced up. Beneath his fedora, his eyes widened, face flushed, and jaw slackened. "Maizie."

"Maizie?" said Remi, trying to look over her shoulder. "I can't see around Nash's hat."

For my part, I wore Timberland boots, a flesh-colored sports bra, and cutoff shorts that would have embarrassed Daisy Duke. My hair had been knotted high on my head in two tiny buns that allowed a cascade of wisps to fall free. A bandolier of bullets was looped over my sports bra and the necklace of shotgun cartridges hung around my neck. I was missing my rocket launcher. Although, that was not an oversight on HG's part. It leaned against the table.

"You don't have to do this," the words tumbled out of Nash's mouth. He cleared his throat. "You shouldn't do this. You'll violate the terms of your probation if they think it's an entertainment stunt."

"Oh, I know. I could go to jail. But I don't think HG cares much about that."

"It's true. I don't care." HG shrugged, making the fringe on his shoulder epaulets flutter. "We're making history tonight. Nothing else matters. When I flip the switch, the internet will no longer be a globally distributed computer network. Everything will run through the Supreme Commander." He patted the black box on the table and adjusted the gold bow.

I wasn't sure if I should be glad the Supreme Commander was the internet and not HG. Naming the World Wide Web after a violent dictator seemed even nuttier. Not to mention creepier.

"That's how you're saving the world?" My lip curled. "Controlling cyberspace?"

"The Supreme Commander will do a better job of policing all the current social difficulties, like cyberbullying and crime. Imagine the next time someone talks about school shootings, arranges human trafficking, uploads child porn, or sends spam to your email, the Supreme Commander will know and report it immediately."

"Kind of ironic, don't you think, that you're using violence to stop violence?"

"I'm fighting fire with fire." HG lifted his chin and smiled.

That was also ironic. Or perhaps literal, considering the stake.

"I want to see what you're wearing," called Remi. "But I'm facing the wrong way."

"I don't want you to see me." The humiliation I was about to face felt too much to bear. Plus, I had a bad feeling about that stake. "Just show me my marks, HG. Then let them leave."

"I think not," said HG. "They should witness history in the making."

"Dammit Gentz," said Nash. "Don't make her do this for a publicity stunt."

"Do what?" said Remi. "Why can't I see?"

HG took my hand, kissed it, and led me to a spot before the screen. "When you get your cue, cross stage right. I'll disarm you and place you on the burning stake. Then I'll talk about the Supreme Commander for a few minutes. All its capabilities and features. On the screen behind us, visual graphics will show how SC will end crime, violence, and bullying on the internet forever. Plus show its awesome speed and search proficiency."

"Are you going to place the firewood right on the tiles?" I said, more concerned with the burning stake than the Supreme Commander's unveil. I'd been counting on a pile of wood. I had a bottle of gun oil and a lighter tucked into my bra. Hopefully hidden well enough behind the necklace and bandolier.

"Of course not." Taking my hand again, he led me away from the stake. "Then I'll release you. You'll jump, clap, and cheer, declaring how Warhead Girl can now resign from vigilantism thanks to the Supreme Commander. We'll embrace and the countdown to midnight will begin. I'll pretend to flip the switch — they actually do that at my office in the valley — and the Supreme Commander will take it from there."

"Lord help me," muttered Nash, gritting his teeth. "I really want to kill this man."

"That's all?" Jumping up and down in a sports bra and shorts on camera was never a good idea, but it was much better than burning at the stake. "And then you'll leave?"

HG looked away. "After you sign some waivers."

"What kind of waivers?"

"That any result in your untimely deaths would not reflect on my company or the Supreme Commander in any way."

I glanced at Nash. His eyes tightened and the scar on his chin seemed to pulse. With renewed vigor, he worked his wrists and shoulders, trying to loosen the binds.

JJ looked up from her monitor. Mascara was smudged beneath her eyes like she'd been crying. "You're on in ten."

New plan. I glanced around the room, homed in on the great fireplace, and decided to work from my old plan. I strode to the hearth. "I'll just wait for my cue here."

"Excellent," said HG, pacing to the table.

I reached for the fireplace remote I'd hidden behind the Elf on the Shelf that sat on the mantle. I pressed the start button. The gas whooshed on, followed by the whump of ignition. Flames flickered, then leaped as I increased the volume of the gas.

"What are you doing?" barked HG.

"Just warming up. I'm in a bra and shorts."

"Did you open the flue?" said Remi.

"Nine minutes to live feed," said JJ. "Get on your mark, HG."

As HG turned back to the set, I yanked off my necklace and bandolier. "Hey HG," I called. "I'm going to blow up your trophies."

He spun around. Red mottled his pasty complexion.

I dangled the necklace and bandolier over the grate and grinned.

"Are their lives worth nothing to you?" HG narrowed his eyes and snapped his fingers. "Don't think you can escape from here."

Grant unclipped his holster and pulled out a pistol.

"That depends on how reasonable you're willing to be. All I want is for Remi and Nash to leave. Alone. Unharmed. Then I'll do your little publicity stunt."

"And what if I refuse? I can shoot you and still force you to act."

I dipped the necklace close to the grate. "Then your Supreme Commander has no prize. You just get me in a sports bra and uncomfortably tight shorts. Sporting bullet holes. Which looks a little like the violence you claim the Supreme Commander will be ending."

A safety clicked. Brian pointed his gun at Remi.

"You shoot them, and I'm jumping in this fireplace," I snarled. "I thought I was going to get burned at the stake, so I've already mentally prepped for the role."

"No," shouted Nash.

HG pushed air noisily from his nose.

I stepped onto the inner hearth. The flames lapped at the Timberlands. The heat scorched my bare legs. "Get Nash and Remi out of here."

HG waved a hand. Brian jerked Nash up from the loveseat. Tied to Nash's back, Remi rose with him.

"Don't do this Maizie," said Nash.

"What's happening?" said Remi.

"Close your eyes, Remi," I said. "Whatever you do, don't open them."

"Eight minutes," said JJ. "What should I do?"

Sweat beaded my forehead. My back had grown slick and sticky. The hand holding the necklace and bandolier felt scalded. I pulled out the gun oil and lighter and tossed them onto the hearth. "Let Remi and Nash go out the patio door behind them. Lock them out. We still have time to do the announcement."

"Brian, wait." HG crossed his arms. "I don't believe she'll really do it."

I didn't want to do it. I wasn't brave like Warhead Girl or as cunning as Julia Pinkerton. But after his ridiculous fight to get the necklace, then to get me to do his stupid reveal, I figured he wouldn't want me to incinerate myself. "Nash. Get Remi out of here."

"No," screamed Remi.

Attached to Nash's back, Remi kicked out, smacking Brian in the nose with her boots. Nash swung around. Snapping his head down, Nash smashed his forehead into Brian's face. Bent over, he barreled into Brian, knocking him backward. The gun flew from his hand and skidded across the granite floor.

Grant's gun exploded, and a bullet smacked into the wood paneling.

JJ shrieked and ran into the foyer.

"Don't shoot, you idiot," screamed HG. "The equipment."

I could hear dogs barking and a door slammed, but my focus was on Nash and Remi.

"Maizie," yelled Nash, crashing his shoulder against the patio doors. The door held. His fingers scrambled, trying to gain purchase on the lock. "Come on, honey. Now."

"My eyes are still shut, Maizie," hollered Remi. "But I want to look real bad."

"Keep your eyes closed, Remi, and no matter what, don't look." My arm felt singed.

"Brian, get off the floor," yelled HG. "Shoot them."

"That's it. Fire in the hole," I screamed, tossing the necklace and bandolier into the fire. Leaping away from the fireplace, I tripped on a cord and slammed onto the granite. Then wrapped my hands around my head, waiting for the necklace to blow.

TWENTY-THREE

#RAIDERSOFTHELASTSNARK

THE GRANITE FELT BLESSEDLY cool on my heated skin, despite my skinned knees and palms. But the necklace didn't blow, detracting everyone from our escape, which had been my great plan. The leather bandolier only smoked, and the bullets turned bright white without a single pop.

When I had given Daddy the necklace, he told me the bullets weren't hollow, just tied to the leather. "What kind of idiot makes jewelry from live ammunition?" Daddy had said. "But thank you, honey, it's real interestin' anyway."

As much as I wanted to cool my singed skin on the tiles, my plan needed some work.

"Grant, you idiot. Use the ash shovel to get the relics from the fire," screamed HG. "Brian, forget about the man and the girl. Help him."

"Hurry, Maizie." Nash had the patio door open. Blessedly frigid air blew in. Outside, dogs barked and people shouted.

"Get Remi away from here." I needed a new distraction.

Springing up, I dashed toward the green screen and grabbed the black box from the table. I yanked hard, ripping it free from the tethered wires, and ran for the foyer. Through the open fireplace, I spied Grant struggling with the fire tongs and Brian reaching for the bandolier with the ash shovel.

Shouting outside the front door caused me to halt in confusion, giving HG time to enter the foyer. "We're live in a few minutes. You're wearing those artifacts. I don't care what it does to your skin. I know what hot bullets feel like." He held up his burned hand. Puffy red and white marks covered his palm.

I backed toward the hall bathroom. I'd gone through enough phones, laptops, and iPads in my teens and early twenties to know exactly what to do with the black box. No amount of rice would save the Supreme Commander.

"Gentz. HG. Whatever. It's over. Listen. It's midnight." Somewhere, dogs continued to howl. "That's the fireworks over Black Pine Lake. They make the dogs go nuts."

"No. It can't be. JJ hasn't given me the cue."

"JJ's gone. Your time's—"

HG pulled his gun from the saber holster, stopping my words. He glanced over his shoulder, then pointed. "Brian has rescued the bandolier. It's scorched, but the significance will have a greater impact. Grant, hurry with that necklace."

On the other side of the fireplace's open maw, Brian held the blackened bandolier pinched between tongs. The brass rings gleamed like white gold and the bullets inside almost appeared to be twitching.

"Look," gasped HG. "It's beautiful."

An explosive pop stopped my words. I fell back, slamming onto the floor. Covering my head, I squeezed my eyes shut.

"No," he screamed. "Not the death necklace."

A series of explosions boomed from the fireplace, sounding like the Fourth of July instead of New Year's Eve. I felt heat zing past me. Abandoning the box, I scrambled on the ground toward the entry. The front door flew open, crashing against the wall. Nash stood in the doorway. In two long steps, he reached me. Scooping me into his arms, he dashed out the door and ran down the drive. His hat blew off, but he didn't stop.

Through the open front door, I heard screams. The screams mixed with sirens, dogs barking, and the pounding of Nash's feet on the drive.

"Remi?" I said, looking over his shoulder at my father's cabin.

"She's with Tiffany and Rhonda in their vehicle on the other side of the gates. The dogs are in the car, too. Your friends called the police when they saw JJ run out of the house. They came here to help us find Remi. When I ran around the house with the kid, they cut us free." He slowed, then turned back to look at the cabin. "We're going to need ambulances, too."

"Did the bullets shoot Gentz and his men?"

"No." Nash carefully set me down but kept his arms around me. "The gasses inside combusted and the metal burst. Flying bits of hot shrapnel." Nash moved us off the gravel and into the grass. Flashing red and blue lights flooded the drive. "It was awful. Like Gentz's face had melted. I don't know what he was thinking, trying to get the necklace out of the fireplace."

"How awful. I didn't mean for that to happen." I shuddered against him. "I was just trying to give you time to get out with Remi."

"It worked but don't ever do that to me again." Nash gently tightened his arms around me. "I've never been so scared in my life. That man's deranged."

"You should meet some of the directors and producers I've worked with." I laid my head against his chest and sighed. "Genius is overrated if you ask me."

"Give me dumb and easy to catch any day." Nash kissed my hair, then pulled away to look down at me. "Back at the hotel, you were very angry at Ms. Wonderly. Why do you think my type is helpless females?"

I shrugged, avoiding his eyes.

"Miss Albright, I've never considered you the helpless type. Maybe when I first met you, but if you remember, you proved that wrong pretty quickly."

"Wait, what?" I looked up.

"You're the opposite of helpless. In fact, I wish you would let me help you just a little. Offering to set yourself on fire? Willingly allow yourself to be abducted?" He gritted his teeth, cleared his throat, and gazed at me. "Maizie, my type is you."

"Me?" Tears bit my eyes. "I'm sorry I didn't trust you. I was jealous. I'm not used to someone always having my six. I'm more accustomed to a guy maybe having my three, but usually they stop at two."

"I don't think you quite understand what watching your six means," said Nash slowly. "But I get it. I've had the same issue with women. And I got your six. And your three, nine, and twelve."

A police car zoomed past us. Another followed, and a third slowed down to shine its lights on us. In the distance, I could hear the faint clanging of church bells immediately followed by the shrill wail of Black

Pine's emergency siren. An explosion of colored lights lit the sky above the lake. And inside Rhonda's car, the dogs howled.

"You're hot, Miss Albright," Nash shouted over the noise. "But it's midnight. Can I kiss you?"

My skin felt too warm to blush. "You're pretty hot yourself, Mr. Nash."

"I meant literally. I was worried about hurting you." He chuckled. "But that, too."

Spotlit by the police car, Nash bent his head. His lips covered mine, and more heat zinged through me. I didn't think I could ever complain about Black Pine's winter weather again.

TWENTY-FOUR
#NEWYEARSREVOLUTION

WITH HG and his people arrested, a government agency had arrived to take away his equipment. Remi, Nash, and I watched them box up the Supreme Commander and all the other gadgets, then remove the wooden crates.

That left us to clean and restore the cabin before my father arrived home. He'd left Brunswick when I called early on New Year's Day to report what had happened.

"I hope Daddy's not going to be too upset about losing his hunting and fishing tree," I said. "But I'm not sorry the necklace was destroyed."

"I'm never touching that fireplace again," said Remi. "But my Grinch traps worked."

"Remi?" I folded my arms, giving her my best big-sister-means-business look.

"I know it was wrong," she said quickly. "But I reset 'em when you and Nash were talking in the kitchen yesterday. I'll never ever do it again, and please, please, please don't tell Daddy."

Peering into the fireplace, Nash reached inside and unhooked the bungee cables. Three dented cookie sheets fell into the fireplace, crashing against the metal andiron. "I guess you did catch the Grinch. The way these were battered, looks like they probably caused some ricochet."

"Don't give her any ideas." I shuddered, but Remi looked pleased.

"Any more bullets in there? I'm afraid of what will happen next time Daddy or Carol Lynn want a fire."

"What will happen?" A booming voice responded from the hall to the kitchen. Looking like a cross between a bewildered Paul Bunyan and confused Santa, my father stood slightly slack-jawed, eyeing the mess in his foyer.

"Daddy," Remi shrieked, bounding over to Boomer Spayberry. "I saved everyone from the Grinch."

He patted Remi's head, then reached into his pocket and passed me a box. "Maizie, I got you a little something while we were in Brunswick."

Inside the box was a small glass ornament. I held it up. "It's a peach."

"A Georgia peach. For your tree next year."

"My tree?" My smile faltered. "Do you want me to move out because of what happened?"

"No, sugar." He slipped an arm around my shoulder. "We'll have four trees next year. At our house, everyone gets their own tree. An oversight on my part this year."

Remi tugged on my sweater. "You can have my ponies if you want, Maizie."

Daddy swung Remi up and pulled her into our hug. I glanced at Nash, wishing I could invite him to join. He studiously avoided us by making a stack of dented cookie sheets.

Nash wasn't much of a hugger. And, I supposed, we hadn't reached the family group hug stage in our relationship. Yet.

Releasing me, Boomer eyed my sister. "You and I are about to have one long talk about the Grinch, Remington Marie Spayberry."

Remi ducked her head. "I was just trying to help."

"Your sister had a fine job saving you from helping." Boomer looked at Nash. "I'll take over from here. I imagine y'all have some paperwork or whatnot concerning the police. I can never thank you enough for rescuing this one from the trouble she's caused."

"Don't be too hard on her," I said. "She had a rough night."

"Oh, I'm fine. It was all so exciting." Eyeing her father's look, Remi changed her expression. "I mean, I'll never try to catch bad guys again."

"I hope Maizie's done catching bad guys, too." Daddy gave me a similar look to the one he'd used on Remi. I didn't like that look. The look spoke of his disapproval of my career choice. He'd had similar looks several times in the past. For example, when I had taken the role of *Warhead Girl.*

But I guess he'd been right about that career choice.

"We'll be going. Police and paperwork and whatnot," I said quickly, grabbing Nash by the sleeve. "Happy New Year, Daddy. And don't worry, all's well—"

"Judging by the way my house looks, I wouldn't say it ended well." His shoulders sagged and he tightened his grip on Remi. "But y'all are safe and sound and I can't really ask for more. Thank you, Jesus."

"Amen," I called over my shoulder and pushed Nash toward the door.

BACK IN NASH'S OFFICE, we collapsed on the sagging couch, then straightened as the office door flew open.

"Maizie, why are you so difficult to find?" Vicki arched a brow. "I've been trying to call you to wish you a Happy New Year since midnight."

"My phone is in a porta-potty..." I stopped. "I thought you were in Fiji."

"That's the thing about vacations. You generally return from them." She strolled to the couch, bending to buss my cheek. "Merry Christmas, Happy New Year, and all that."

"Happy New Year, Vicki," said Nash drily.

"Yes, you, too. I have some news for you." She glanced around, wrinkled her nose, and carefully placed her Bottega Veneta pouch on the coffee table. "It's remarkable that you've had any clients at all with the lack of seating in here. Not to mention the dust."

"We have news for you, too." I leaned back on the couch and crossed my arms. The old Maizie would have hopped up and offered her my seat, but Vicki had broken the proverbial straw this time. "The *Warhead Girl* cartridge necklace has been destroyed. You can't have it. Your mission failed."

"What mission?" Vicki laughed. "What would I want with that necklace?"

"To sell it to HG? Horatio Rudolph Gentz, the billionaire tech giant." I stared at her. "You went to all this trouble to get the necklace, sending Ms. Wonderly here. Having Gordon find me. Destroying their lives when they should have been spending the holiday with their families."

"I paid them well for their troubles." Vicki rolled her eyes. "And I wasn't going to sell the necklace to HG. He's a lunatic. Brilliant. A genius. But a lunatic. Everyone knows that. He's driven me crazy for years, wanting baubles from your odious movie. When Manganoid Pictures decided to do the sequel, HG grew more erratic. I finally paid Manganoid fifty thousand to get out of my production contract. If anything, I want to get rid of that damn necklace."

I darted a look at Nash. He glanced at me, then rested his icy blue eyes on Vicki. "So you were trying to protect Maizie from HG by tricking us into giving the necklace to you?"

I threw my hands into the air. "Why didn't you just tell me about HG and what he wanted with the death necklace?"

"You gave your father that necklace. Would you have given it to me, even if I told you about HG? The truth was so ludicrous, you'd think I was doing it to spite Boomer."

It was true. She had a history of trying to spite my father. Often times in ridiculous circumstances.

Vicki studied the emotions flitting over my features that I hadn't bothered to hide. "Exactly. You're welcome." Vicki grabbed her purse and dusted the bag. "By the way, you have one week to move from this office. I stopped paying the lease on this grungy dive. It's not befitting our purposes."

"And what purposes would those be?" Nash's voice had all the warmth of a January blizzard.

"Private investigations for celebrities, of course. You'll move into the office I secured on the next block. They're putting shiplap on the brick walls as we speak. With my connections, this company will be in the black in three months. From now on, all cases have to be approved by me first. Ms. Wonderly was the last client you'll take without my approval."

Nash opened his mouth, then firmed his lips into a tight line, making his scar pulse.

"Vicki," I said. "This isn't fair."

"I have the controlling interest in this company, how is that not fair? I'm paying off debts and back taxes. Giving you health insurance and other benefits. Company car and phones, Maizie. Mr. Nash can stop living in his office. Pay off his numerous bills."

Nash jerked his head up. "Hey, that's not any of your business."

She gave him a quick, cool glance. "You're not the only one who can do due diligence. You see, I'm saving this godforsaken rattrap you call a business. For my daughter. Not for you. I don't care about you."

"The feeling is mutual," growled Nash.

"But you will benefit financially. And as long as Maizie stays, I'll continue to manage this business. In two years, her apprenticeship finishes, and she can fulfill her absurd dream of becoming a private investigator. Or not. Then, Mr. Nash, you're on your own to let the business go to hell once again."

Nash folded his arms. The way he clenched his biceps, it wasn't hard to guess who he prevented himself from choking.

"And Maizie." Vicki sighed. "I have spent all my adulthood trying to do best by you and your career choices."

"At age three, I don't think the choice was really mine—"

"But, since following you back to Black Pine," she continued, "I've learned I can wait out this purgatory. Two years is nothing. Well, not in the entertainment world where they forget you in a heartbeat. But if you insist on staying out of the industry for that time—"

"A judge insisted I get a new career as terms of my probation."

"Whatever. That should be up in two years, too." She waved a hand. "I'll be here when you're done."

She walked out.

Nash and I sat in awkward silence, staring at the floor.

"What did she mean by that?" I muttered. "She'll be here when I'm done?"

"I have to move out? In a week?" He muttered. "I can't choose my clients?"

I gazed at him. "Are you sorry you met me?"

"What?" He regarded me wearily. "Why would you say that?"

"Since I first walked into this office, I've caused you nothing but trouble. Particularly because of all the baggage I bring with me. Like crazy celebrity stalkers. And manager-mothers who take over your business and kick you out of your office."

"I'll tell you what." Nash slid toward me.

"What?" I met his slide with one of my own.

"I'll take on your trouble if you stop getting yourself almost killed." He waggled his brows. "And you can take care of me some, too. Watch my six, you know."

I smiled. "It's a deal."

"It's a new year." He drew me towards him. "Change can be good."

"You told me once that you don't like change."

"And then I hired you."

The End.

(Until you read 18 CALIBER)

(And if you keep reading, you'll find a one-chapter preview of 18 CALIBER).

A ONE-CHAPTER PREVIEW OF 18 CALIBER

MAIZIE ALBRIGHT STAR DETECTIVE
BOOK 6

MAIZIE'S GOT ONE MOTHER OF A CASE. HER OWN.

MAIZIE'S MIXING with international stars, spies, and her mother's dark past in her sixth case in The Wall Street Journal bestselling series.

"Full of hilarious banter, wry observations, and tantalizing hints of romance."

CYNTHIA CHOW, KING'S RIVER LIFE MAGAZINE

ONE
#EyeSpyANotSoDeadGuy

You'd think with the explosion of DIY home security, Nash Security Solutions would lose a lot of clients. Not so when a celebrity management company acquires your private investigations office. Our clients — rich and posers alike — wanted to hire someone to set up their Ring and Google whatnots. Except for the paranoid few who want their homes to look like a *Mission Impossible* set, most were content with the self-service models, not the high-tech systems we specialized in.

We — Wyatt Nash, a professional PI, and me, Maizie Albright, his apprentice — had gone from private investigations and security specialists to handymen. Or handywoman in my case. Makes me miss cheating spouse surveillance.

Still a paycheck is a paycheck.

"Hand me the screwdriver, Miss Albright. Phillips." His eyes on the door of a trailer, Wyatt Nash held out a hand. A large hand. Calloused. Pocked with a few small scars. But with long, nimble fingers capable of a gentle touch.

A touch that can induce feelings of wondrous and rapturous delight, I might add.

Nash glanced at me. "The one you named Phyllis."

I grabbed the screwdriver from his adorable red metal box and placed it in the center of his big hand. Then dragged my fingers across his palm before he could close it.

His ice-blue eyes darted to my sea glass greens. "Miss Albright. We're working."

Holding back a pout, I examined the bright blue sky with bare puffs of clouds gliding on the horizon. Winter in the North Georgia mountains was much colder than winters I'd experienced in LA, naturally. But there were days like today, when the sun changed the temperature from chill to brisk. The blue and gold sky lit the tops of the tall Georgia pines, disguising all the dull brown that became more apparent with gray skies.

The sun made me hopeful. I looked back at Nash, who concentrated on screwing in a peephole camera. The tall, muscular body leaned toward the door. The sleeves on his flannel-lined denim jacket straining to accommodate his biceps and chest. Levi's fitting him snugly in all the right places.

I gave into a pensive and mournful sigh. Wyatt Nash was no longer my boss. Officially, I had dibs on him romantically. But he was still the southern gentleman through and through. Which meant a strong division between work and play. Stronger than concrete, steel, or diamonds. And not even flexible-strong like bamboo or spider silk.

He was carbon fiber among men.

And it wasn't just because our boss, Vicki Albright — still-owner of Always Albright Celebrity Management and new-owner of Nash Security Solutions — made clear the rules for our working relationship clear. No hanky-panky on the job site.

As if.

Nash had been offended she'd even raised the issue. And I had morals and ethics and all that. Even after growing up in Beverly Hills.

Sort of, anyway. The more time I spend in Georgia, the more I wondered about my prior values.

The real problem lay with Vicki's celebrity connections. We worked non-stop. Which is totally awesome if you're trying to re-establish a foothold in the once slippery position of private investigations and security systems in our town of Black Pine, Georgia. Not so awesome, if you want to date your co-worker and you're working twenty-four-seven-three-sixty-five.

Not that I was working. Not at the moment, anyway. We'd split up the trailers and I had finished my jobs. Yay me for grabbing the electric screwdriver first.

"I'm going to check the special case," I said to Nash. "See what extras were added to the list."

He nodded and continued to screw the camera into the door.

Times like these made me jealous of Phyllis.

I hiked my Golden Goose sneakers across the backlot's pavement. The trailers were rented by a new production — some kind of martial arts action film — and would be hauled to various locations in the mountains when they weren't sitting behind one of the big sound stages that took a large chunk of land on the outskirts of Black Pine. Black Pine Studios was new to the area, although the land had been bought and construction started several years ago. The film industry had recently exploded in Black Pine due to Georgia's generous tax shelters, cheap land, and cheaper labor.

I entered the three-room trailer. Checking the clipboard lying on the table near the door, I noted their security needs. Nothing over-the-top — not like the retinal scanners we'd recently installed in a producer's rented home — but it would need more work than the others. Alarms on all the windows. Emergency button in the bathroom. Scan for hidden cameras and microphones.

I made a quick list of supplies we'd need, then began my walk-through for the alarm count. Like their security feature wish list, the trailer was lavish but not outrageous. The roomy living area had a galley kitchen featuring an eat-in peninsula. Cherry wood and marble. Below a large flatscreen was an inset fireplace. In the mountains, Georgia did get cold this time of year. Large makeup station in the bathroom, complete with Hollywood lighting. King-size bed in the bedroom.

Where a man lay dead.

"Holy Hellsbah," I shrieked and backed out of the room. "Not again."

The dead man rolled over, then sat up.

"Thank God." I slapped a hand over my heart. "You're not dead."

From the doorway, I examined the youngish man. Dressed in (rumpled) trendy clothes with sandy brown hair, he didn't look like a derelict. But if he worked in the business, he would know he shouldn't be in the trailers. "Why are you sleeping here?"

"I was tired." He had an impish smile. "Why did you assume I was dead?"

"Long story but mostly bad luck." I folded my arms. "You can't sleep in these trailers. And you shouldn't be on-set without permission."

Sliding across the bed, he grabbed a lanyard from an end table and held up a plastic badge.

"Then you should know you can't sleep in these trailers." I raised my chin. "Who are you?"

"Jeff Johnson." He grinned. "Who are you? Besides a ginger with a nice…clipboard."

I narrowed my eyes. "What are you? I mean, what do you do?"

"Awesome." He waggled his brows. "And wouldn't you like to know."

"I would. Like to know. Considering I'm installing the security in this trailer."

"No worries, doll." He slid to the edge of the bed.

I wasn't security-security. I was a contractor who screwed in doorbell cams then uploaded the app to the client's phone because they were too busy (lazy) to do it themselves. However, I should report Jeff Johnson. For unofficial napping.

"Before you go, let me see your badge." I used my official security voice, one I'd developed for a *Julia Pinkerton, Teen Detective* movie that went into production but was abruptly canceled after the producers (and their marketing department) decided the script wasn't pro-STEM enough. Julia had already graduated from high school and the writers decided as a vigilante she'd major in pre-law.

Instead of engineering as the marketing department would have liked.

At the time, I had majored in criminal justice at U Cal Long Beach, so pre-law made all kinds of sense to me. But what did I know about pre-teen demographics? Anyway, I'd had a two-year hiatus from starring in the *Julia Pinkerton, Teen Detective* TV show, and thought for the movie, I could make her more edgy with a scholarly, pandering raspy drawl. I had the college sneer down pretty good, too. Now I used it with on-the-job pests.

I loved finding new uses for old character traits. Recycling always made me feel like a productive citizen.

"Badge," I repeated, extending my hand.

"I'll show you mine if I can see yours." Jeff Johnson countered my collegiate sneer with a frat boy smirk. He crooked a finger and deepened the smirk. "Show and tell time."

"Yours first." I'd reverted from collegiate to grammar school.

Jeff chuckled and held out the badge. "Feisty. I like that."

Instead of calling him something that would lower me to his standards (and possibly get me in trouble), I snatched the badge from his hand and examined it.

"You're a visitor for *Unlucky 18*? The martial arts movie? How did you get this?" I handed him the badge. "They haven't started filming. This is pre-production. You shouldn't be here."

"That's an all-access pass. Ask around. Everyone knows me."

"Visitors have restrictions. Someone from the set should be accompanying you."

Looping the lanyard around his neck, he winked. "You know what they say about all work and no play. Are you always this strict, doll?"

"Yes." Not really. Only with this dude. I folded my arms. "These trailers are under surveillance. I'd advise you to find whoever got you the pass and stay with them."

"All right. No harm, no foul, right? Can't blame a guy for trying to find some peace and quiet with all the banging on set." He chuckled and repeated "banging" to himself.

Frat boy humor.

"Just get out of here." It was difficult to nap during pre-production. I'd longed for many a nap on-set. But I wasn't telling him that.

Jeff exited. I resumed my checklist, then straightened the bed. I didn't want anyone to think we'd been napping on the job. Exiting the bedroom, I heard the trailer door open and scurried into the living area.

Nash glanced around, scowling. But that was his MO. Which made his smiles even sweeter, IMHO. "Did I see a guy exiting this trailer?"

"Jeff Johnson had a visitor badge. I kicked him out. Caught him napping." I pointed to the clipboard. "We're going to need some extra equipment for this one. I guess that's why Vicki told us to do it last."

Nash peered over my shoulder. "They want this swept for bugs? We've not done that before. And a camera on the roof? What the sam hell? Whose trailer is this?"

"Maybe it's for a producer or director. They can get a little paranoid about leaks."

Nash rolled his eyes. "This industry."

"A billion-dollar industry. *Unlucky 18* is a big-budget action movie. Vicki said the production company teamed up with an international consortium. There's a lot of money at stake, so they're just being careful."

"Why do you always defend the dopey decisions these movie people make?"

"I'm explaining their reasoning. It's why they hired us. In their minds, it's important." I shouldn't defend them. The entertainment industry had eaten me up and spit me out like a polar bear on a baby seal. At the same time, this was the work we were given. By Vicki.

I loved polar bears. My favorite animal to watch at the zoo. But on a documentary, I'd seen a polar bear play with a seal before ripping off the head, devouring the meat, and tossing the carcass for fish food. Poor baby seal.

At least its mother hadn't auditioned him for the polar bear.

"And Vicki. You're always making excuses for her." Nash folded his arms. "You don't have to pretend this situation is okay. It sucks. For both of us. You more than me."

"It's not that bad," I pleaded. "We're working."

"On stupid projects. And dealing with obnoxious people."

"We've dealt with obnoxious people before. Most of the people we know are obnoxious."

He picked up the clipboard. "I have a scanner in the truck. I'll see if it picks up any interference from hidden mikes or cameras. Why don't you start installing the sensors?"

I nodded, glad to ignore the elephant — or polar bear — in the room. Nash hadn't wanted an ex-actress as an apprentice. I'd won him over then ruined his career by bringing media attention to a splashy case. Cost him his credibility in the community. He lost jobs then his company. In that situation, I wasn't exactly the polar bear. But I'd accidentally unleashed the real polar bear on him. Vicki. He said it wasn't my fault. He'd had some bad luck. Also an ex-wife with her own ursine qualities. Grizzly, IMHO. Jolene gladly traded her half of Nash's company to Vicki for a hefty catch. Money not salmon. Although Jolene would have eaten the baby seal if given the chance.

After a lot of good breaks as a child star, I'd had nothing but bad luck as an adult. I couldn't help but feel I'd jinxed Nash. And I only knew one way to make it up to him.

Well, two ways. But the one I could do at work was to stay positive.

While I attached sticky-backed sensors to the windows and doors, Nash returned with a hand-held gadget that looked like a TV remote. He moved through the trailer, playing hot and cold, listening to the crackling sounds turn to beeps. It squawked next to a lamp in the living area.

Hidden mike.

We found a pinhole camera inside an empty screw hole in the thermostat panel. And in a wall socket next to the makeup station, another mike.

"Wow." I followed him into the master bedroom where the beeping intensified. He found the bug and a tiny fisheye camera in the overhead ceiling light.

"Nash, that Jeff Johnson. I don't think he was napping." I swallowed hard and sank onto the bed. "Hells. I caught a spy."

"Caught?"

"You're right." I blew out a long, slow breath. "More like let him go."

LARISSA'S SERIES

THE MAIZIE ALBRIGHT STAR DETECTIVE SERIES

15 MINUTES

16 MILLIMETERS

NC-17

A VIEW TO A CHILL

17.5 CARTRIDGES IN A PEAR TREE (novella)

18 CALIBER

18 1/2 DISGUISES

19 CRIMINALS

20 CARATS (novella)

21 GUNS

"Child star and hilarious hot mess Maizie Albright trades Hollywood for the backwoods of Georgia and pure delight ensues. Maizie's my new favorite escape from reality."

GRETCHEN ARCHER, *USA TODAY* BESTSELLING AUTHOR OF THE DAVIS WAY CRIME CAPER SERIES

Ex-teen TV and reality star, Maizie Albright, returns home to Black Pine, Georgia, determined to start a new career as a private investigator, modeled after her childhood starring role as *Julie Pinkerton, Teen Detective*. Unfortunately, Maizie's chosen mentor, Wyatt Nash of Nash Security Solutions, is not a willing teacher and her learning curve includes becoming her own person after spending a life under the thumb of managers, directors, and producers, particularly her stage-monster mother.

A CHERRY TUCKER MYSTERY SERIES

A CHRISTMAS QUICK SKETCH (prequel)

PORTRAIT OF A DEAD GUY

STILL LIFE IN BRUNSWICK STEW

HIJACK IN ABSTRACT

THE VIGILANTE VIGNETTE

DEATH IN PERSPECTIVE

THE BODY IN THE LANDSCAPE

A VIEW TO A CHILL

A COMPOSITION IN MURDER

A MOTHERLODE OF TROUBLE (novella with Carolyn Haines' Trouble the Cat Detective)

Meet Cherry Tucker, big in mouth, small in stature, and able to sketch a portrait faster than kudzu climbs telephone poles! The Cherry Tucker Mystery series (Henery Press) begins with Portrait of a Dead Guy, a 2012 Daphne du Maurier finalist, a 2012 The Emily finalist, a 2011 Dixie Kane Memorial winner, and a Woman's World Magazine book club pick for 2018!

"An entertaining mystery full of quirky characters and solid plotting… Highly recommended for anyone who likes their mysteries strong and their mint juleps stronger!"

JENNIE BENTLEY, NEW YORK TIMES
BESTSELLING AUTHOR OF *FLIPPED OUT*

———

FINLEY GOODHART CRIME CAPERS

"As fun as it is moving and at times heart-breaking, never the more so when the final page comes and readers are only left wanting more."

CYNTHIA CHOW, *KING'S RIVER LIFE MAGAZINE*

THE PIG'N A POKE (prequel, short story)

THE CUPID CAPER

THE PONY PREDICAMENT (coming soon!)

THE HEIR AFFAIR (coming soon!)

Ex-con Finley Goodhart finds her criminal past – and criminal ex-boyfriend –
useful in catching crooks. Can she make up for her past by helping victims
double-cross their swindler? More importantly, can she convince Lex that going
straight is the best (and most challenging) hustle of all?

*"Faced paced, bold, heartbreaking, this book has it all. It takes us deep into the
world of hustlers, cons and dirty business. Highly recommended for lovers of
mystery and thrillers."*

ABOUT THE AUTHOR

Wall Street Journal bestselling and international award-winning author, Larissa Reinhart writes humorous mysteries and romantic comedies including the critically acclaimed Maizie Albright Star Detective, Cherry Tucker Mystery, and Finley Goodhart Crime Caper series. Her works have been chosen as book club picks by *Woman's World Magazine* and *Hot Mystery Reviews*.

Larissa's family and dog, Biscuit, had been living in Japan, but once again call Georgia home. See them on HGTV's *House Hunters International* "Living for the Weekend in Nagoya" episode. Visit her website, LarissaReinhart.com, join her VIP Readers Group, and get a free short Finley Goodhart story.